RAW MATERIAL

JJ MARSH

D0950423

TRISKELE BOOKS

Cover design: JD Smith

Published by Prewett Publishing.
All enquiries to admin@beatrice-stubbs.com

First printing, 2012

ISBN 978-3-9523970-4-6

To Janet and Terry Marsh – for being you

Chapter 1

Twenty minutes after the alarm blasted her out of a profound sleep, Fernanda dragged on her uniform and locked the flat. Her eyes were open but yet to wake. She trudged down the path in the dark, squeezed past the wheelie bins and out onto Biggerstaff Street. The cleaning contractors' depot was a good half hour away. Thirty minutes walking in the cold would liven her up, as it did every morning. Not much movement on Fonthill Road. She gave a long, creaking yawn, before getting into a determined stride towards the Tube station. Her teacher had taught the class a new expression this week – *no rest for the wicked*. She liked that. Sounded like there was some fun involved.

Despite her fatigue, her main feeling was one of relief and optimism. Luis would sleep until she returned. His fever had broken and now came the easy part. And Rui could answer any fretful calls. He was a caring man. A fine father and such a kind husband, insisting she go to bed at midnight and taking over the watch. She was grateful; three hours' sleep was better than none.

The railway bridges loomed above and Fernanda picked up her pace. These new lights meant you could see the length of the tunnel, check there was no one waiting in the shadows – no one following some paces behind – and relax as you walked. Fernanda never relaxed. She scurried under those bridges as fast as she could without running. Denim on her inside legs brushed a regular beat, while her heels ticked in syncopation. The street lights at the other end beckoned her to safety and her breathing was short. She was awake now – eyes, ears, everything. Clearing the last of the bridges, some of her tension dissolved and she began to climb the ascent to the main street. That was when she heard the voice.

"Hello. I've been waiting for you."

She snapped around, her breath tiny, fearful puffs. There was no one behind her. The sodium light created shadows on the banks rising from the underpass, but she could be sure no human shape hid there. Electric pulses buzzed through her, even between her fingers. She turned and began hurrying away, just short of a run.

"Aren't you even going to say hello?"

She whipped back, the voice so close, so intimate. A light clicked on. Her eyes flew upwards. Balanced on the railway bridge, above the security camera, a man stood with a torch in his hand. A baseball cap kept his face in darkness, but his naked white thighs and abdomen were exposed in the torchlight. One hand provided the illumination, the other worked rhythmically at his groin. The images took their time to reach Fernanda's consciousness. He grunted, like Luis passing a stool, and something spat onto the tarmac near her feet. These random elements connected in her frightened mind and she realised what she was watching.

Her stomach contracted and bile rose. She turned to run, tears of shame filling her eyes, when she heard his satisfied voice.

"Thank you, darling. See you tomorrow?"

She finally stopped running on Seven Sisters Road and vomited at a bus stop. The birds were singing.

Chapter 2

Surf and snoring, in a perfect call and response rhythm. Soughs and sighs, breaths and breakers. Deeply soothing. The creaking of the wooden ceiling added an irregular percussion to the symphony. Nothing could be more conducive to relaxation. A long weekend by the sea, Matthew asleep by her side and an excellent forecast for the day. Beatrice looked at the clock. 05.03. She'd slept a full six hours. The sea air must be having the right effect.

She shifted onto her side and gazed at the moonlit contours of Matthew's profile. The slope of his forehead, bulb of his nose and bump of his chin were striped with pale grey; eye sockets, cheeks and mouth in shadow. She squeezed her eyes almost shut and wondered, if his profile were not so dearly familiar, what he would look like. The chiaroscuro hinted at Radcliffe's murderous monk, or Bronte's brooding Heathcliff, or a lantern-jawed swashbuckler called Cliff Hanger ... He stopped snoring. His eyes remained closed as he spoke.

"Why are you staring at me?"

"I was imagining you as the hero of a Gothic romance."

He opened his eyes, looked past her to the digits on the clock and returned his blinking gaze to her. "How did I do?"

"Marvellously. Murder, passion and swordfights, but tragically you fell off a cliff."

"Could be worse. Can't you sleep?"

"No, but you can. I'll get up and read awhile. It'll be light soon." She threw back the heavy eiderdown and dragged on her bathrobe. Cool air chilled her ankles.

Matthew heaved himself up on his elbows to look out of the window. "It could be a glorious sunrise. Should we get down to the beach and *carpe diem quam minime credula postero*?"

"What a lovely idea! I'll go along with the seizing the day bit, but I'm afraid I insist on keeping my belief in the future."

He stretched and yawned. "As you've just fantasised about pushing me off a cliff, that sounds rather ominous."

"I didn't push you, you fell."

"That's what they all say." His martyred expression, in the half-dark, made Beatrice snort with laughter.

The expedition was precarious. Although the Pembrokeshire Coastal Path was immaculately kept, it was intended for those who walked by daylight. A bright flash in the sky made them both stop and listen for thunder, but none followed. Probably car headlights on the other side of the bay. Being caught in a storm in the dark on top of a Welsh cliff ... Beatrice could imagine the 'stupid tourist' headlines.

Birdsong anticipated the dawn, yet the sandy path and its attendant obstacles were lit by nothing more than the moon and Matthew's Maglite. Beatrice appreciated the faint glow as she navigated the metal steps leading down to the bay. The scent of surf hit her at the same time as the saline dampness in the air. Her hair would be uncontrollable. She dismissed the thought and embraced her irrational excitement at the pull of the sea. When they finally reached the sandy cove, Beatrice slipped off her shoes, wriggling the cold, damp grains between her toes. She hunched her shoulders against the wind and smiled at Matthew.

"I feel practically pagan."

He shook his head and smiled. "Don't take this the wrong way, my love, but at this moment, you look it."

Beatrice laughed and moved into his arms to watch the paling moon, its reflection in constant flux with the restless sea. The white tips of the waves, black headland, and opalescent moon gave the impression of a silver lithograph in motion. As the sky expanded, the sea began changing from black to grey, as if someone were adjusting a monitor. The density of the cliffs took on shapes, a large mass separated and became individual rocks, and clouds on the horizon basked in rosy light. Vapour trails scored the growing saffron glow from behind the cliff. The smoky swirls of clouds, the immense canvas of colour, the shades of hope and morning inevitably brought Turner to mind. Beatrice resolved to visit the Tate on her return home. As the sun hit the sea, flashes of precious metals refracted back to the beach. Coarse calls of seabirds announced the start of the day.

"Worth getting out of bed for, I'd say," Matthew murmured. "Would you pass me the camera?"

She rooted in her bag and handed him the dinky device. "You won't do it justice."

"Certainly not. But I might be able to capture the essence of pagan Stubbs. Look at me."

Beatrice did so, her smile already in place. He stood in the sand, legs apart, took a shot, fiddled with the settings and took another. His hair blew upward in a spectacular peak, tipping his appearance towards the rakish.

"My turn," she called, and caught a couple of inexpert shots on her phone. Matthew with mad hair, the sunlit beach, a boat in the distance and a seagull overhead. Perfect.

They compared results. Beatrice was unimpressed with her photogenic qualities – the face of an ancient Celtic warrior in a jumper from British Home Stores.

Matthew examined the small image of himself on the screen. "Oh dear."

Her stomach gurgled. "Yes. Photographic proof that Professor Bailey has bad hair days. Now, shall we head back? I've worked up a tremendous appetite."

"How unlike you. Would you put the torch in your handbag? I'll hang onto the camera."

"You use me like a pack horse."

"I think of you more as a kangaroo. A female with a handy pouch."

They retraced their route back up the metal steps, which was brighter, warmer and far steeper. Conversation was limited to the odd grunt as they neared the top. On their final ascent, a vehicle stopped on the lane above. Seconds later, a hooded youth appeared, making his way downwards. His face was barely visible. Hot and out of breath, Beatrice offered no more than a nod as he passed. A sudden wrench threw her sideways and she slipped down several steps. Her hip hit steel and she let out a cry. Matthew hurried back.

"Beatrice! Are you hurt? What happened, did you fall?"

"My bag! Matthew, he's got my bag!"

Beatrice lay awake, frowning.

I always like talking to drivers and people when I'm here. Very Welsh thing.

It was 03.22, pitch dark, and a line from her book looped through her mind. Beside her, Matthew slept the sleep of the just.

I always like talking to drivers and people when I'm here. Very Welsh thing.

Amis was right; she wouldn't have the time or inclination to make small talk in London, but as soon as she was on holiday – bar staff, shopkeepers, taxi drivers – she became loquacious in the extreme.

Especially with that policeman. PC Johns of the Fishguard force had stayed a good hour, drinking tea and comparing notes on their respective jobs. Someone had found her handbag in a rubbish bin and taken it to the station. PC Johns kindly returned it to its owner and with the proud air of achieving a precedent, said it was the first case of physical mugging he'd ever seen. Beatrice rifled through her bag, which looked considerably more battle-scarred than when she'd last seen it. Apart from eighty pounds in cash, nothing was missing. A friendly sort of chap, with a steady sense of procedure, PC Johns ensured the paperwork was complete before accepting Earl Grey and a Hobnob and asking fascinated questions about life with the Met.

Beatrice sighed, pondering the experience once more. A mugger, on a remote Welsh beach just after dawn. Did bad luck simply follow her around? Why them? Why then? Local hoodies preying on dopey tourists. *The first case of physical mugging I've ever seen.* No, it made no sense at all. Assaulting someone on cliff steps was foolhardy in the extreme. A simple bag-snatching could result in serious injury to either party, or even a fall and subsequent murder charge. It was personal. That hoodie wanted her handbag and took an extreme risk to get it. What on earth for? Her eyelids drooped. Matthew's breathing had a soporific effect, so Beatrice ordered her mind onto standby and wriggled back down under the duvet. Bloody mugger wouldn't rob her of sleep as well as eighty quid.

Her eyes flew open again at a noise from the kitchen. Something breaking. Or rather, somebody breaking something.

Beatrice tensed and drew shallow breaths. She replayed the sound to find an explanation while listening for more. Broken glass, certainly, but more of a crunch than a shatter. Waves hushed and rushed outside, yet the house remained silent. It was not her imagination; she'd heard it whilst wide awake and repeating a line from *The Old Devils*. She nudged Matthew, whispering in his ear, in case he woke with one of his Lazarus-type gasps.

"Get up. Quietly. There's someone in the kitchen."

After a moment's blinking, he obeyed, easing out of bed and retrieving the Maglite from her bag. She picked up her phone and followed him to the landing. No light, no movement, no sound from below. But she knew with total certainty someone was down there. Matthew clutched the heavy torch more as a weapon than for illumination and they listened from the landing. Beatrice breathed through her mouth and waited.

Someone banged into a chair. Unmistakeable! The graunching of wooden leg on tile, followed by an intake of breath. The tiny hairs on her scalp rose in fear and anger, as Matthew charged down the stairs, wielding his torch and bellowing.

"Get out of my house, you bastards!"

As they rounded the corner to the kitchen, a figure fled out of the kitchen door, knocking over a chair. He glanced over his shoulder, revealing himself as a frightened young man, rat-faced with a weak chin and the oddest haircut. Short and dark at the front and long at the back with blonde highlights. He looked ridiculous. Like an 80s pop star.

Matthew lurched into a half-hearted pursuit, but Beatrice grabbed his pyjama top. They stood still, panting, as the sound of running footsteps faded away. Although her hands still trembled from the rush of adrenalin, all Beatrice's fear had evaporated after that glimpse of the intruder's face.

Matthew locked the door with a wry look. She'd left the key in the lock. All a burglar needed do was break the glass and he was in. How incredibly stupid of her. She righted the chair and checked for losses as she dialled the police for the second time that day. Her handbag and laptop were safely upstairs; their keys, her Kindle, Matthew's iPod and his mobile still remained on the kitchen table. But the camera had gone.

"Dyfed-Powys Police?"

"Good morning. I'd like to report a burglary. My name is Detective Inspector Beatrice Stubbs."

Chapter 3

"Good weekend, Beatrice?"

"Not exactly. How was yours?"

Melanie's face softened. "Oh, it was lovely! We went to Bluewater on Saturday and looked at bridesmaids' dresses. On Sunday, we went to my mum's for lunch and finally worked out the guest list. So I spent Monday designing invitations. I am so excited, it feels real now."

Beatrice smiled at the team's admin assistant. Melanie was never anything but perennially delighted. A ray of continual sunshine whose whole life was filled with plans, hopes and happiness. Pollyanna of the Yard.

"I imagine it would. It's only fourteen months away. Shall we have a cup of coffee and you can tell me all about it before I make a start on my emails?"

"You haven't got time. Hamilton wants a meeting at nine." Melanie pointed a decorative nail at the whiteboard.

COOPER, RANGARAJAN, STUBBS, WHITTAKER – MTG TUES 9AM <u>SHARP</u> – REALLOCATION OF RESOURCES

Beatrice didn't like the look of that.

Dawn Whittaker was the only person in the meeting room.

Something to be grateful for. Busy composing a text message, Dawn looked up from her mobile and greeted Beatrice with a sad smile. As always, she looked like an abandoned Labrador. Only a few years younger than Beatrice, but saddled with a plethora of personal problems, Dawn's face had prematurely aged. Despite her worry lines, she had a gentle air one couldn't help but trust. Her straight grey bob and smart suit should have been intimidating, but her face radiated kindness and sympathy. Small wonder she had achieved such success in her campaign to encourage rape victims to come forward. Dawn was the closest thing on the force Beatrice had to a friend.

"Hello Beatrice. Did you have a fun weekend?"

The graze and bruises on Beatrice's hip seemed to flare up as a reminder of her 'fun' weekend. "Don't ask. How about yours?"

"Similar. Any idea what this is about?" She stuffed her phone in her bag as Beatrice sat beside her.

"No clue. I've been with Cooper and Ranga for the last few weeks. Maybe you're the extra pair of hands we need for the knife crime op?" Like every other officer involved, she refused to call it by its formal title.

The door opened and DS Cooper entered, followed by DS Rangarajan. They both raised eyebrows but said nothing – a tacit signal to indicate the presence of an authority figure. Hamilton strode in behind them, closed the door and began the meeting while walking to his seat.

"Good morning everyone, hope you're all refreshed after the Bank Holiday. Thank you for attending so promptly. Situation is, we need to rearrange personnel. Whittaker, taking you off the missing twins case. You're to join Operation Sheath."

Dawn seemed lost for words; a state of affairs Russell Cooper had clearly never experienced. He leant his arm over the back of his chair. "Good news, for a change. Thank you, sir."

Hamilton fixed Cooper with cold eyes. "You will remain a team of three. Stubbs is coming off the team and joining a special project with British Transport Police."

"But sir!" All four voices rose in protest. Cooper, the loudest and deepest, won.

"Sir, with all due respect, if a female detective is required by BTP, why not Whittaker? It makes no sense to replace Stubbs at this stage. No offence, Dawn."

"None taken. I agree with you. Is there a reason for this, sir?"

Deep creases appeared between Hamilton's brows and his voice was low and acidic. "What do you think, Whittaker?"

Dawn looked away and shot a sympathetic glance at Beatrice while Hamilton waited for further protests. Beatrice noted his brick-wall expression and accepted defeat. Any arguments would be wasted. Exactly what she needed after a bloody awful weekend.

Ranga hadn't yet given up. "Sir, although Whittaker is one of our sharpest minds, it will be time-consuming to bring her up to speed. We have made significant progress on this case and arrested three suspects already. It would be quite a blow to lose Stubbs now."

Hamilton seemed unmoved. "I'm sure you'll manage. Incidentally, three arrests in six weeks is not what I call significant progress. Now look here, Stubbs is the right person to work on this transport case for two reasons. First, she has a record of successful collaboration with other agencies. And secondly, her counterpart in this investigation will be Virginia Lowe. So, does anyone require any further explanation?"

Ranga, Dawn and Beatrice dropped their heads in an embarrassed silence. Cooper, who had only been promoted to Scotland Yard a year ago, looked from one to the other in confusion.

Bomb dropped, Hamilton rose from his seat and leant forward on his hands. "Thought not. I suggest you brief Whittaker this morning, so she can work alongside you this afternoon, and be ready to take over as of tomorrow. Stubbs, my office after lunch. Shall we say one o'clock?"

One o'clock was *after* lunch? He who pays the piper calls the tuna sandwich.

"Yes sir." She knew she sounded like a sulky schoolgirl.

Hamilton fulfilled his part by giving her a headmasterly stare. "You may as well start by updating Cooper. Good day to you." He picked up his papers and left the room.

Beatrice ached in sympathy for Dawn. How many times would this come back to haunt her?

Cooper looked across the table at the two women, while Ranga shifted awkwardly beside him. Dawn heaved a huge sigh.

"I'm sure the PBA story even reached as far as West Yorkshire."

Cooper frowned and shook his head. His puzzlement was genuine, Beatrice could see.

Dawn sighed again. "In 2008, the Police Bravery Awards were held in London, at the Dorchester. Chief Superintendent Davenport was on crutches after his knee operation. So he made use of the disabled toilet. As he opened the door, he discovered a man with his pants round his ankles and a woman with her mouth full. The woman was Virginia Lowe. And the man was Ian Whittaker. My husband."

Cooper winced. "Shit. Sorry."

Dawn shrugged with her eyebrows. Ranga and Beatrice kept their heads down.

Attempting to recover, Cooper spoke. "Look Dawn, I hadn't heard about that, but I'm glad you explained. So Hamilton thinks he's doing you a favour by giving the gig to Stubbs?"

"Doing Lowe a favour, more like. He knows I'd shove her under a Tube."

Beatrice looked up with a grin. "But you'd make it look like an accident?"

Dawn met her eyes. "Why not? I have the expertise. And so do you, for that matter. Beatrice, we've been mates a long time. I can't exactly offer you hard cash, but if you could see your way clear to pushing that predatory bitch onto some electric rails, I would consider you a true and loyal friend."

Ranga laughed and the tension eased. "Shall we get coffee and start the handover? Beatrice, you OK with this?"

"No. But what choice do I have? Hamilton's right, much as it pains me to say it. And Dawn's going to be a real asset to you. Will you keep me updated, though? I've invested a lot in this operation."

Dawn patted her shoulder. "Believe me, you're going to get so much 'updating' that you'll tell me to piss off. By the way, I think you should wear your skirt suit for this assignment."

"My skirt suit? Why's that?"

"She'll have anything in trousers. That's what they say about Virginia."

Beatrice grinned and shook her head. "Was ever a woman so unfortunately named?"

One o'clock was an absurd time for a briefing. Instead of lunching with her colleagues in the canteen, she grabbed a sandwich and returned to her desk to complete her paperwork. She hated eating at her desk. So uncivilised. And messy. At one minute to one, she knocked on his open office door. Hamilton gestured to a chair and commenced without pleasantries.

"Yes, awkward business really. Wouldn't pull you off Operation Sheath otherwise."

Beatrice knew that was as close as he was likely to get to contrition.

"Fair enough, sir. Needs must. The British Transport Police case?"

Hamilton cleared his throat and shuffled some papers. He looked most uncomfortable. Whatever was the matter with the man?

"Yes, well, it's all rather unpleasant. Have you heard anything at all in the media about the Finsbury Park Flasher?"

Beatrice gritted her teeth. He was pulling her off a major case involving serious weapons for a dirty old man? "Can't say I have, sir."

"Thing is, this chap does a bit more than just exposing himself. He seems to be targeting his victims quite carefully and sometimes threatens or even gives a repeat performance. Psychological profiler fellow says a pattern is emerging. Looks like this man is growing more confident and is highly likely to commit a sexual assault. We have agreed to collaborate with BTP on a preventative exercise. See, Stubbs, this is political. After the Reid case, not to mention that taxi driver, this one needs to be handled correctly. Whittaker would have been the obvious choice. Used to working with victims of sexual aggression, but under the circumstances ..."

"You don't think this is simply a matter of surveillance, sir?"

"You don't think this is a matter of Bloody-Stupid-Questions, Stubbs? Would I pull a senior detective off a crucial, not to mention media-friendly, case if it were? No, I do not think it is a matter of surveillance. It is a case for experienced, intelligent minds to analyse and resolve. Hence yourself. Now, please take the case file and study it well. A meeting has been arranged up the road, BTP HQ, tomorrow at nine o'clock sharp. DI Lowe will give you the background."

"Yes, sir. Am I to be based there?"

"That will be something for you and DI Lowe to decide. This is a joint effort, so should you wish to work here, that is acceptable. Now look here, Stubbs, I hope you will not allow personal feelings to cloud this case. We all make mistakes, and DI Lowe has atoned for her transgression."

Heat rose to Beatrice's cheeks. "An official reprimand and missing out on a promotion? Sorry, but I don't see that as atonement, sir. Not only was DI Whittaker's marriage wrecked, but she has had to live with the humiliation ever since. She was forced to rehash it again today, for example."

"Dispense with the dramatics, Stubbs. Whittaker is not on this case. You are. Do you think you will be able to remain impartial?"

"Yes, sir. My professional opinion will not be influenced by my personal view of that woman."

Hamilton studied her for a moment, exhaled and shook his head. "The case file, if you would. And you're meeting *that woman* at nine am sharp tomorrow. Good day to you."

Beatrice returned the wishes, picked up the file and headed back to her desk. Bloody Hamilton. Bloody flasher. And bloody Virginia bloody Lowe.

Chapter 4

After a long weekend with Matthew, the first few evenings at home always held the lurking chance of an emotional trough. Today was no different. The flat seemed empty, work looked bleak and uninspiring, and she still felt cheated of her relaxing Bank Holiday by the bag-snatching and burglary. Life could be very unfair at times.

In an effort to prevent a self-pitying spiral, she took a trip to Marks and Spencer's, where she bought far too much food and a bottle of decent Chardonnay. After performing the minimum of household obligations, Beatrice prepared her meal and listened to *The Archers* while enjoying pasta puttanesca. She was reluctantly dragging out her paperwork when the doorbell rang. She leapt up with relief. Anything to delay the flasher file.

"Hel-lo?"

Adrian's familiar voice crackled through the intercom. "It's me. Has *The Archers* finished?"

"Hello you. Yes, it has. But I have work to do."

"Can I come up for half an hour? I've brought you some wine to replace what I tucked away last night, and also, I've had a thought."

Beatrice beamed and pressed the buzzer. Adrian was a godsend. Yesterday evening, the poor boy had happily listened to her letting off steam about her spoilt weekend, so long as she kept his glass filled. He offered sympathy and outrage as required, invariably on her side.

She opened the door as he arrived on the landing. He bent to kiss her cheek and she felt the lightest graze of stubble, accompanied by a whiff of something fresh and lemony.

"I really will only stay a half hour. I've got choir practice at eight-thirty and I need to shower before I go. Here."

He thrust an Oddbins bag at her.

"Ooh, two bottles. Thank you."

Adrian hung up his coat. "Don't just say 'two bottles' – look at the label."

"Sorry. Ooh, two bottles of Chablis Premier Cru Beauroy. Lovely."

"It *is* lovely. Very fresh, with complex layers. I want you to save at least one bottle to drink with Matthew. Accompany it with seafood, or cheese. How was work?"

"Vile. Let's not talk about it. Thank you for the wine. How was your day?"

"Good. Bank Holiday weekends are always a boost for trade. But I spent most of the day pondering your adventure." He arranged himself on the sofa and looked at her expectantly.

"What? Oh. Would you like a glass of wine, Adrian?"

"Why, that would be marvellous, Beatrice. Thank you. Don't open the Chablis. You're bound to have some supermarket tat in the fridge, so I'll suffer a glass of that."

Beatrice laughed as she poured him a Chardonnay, already anticipating his wrinkled nose and pained expression. He was awfully handy to know, not just because he ran the local Oddbins, but as a kind, entertaining neighbour. He'd moved in downstairs six years ago and they'd never had a cross word. She returned to the living-room, handed him his glass and settled in the armchair opposite.

"You said you'd had a thought," she prompted.

He sipped, but did not grimace. "Where is this from?"

"M and S. Don't start."

"I'm not. It's actually drinkable. Unlike that foul brew you plied me with last night. No wonder my head was mush until lunchtime."

"That may have been more to do with quantity than quality. Now, what did you want to tell me?"

"Yes. You see, I was thinking." He hitched up his grey trousers and leant forward. Adrian always dressed beautifully. It helped that he was tall, lean and catalogue-man handsome, but he also possessed natural style. His suit today was marl-grey and the black polo-neck beneath framed his strong jaw. He reminded Beatrice of a Crufts champion. Pleasing to the eye, yet highly impractical.

"The maniac who stole your bag. The one who broke in and half-inched the camera."

"We can't be sure it was the same man. I can recall nothing of the hoodie's face and we only caught a tiny glimpse of our intruder."

"I'm quite sure it was the same man. And I think he was looking for something. Listen, the mugging was just after dawn. What was he doing hanging around at that hour? Hmm? Let's work backwards. You and Matthew arrive on the beach, take some photographs and climb back up the cliffs. A man suddenly appears from nowhere and races off with your handbag. Why would he do that?"

The same thoughts had occurred to her, and to Matthew, and to the Dyfed Powys police force. But she played Devil's Advocate, just to see what conclusions Adrian would reach.

"You're making too much of it. I don't know what he was doing, but I'm pretty sure the mugging was opportunism."

Adrian exhaled a scornful huff. "You disappoint me, Detective Inspector Stubbs. Think about it. What were you doing before that punk assaulted you?"

Beatrice smiled at his hardboiled tone. "We were watching the sunrise. Taking photos and nothing else."

"Exactly. So you take some photographs on the beach. Then, just after the sun comes up, a car happens to drive along the top of the cliff, stopping at the end of the same path you are following. They drop off a hit-man, who steals your bag and tries to push you off the steps. He runs down to the beach with his booty, meets his accomplice in a cave and they search your handbag. But the search is fruitless." Adrian took a sip of wine and looked intently at Beatrice. His dark eyes were full of drama. "And they still haven't found what they're looking for."

"Adrian ..."

"Wait, I haven't finished. Despite almost killing an innocent woman, these people refuse to give up and they come back, in the dead of night. Ruthlessly, one of them breaks into your cottage, terrifying the poor woman inside – that's you – and snatches his prize. At last, he succeeds in obtaining the camera. The evidence."

She adopted the same cynical tone Matthew always used when she got carried away. "What on *earth* have you been reading? Firstly, I suffered nothing more than a slight graze. Secondly, I was not terrified. Thirdly, I have no reason to think the burglar was the same man. And even if he was, why would he want Matthew's camera? It's nothing special."

Adrian relaxed back on the sofa, pressing his fingertips together as if he were a prosecution lawyer about to sum up.

"The camera may be nothing special, but what of its contents? Did you take a few carefree snaps of something rather less than innocent? Sadly, we'll never know, as any incriminating images are probably swimming with the fishies." His eyes flashed, he crossed his legs and clasped his hands together in satisfaction. Beatrice gazed at him in amusement. Such a wonderful-looking man, all sharp planes and dark features, rather like Montgomery Clift. Yet his mannerisms reminded her of no one more than Ronnie Corbett.

She assumed a serious face. "You think like a detective, Adrian. I've been wondering the same thing. But all is not lost. We can test your theory. I downloaded the pictures onto my laptop before we went to bed that night."

His mouth opened, his eyes widened and he broke into a triumphant grin.

"Beatrice! I always forget your training. You are a star! Let's check them now, I have a programme downstairs for refining images and we can find exactly what it was they were trying to hide."

"I've already looked. I can't see anything. But who knows, perhaps your whizzy technology might shed some light. There might be something, I suppose. Look, let's do it tomorrow. I'll bring them down on a memory stick. However, tonight you have Gay Men's Chorus and you're going to be late. And I have to familiarise myself with a flasher."

He glanced at his watch, torn. "OK. Any other day, I'd give it a miss for something so thrilling. But *Oklahomo!* opens on Saturday and tonight is a key rehearsal for the soloists. I have to go. But tomorrow evening, we're gonna uncover the shady plot behind all this. I'm riding piggyback as your rookie, but don't worry, boss, I know when to button it."

Adrian's accent was woeful. Beatrice hoped his Midwest cowpoke was better than his Detroit dick.

"Thanks, Cagney."

His face dropped. "I was aiming more for Jimmy Stewart than Jimmy Cagney."

She picked up his coat and kissed him on the cheek. "And I was aiming more for Cagney as opposed to Lacey."

Adrian gave her a radiant smile. "That changes everything!"

"Have a great rehearsal and thank you for the wine. By the way, you smell gorgeous. Don't worry about the shower."

He shook his head with a devilish grin. "I always shower. Because, Beatrice, you never know what might happen. Night, night."

"Goodnight, Adrian." Gratified by his interest but relieved that he had been successfully deflected, she closed the door.

After refilling her glass, she resigned herself to spending the evening with a dirty old man. She'd probably need a shower herself. Maybe just a quick call first.

Chapter 5

"Inspector Howells, how can I help you?"

"Good evening, Inspector. DI Beatrice Stubbs here, from the Met. We spoke at the weekend, if you remember."

"Oh yes. I remember. The bag-snatching and the break-in. Has something new come to light, Detective Inspector?"

"No, nothing new at this end. I was just calling to see if you have managed to make any headway with this case. Hear your latest report, as it were."

No response.

"Inspector Howells? Are you still there?"

"If you mean am I still at work, then no, I'm not. It's almost eight o'clock in the evening. I'm at home and about to have my tea. As I told you on Sunday, I will call you if we find anything to connect the events in question. Until then, there is no case, and there will be no reports. DI Stubbs, you were involved in two separate incidents this weekend. I have no doubt you feel a personal involvement, but I don't make a habit of calling witnesses to keep them updated with my enquiries. Regardless of their position."

Warmth flared in Beatrice's cheeks.

"I apologise for disturbing you. However, I would describe myself as a victim of two connected crimes, rather than a witness to two separate incidents. I don't think you will find anything more about the two events by treating them as unconnected petty crimes. You said yourself, the thief, or thieves, wanted the contents of that camera. Therefore, as I mentioned, regular surveillance of the beach might well throw up something more concrete. I'd strongly recommend a proactive approach in this situation, Inspector."

"Thank you for the advice. The likes of us bumpkins are eternally grateful. Now, if it's all the same to you, I'd like to eat. Goodnight, DI Stubbs. And next time, I'll call you."

Beatrice stomped into the kitchen, opened the fridge and closed it again. She walked back to the living-room, picked up the phone and put it down again. Pacing around the flat, she wrestled with her indignation.

It was grossly unfair to assume she was interfering. As the victim of two robberies in twenty-four hours, she had a right to know where the investigation was heading. Howells was out of line speaking to her like that. All she wanted was information.

She pressed her forehead to the window and fumed. The bustle of Boot Street went unnoticed as she rewound the conversation. Of course, she understood that persistence on the part of those affected by crime could be an annoyance. And she might have been wiser to call him at the station than at home. But to dismiss her as a supercilious busybody was quite intolerable. It wasn't as if she was trying to teach the man his job.

I'd recommend a proactive approach in this situation.

She picked up the phone again, dithered and finally pressed speed dial one.

"Good evening. This is Professor Bailey."

"Matthew, do you think of me as patronising? An interfering old biddy? Am I unreasonably demanding in my curiosity?"

"Well, this is merely my subjective opinion, you realise. But I'd say generally no to the first, absolutely not to the second and quite possibly to the third. However, the answers will very much depend on who you're asking. What's up, Old Thing? Have you upset someone?"

"No. Yes. I don't know. But that police inspector in Wales was very short with me this evening and said that next time, he'd call me."

"There you are then. Don't call him again and let those people do their job."

"That's all very well for you to say. What if they aren't doing it properly? They should have people watching that beach every morning. It's obvious something untoward is happening. Why won't he take it seriously?"

She could hear Matthew stretch and yawn. "If a police detective from, let's say New York, was in London for the weekend, reported a crime and then called you daily for an update, how would you feel?"

"That's not very supportive of you."

"But you see my point? Leave them alone to get on with it. You have enough on your plate with knife crime."

Beatrice's mood sank still lower. "No, knives are no longer on my plate. Instead, I'm working with British Transport Police on apprehending a flasher. And my partner on this one will be none other than the man-eating Virginia Lowe. I tell you, I'm dreading every minute of this, especially when I could be in South Wales or Lewisham, assisting with serious and worthwhile investigations."

"A flasher? I thought they'd rather fallen out of fashion. Isn't it all stalking and cyber-porn these days? And I feel sure the Welsh police have their investigation under control. From what I saw, they're keen, young and enthusiastic. You get on with your job and leave them to theirs."

"Doesn't seem like I have a choice, does it? That inspector has some sort of regional inferiority complex, in my opinion. Anyway, as far as I've gathered, the flasher is also a stalker and may well have a penchant for cyber-porn. I really ought to knuckle down to this case file. See? I called you to soothe my conscience but now feel doubly guilty."

"Marvellous! So pleased to have been of assistance. Now, I

should begin chopping my stir-fry and put the rice on. And you should focus on the task in hand. Goodnight, Old Thing. I'll call you tomorrow to hear about your first day."

Beatrice said goodnight, made a herbal tea and returned to the folder, still vaguely indignant.

Keen, young and enthusiastic was all very well, but no substitute for experience.

Chapter 6

"No horror movies tonight, you said. Well, that was the most horrific thing I've ever seen. I feel a small part of my life was wasted ..."

Laure caught Ayako's eye and grinned; there was no stopping Urtza declaiming her opinions, positive or negative. Ayako hugged her knees and laughed. Small, tinkly noises came from both her mouth and her clothes. Urtza paced the two metres of the lounge, throwing an exasperated arm at the television as she ranted. Laure's flat always seemed smaller with Urtza in it.

It was four minutes past ten.

" ... a terrible waste of all that talent! That is the real shame. Cheap, and a copycat. That makes it worse! If you do such a rip-off, you choose a brilliant movie. *Love, Actually* is not a brilliant movie, it is average. And a lot of the writing is very bad. *Love, Actually* was saved by the actors. Here, the acting ..."

"Come on, Urtza," Laure interrupted. "Eric Dane was amazing. And Jessica Biel surprised me."

Urtza stopped her pacing, glared at the two on the sofa and placed her hands on her hips.

"Laure. Oh Laure. Are we going to have the same argument again? Beauty does not equal talent. There was much beauty in *Valentine's Day*, but as for talent? Ayako, don't tell me you agree with her?"

Tiny Ayako, with her asymmetric bob, abundant hair-grips

and predilection for pink, nestled further into the cushions. Her knee-high socks were striped pink and purple, and white tights kept her thighs decent below the frilled micro-skirt. She leant her head onto one side and widened her eyes.

"I liked it. Fun and pretty to watch. Not every movie has to be art, Urtza. And what did you expect? It's called *Valentine's Day*, not *Valentine's Day Massacre*." She was already giggling at Urtza's outraged expression.

The pairing of these two inevitably drew attention and Laure still wondered what drove their friendship. Urtza, size 18, voluble, passionate, committed to classic black and silver jewellery. Ayako, size 6, shy, precise, almost hidden under multi-coloured Harajuku layers and childish accessories. They now shared a flat in Highbury, spending all their free time shopping in Camden Market or watching movies and disagreeing.

"Even now, after I know you for over a year, you still shock me, Ayako. 'Fun and pretty to watch?' This is the opinion of a teenager."

Ayako's piping laugh rang around the cluttered room. "I *am* a teenager! And so are you, but secretly, you want to be middle-aged."

Urtza attempted to take outrage to an operatic level, but the effect was too comic. Even she succumbed to laughter and deflated onto the sofa between them. Laure laughed and laughed and forced herself to keep laughing longer than felt natural. Laughing was good.

It was twenty past ten.

In a way, the closeness between the three would not have happened anywhere else. In London, she was free to choose, making friends on the basis of shared interests, and personality. So what if they were a quirky Japanese girl with startling dress sense, and a large, loud Spaniard with a natural theatricality. Both enjoyed cinema, food and markets, therefore they were the perfect people to be her friends. In Lille, Laure had a close circle of well-dressed, well-read and understated associates, assembled on the basis of education and family connections. Nearly all were blonde. Introducing them to Ayako and Urtza was unthinkable. Laure started laughing again.

Urtza emptied her glass and Laure reached for the wine bottle. Mouth full, Urtza placed her hand over her glass and shook her head.

Ayako heaved up her bag. So adorned with baubles and trinkets, it was practically a percussion instrument. "Yeah, we should be going, Laure. Thanks so much for the dinner. You are a fantastic cooker. And I enjoyed the movie, even if she didn't."

Panic began to rise.

"Listen, Ayako, Urtza, thank you so much for coming over. It is impossible for me to say how much ... it's wonderful for me, you know, just ... just not thinking."

Urtza opened her arms in a dramatic embrace. The scent of cigarettes, Narciso Rodriguez and sweat made Laure tearful, as her cheek pressed against Urtza's décolletage.

Ayako's childlike hand stroked her shoulder. "Laure, we will come again tomorrow. We will come every night until you are ready to go out. We are your friends." Her sweet voice was accompanied by the miniature bells on her white leather jacket.

Laure swallowed and stopped the flood. "Thank you. You two are very kind to me. OK, you should go. You need to catch the bus. See you both tomorrow. Safe journey!"

It was half past ten exactly.

She watched them down the stairs, listened to the tinkling and heard the front door close. Then she locked and bolted the door. For the fifteenth time that day, she wondered how she could find herself a flatmate, a friendship just like theirs, without exposing herself to any more psychos.

Picking up the rest of her drink, she moved to the window and watched Ayako walk away from the block of flats. Tears filled Laure's eyes. Again. If only they could stay. The doll-like figure stopped to pick something from the path. Where was Urtza? Ayako turned, showing something to the darkness. A hand came out of the black and took the object. Urtza's colouring and camouflage would make her a perfect cat burglar. Laure smiled at the thought. Ayako was laughing and Laure wished she could hear it. Six floors up and double-glazed, there was no chance of that.

Ayako stepped into the street, her colours turning acidic under the sodium light. Laure could just make out Urtza, still in the shadow of the hedge, lifting the lid of a wheelie-bin. What had they found? She would check on the way to school tomorrow.

Across the street, a shape moved. Laure recognised it, dismissed it as an overreaction and acknowledged she was right, all in under a second. In a reflex, she clenched her hands. The TK-Maxx glass shattered, pain and liquid registering somewhere, as her eyes strained to see the street.

Crossing the road with a clear purpose, he approached Ayako. Blood and wine stained the pane as Laure struggled to open the double-locked window catch. Not enough time. She began beating on the glass, screaming three syllables, blurring her view of the scene with tears and blood.

Laure watched as he said something to Ayako. Where was Urtza, where the hell was Urtza? That was when he opened his coat. Ayako recoiled from his jerking body, horribly close to her. Almost touching. Oh God, if he got off, it would hit her.

Six floors up and double-glazed, but she could hear Ayako's scream; it mingled with her own. Their harmony developed a bass tone – a roar. His jerking body sprang backwards as a black mass barrelled its way out of the gate, arms flailing. Urtza missed him and whirled to grab his coat, but he'd already begun to run. She charged after him, shouting curses in Spanish, and Laure realised he might get away.

Again.

Dialling 999 left-handed on her mobile, she unlocked the door with her bloodied right, and tore down the stairs to Ayako.

Him. Outside her house. Waiting. He knew where she lived.

No horror movies tonight, she'd said.

Chapter 7

Wednesday morning, and the weather refused to chime with Beatrice's mood. Her rush hour journey on the Northern Line, including a change at Bank, compounded her sour sense of resentment at the injustices of this world. Yet as she ascended from St James's Park station, strangers smiled, glorious sunshine lit the streets and it took a real effort to hang on to her black cloud.

She was early, so sat in the window of Prêt-a-Manger and drank an excess of coffee. Her eyes absorbed the human traffic – short sleeves and summer dresses, sandals and exposed skin, sunglasses and already-sweaty shirts – but her mind was picking away at a problem like a child at a scab.

Assuming the rat-faced man with the terrible hair was either the same person as the mugger, or a close associate, he was determined to get those Pembroke beach photographs. Surely, he'd achieved his wish. His first attempt at retrieving them, with snatch and grab, had failed, so he came back at night. Having successfully taken possession of the camera, he was free to destroy anything incriminating. He couldn't possibly know she'd already downloaded the contents, so that was the end of the story. Yet a low-level discomfort came from the awareness that the thief had pictures of her and Matthew on the beach, of Matthew's family, of Matthew's work. Nothing revealing in those shots, so it shouldn't make any difference. But she couldn't shake the feeling that it did.

Five to nine. She should shift herself. Draining the coffee, she hurried towards the TfL building on Broadway, hoping it was Hamilton who'd insisted on nine a.m. sharp. She really didn't want to be late. Partly due to politeness, but mainly because she wanted to retain the moral high ground. It's hard to look down on someone when you have to start with an apology.

She waited for seventeen minutes in reception before a large fair man approached with a crew-cut and a grin. Beatrice guessed he played contact sports.

"DI Stubbs, nice to meet you. I'm Sergeant Ty Grant."

They shook hands and he gestured up the corridor. Tie? What kind of a name was that? And his hands were sweaty.

He glanced back. "Have to apologise for Virginia. Several incidents overnight added to the morning briefing. Result? Total overrun. She's down as soon as. Get you a coffee?"

Beatrice picked up her bag, her irritation at boiling point. Was he incapable of speaking in full sentences?

"Thank you, but I won't just now. I reached my caffeine limit half an hour ago. Do you have any idea how long DI Lowe might be?"

His security badge unlocked a door to an open-plan room, filled with messy desks and people staring at computers. No one looked up. Grant indicated Virginia Lowe's office at the end and lifted his substantial shoulders.

"Five? Ten? Why don't you park yourself? She'll be as quick as poss. Sure you don't want anything? Just get myself an espresso. Back in a flash."

What a well-chosen expression.

Evidently an insensitive fool who could only converse in txt-spk. One ought not to judge on appearances, but he looked just the type to suffer from foot-in-mouth.

This was altogether a very poor start. Beatrice withdrew her case notes, pulled out a pen and practised variations on a displeased expression. Her eyes scanned the display board to her right, taking in the map, featuring locations of the women who'd reported incidents, and the identikit image of this shadowy lurker which gave them precious little. He looked like 'some bloke'. Her annoyance diminished and her interest grew.

Who is he? What on earth makes these vile men expose their genitalia to strangers? Why do that to solitary females in darkened pockets of the city? They must know how they frighten their victims, how they instil a fear of the streets in these poor women. Throwing an ugly shadow over their lives, for what? What possible satisfaction could this filthy little toe-rag get from rubbing himself in front of barely-awake cleaners, harassed teachers, foreign students and coffee-shop workers, whose lives were hard enough? Beatrice tried to imagine the sexual frustration behind the act. The man deliberately picks on the vulnerable, those whose resources are low. He knows. None of the recipients of his performance have been strong, confident women who might laugh in his face, give chase or fight back. He is an awkward individual, with a conviction that he must be seen, even if he has to force it. Weak and ignored in his everyday life, he finds another way of raising his profile.

The door burst open, making Beatrice jump. The tall woman reaching for her hand looked completely unfamiliar. Short peroxide spikes, a white shirt-dress and court shoes reminded Beatrice of the 1980s for the second time in a week.

"Beatrice! You've been waiting ages. I am so sorry!"

"Virginia Lowe?"

"Yep, that's me. We have met before. You don't remember?" she asked, in evident disbelief.

"Of course I remember. But I wouldn't have recognised you."

"Oh, the hair! Yes, I had the Veronica Lake stuff hacked off two years ago. Going grey, you see. So bleach and hair gel are back in my bathroom cabinet, after an absence of twenty years. Did no one get you a coffee?"

"Everyone offered, but I've had quite enough, thank you."

Virginia sat opposite and looked directly at Beatrice. She'd aged a little since their last meeting; her face was somewhat fuller and noticeable lines scored her forehead, yet she still made quite an impact. Her blue eyes were sincere.

"Of course. You've been waiting half an hour. Apologies. We had an extended briefing this morning. Amongst other things, it looks like our flashing friend has been at it again. Look, Beatrice, this is a shitty way to start and I'm sorry I kept you waiting. Honestly, it wasn't deliberate. So, let's waste no more time and get down to business."

Her open approach spiked Beatrice's hostile guns. "Fair enough. I know how these things are. But I admit I'm impatient to get started."

"Me too. As it stands, this is a preventative exercise. There's a serious danger of it becoming a sex offence if we don't move quickly. He took one step closer last night ..."

The door opened and the rugby player returned.

"You're here! Brought you a coffee. DI Stubbs didn't want anything. Can I do anything else for you, ladies?"

Beatrice watched the transformation in awe. Virginia's movements became languid and slow and she looked sideways at him. Her voice dropped as she held out her hand for the paper cup with a lip-parted smile. "That's very sweet of you, Ty. But I think Beatrice and I are just fine for now."

The look that passed between the beefy suit and his boss made Beatrice thoroughly uncomfortable. She recalled the same feeling in a hotel room once, when flicking through TV channels, she'd stumbled upon something involving moans, slapping flesh and pinkish close-ups.

The lump retreated with an expression just short of a leer. Beatrice's hackles rose. But after the door closed, Virginia snapped back to business like an elastic band.

"The file I gave Hamilton contains all the details on incidents so far. But last night, we think he did it again. Apparently, a student at the international school in Lennox Road was approached by a man who told her he'd been mugged. She offered to help and asked what had been stolen. His cue, naturally. 'They took all my clothes!' He opened his coat and began masturbating. The girl screamed and her friend, who was still some way behind, took off after him. She didn't even get close, but it must have given him a fright. Two real concerns result from this. One – this is the first time he's tried it with more than one person. Bad sign. Two – they were leaving a friend's place."

"And why's that another bad sign?" Beatrice asked.

The white-blonde head bent to check the files. "Their friend, Laure Marchant, was the third person to report an incident. Last night's victims were visiting her flat – she's a student at the same school. Or at least she was. After what happened yesterday, she's decided to go back to France. He seems to be following certain women, exposing himself more than once to the same person, or their friends and relatives. He's not just a flasher, he's a stalker, and that leads us to the conclusion that sooner or later, he'll go that much further."

"Is that how it works?"

"Not always. But repeat offenders are more likely to assault or attempt to rape. This guy's following the pattern as if he's read the manual."

Beatrice turned and considered the map. "Lennox Road. A hop and a skip from Finsbury Park station, as the stone flies. He's not too adventurous, is he?"

Virginia shook her head, slugged some coffee and moved to the meeting table and display board.

"No, he's not. On the mapped area, the red dots signify incidents. Nearly all these happened on the park side of the railway tracks, but Marchant's experience, and that of her colleagues last night, took place the other side. So I need to add one."

As she bent over her desk to retrieve her stickers, Beatrice noticed that Virginia's white shirt-dress was made of linen, rendering her underwear clearly visible through the fabric. So clearly that Beatrice saw she favoured those cut-away pants which looked terribly uncomfortable. Surely she must realise that white knickers would show through her dress. Why hadn't she chosen flesh-coloured? It would be nothing short of churlish to imagine she had done it on purpose.

Virginia stuck the dot onto the map. "Just here. So this pattern tells us he probably lives somewhere between the park and the reservoirs and definitely close to the Tube."

"And not once has he appeared on CCTV?"

"Nope, he's not daft. I've got Fitch scanning the Lennox Road data as we speak, but so far this guy's thought it through and made damn sure he's not on camera."

"What about the victims? Is there any connection that might hint at how he selects them?" Beatrice asked.

"I can't see anything, but maybe two heads are better than one. Want to go through the notes together?"

"I think we should."

They sat side by side at the table and spread the files. Virginia smelt of flowery perfume, and strong coffee. Her nails were perfectly manicured, with long white tips. Beatrice wondered how she managed to type.

"The likelihood is that we know less than half of it." Virginia leant her face on her hand as she stared at the paperwork, her expression disconsolate.

"I thought that too. It stands to reason that if the number of unreported rapes is huge, those who simply dismiss a flasher must be far greater."

"And we've all dismissed a flasher, right? I know I have. We're receiving a noticeable number of reports, which means he's doing more than a noticeable amount of harassment."

With a mixture of gratitude and a small sense of exclusion, Beatrice realised she'd never been flashed. She opened the details of the first incident.

"Right, it's time we put a stop to that."

The bar was already busy with civil servants and off-duty officers as Beatrice pushed open the door of The Speaker. To her relief, Dawn had bagged a table by the window, where late afternoon sunshine spotlit two large glasses of white wine.

"A sight for sore eyes!" Beatrice said, tucking her laptop bag under the table.

Dawn smiled and handed her a glass. "Cheers."

"Cheers." Beatrice took a sip. "That hits the spot. Thank you."

"Thank you for meeting me. I told you I'd be a pain in the arse till I settle in."

Beatrice maintained the pretence that the rendezvous was work-related. "Not at all. As I said on the phone, you can pick my brains whenever you feel the need."

Dawn gave her a sheepish look. "Tell the truth, I'm more curious about how you got on, working with that predator."

"I'd never have guessed," Beatrice laughed. "Actually, it wasn't too bad. She's like a split personality. Focused, intelligent and professional, unless there's a man in the room. Is there such a condition as a pathological flirt?"

"She's always been that way, apparently. But I heard she turned forty last year, and she recently got married. That's had no effect?"

"Not so as you'd notice. Colleagues, senior officers, the chap serving pizza in the canteen, she can't seem to help herself. And they all seem to lap it up."

"I'm sure they do." Dawn tore a corner off her beer mat.

An odd need to justify her new colleague prodded Beatrice.

"Maybe it's her way of coping. We all have strategies for working in a male-dominated environment. Ice queen, one-of-the-lads, ball-breaker, girlie-girl ... Jessica Rabbit could be Virginia's work persona."

"I wouldn't mind betting she's a rabbit in her free time as well. How about the case?"

"It's a pre-empt. We have to catch him before he goes any

further, which will provide some excellent marketing both for us and them. May even earn us a Tilley Award for crime prevention. "

Dawn lifted her eyes from the shredded bar mat. "Super. We all know how Virginia enjoys her award ceremonies."

"You have a grim sense of humour, DI Whittaker. Tell me what happened today on knife crime."

On her way back from the toilet, Beatrice glanced at her watch. By the time she got home, it would be almost eight and Adrian would be impatient. She ought to get her skates on. She shoved her way through the crowded bar and back to their table. Dawn was gazing out the window with a vague smile.

"What's tickled you?" Still standing, Beatrice drained her glass.

"Just feeling my age – observing the latest trend in haircuts – what *do* they think they look like?

"Reminds me, I have a story to tell you. But right now, I must make a move. I'll buy you a drink on Thursday. Good luck with surveillance tomorrow." She hooked her handbag onto her shoulder and reached under the table for her laptop case.

"Thanks. It'll be a long, boring day, full of Cooper's bullshit and ... Beatrice? What's the matter?"

"My computer. It's not here."

It took a thorough search, an appeal to the bar staff and a check that none of their neighbours had made an innocent mistake before Beatrice faced facts. From the pub well known as the watering-hole of the Metropolitan Police, from under the feet of two senior detectives, someone had stolen her laptop.

Chapter 8

Amber was still talking. Zahra pressed the button on the pelican crossing, hitched her bag higher on her shoulder and listened. It wasn't as if she had a choice.

"... asks me if I'll miss her. So I'm like, I guess so. And she says, is that it? So I'm like, yeah, pretty much. And she goes all quiet and walks off. I mean, whatever."

"She gets like that." The beeps signalled they were safe to cross. Zahra kept an eye out for speeding cyclists. "She'll be back to normal by next week."

Crossing Green Lanes without incident, they headed for the river. Almost home, and tonight Dad was doing a barbeque. Zahra picked up her pace.

Amber was still talking. "Don't care if she is or she isn't. I mean, what is she like? Does she want me crying my eyes out and begging her not to go? As if. I mean, yeah, I'll miss her, but life goes on, and anyway, it's not like we're not linked up. We so totally are."

Turning onto the river path, they left the noise of the traffic behind. Green verges, daisies and dandelions. You could almost imagine it was the countryside. Nearly home. The only cloud on the horizon was Amber. Her friend's bitching could really ruin a good day.

Zahra switched subjects. "Aren't you getting nervous about the show? I think I'm the nervousest I've ever been about anything in my whole entire life. But it's the first time in my whole entire life I've ever had a solo."

"When you've had a few solos, you don't get nervous anymore. You know what? Miss Rice told me I shouldn't be over-confident. She said a few nerves are good for you. And I thought to myself, what would you know? I mean, if she was any good as a dancer, she'd be doing it. Not teaching it. She gets on my nerves, always going on about her performances. Like, living on past glories, know what I mean?"

The sun sank below the houses and long shadows stretched across the river. The water, sparkly and fresh in sunshine, revealed itself as dark and filthy, littered with beer cans, polystyrene and a floating nappy.

"And anyway, when you've rehearsed as much as we have?" Amber went on. "Like. Every. Single. Day? We should be confident. You know what I mean? I'm full of it, I really am. God, I hope you're not gonna get stage fright, Zahra. That would be SO embarrassing."

Her words stung. "Of course I won't. I am totally going to give my best performance ever. If I do mega well, my parents might just think about letting me go to stage school."

"Stage school! You're so funny. Whatever. I'm giving it everything I've got in case there are any casting agents in the audience. Most def. I mean, next year I'll be fourteen, and I need to make choices about my career direction."

They turned the bend in the path. Halfway along the next stretch, a man crouched, looking at the ground.

"Victoria Beckham went to stage school," Zahra replied, kicking a stone into the water.

"Victoria Beckham also did every audition going. You don't get anywhere without ambition, Zahra. What's that bloke doing?"

Zahra looked up. The man peered at the grass and made little kissy noises. He seemed searching for something, although any kind of animal he hoped to find along the canal was bound to be rank. He wore a big black coat which was well tatty; his legs were bare apart from some even tattier trainers and he had a baseball cap pulled down low. As the girls approached, he stood up.

"Hello, girls. I don't suppose you've seen a ferret along here? I've lost Ginny, my little furry friend."

Zahra didn't want to speak to the bloke. Amber obviously wasn't bothered.

"A ferret? No. What are you doing out here with a ferret anyway?"

"She comes with me when I go fishing. She normally sleeps round my neck, but she's wandered off and I can't find her. I'm getting a bit worried. It'll be dark soon."

His words acted as a trigger for Zahra. "Hope you find her. We have to get home. Bye."

Amber didn't move.

"Am-ber!" She spoke through clenched teeth and boggled her eyes.

"Zah-ra!" Amber mimicked her. "Let's help the guy look for his ferret. We're doing a good deed."

"No. Ferrets bite. And I want to go home."

"This one's tame, love. Had her four years and not so much as a nip."

Zahra didn't look at him. "Amber, I'm going. Come on!"

"Bye then." Amber put her bag on the path and began looking along the verges. The man joined her, making the kissy noises again. Zahra's frustration built. She should just go. It would teach her a lesson. But she couldn't and it wouldn't. Leave her friend by the river, with some weirdo? No way. But she wasn't helping them look for any crappy ferret.

The smell of a barbeque wafted across from the back gardens on the opposite bank. Zahra heard voices, laughter. She was hungry. She wanted to go home. The ferret-friends moved further away from her. Amber was still talking, firing questions at him about the colour, housing arrangements and eating habits of the animal. Zahra frowned. Why did he need that long black coat? If it was warm enough to wear shorts, why did he need a massive great coat over the top? Where was his fishing stuff? He should have a rod, and bait and that. And what did he expect to catch in New River? A nappy? The man stood up.

"Well, thanks for the help, but I think she's lost." He put his hands in his pockets and burst into a laugh. "I don't believe it! Here she is! She was curled up asleep in my pocket all the time!"

Amber's face broke into a curious grin. "And you didn't notice?"

"She's so light. Put your hand in and you can feel. You can stroke her." He gestured to his coat. There was something funny about his eyes.

Zahra's whole body flooded with fear. "No! Amber, no!"

Amber glared back at her. "Zahra! Who died and made you boss of me?" She approached the man, who was smiling and holding open his pocket.

"She's all warm and furry," he said. "Come and feel. She won't bite."

Amber hesitated. Blood pounded in Zahra's chest. She rushed forward and snatched at Amber's arm. "We're going. Now!"

The man's voice changed. "I don't think so."

Shoving Zahra away, he caught Amber's wrist and tried to force her hand into his pocket.

In her family, Zahra was known as The Screamer. When she was only eighteen months old, her shrill shriek could force both her brothers to flee the room, hands over their ears. At thirteen, her voice was louder, lasted longer and could shatter glass. Landing on her backside beside the river, she let rip.

The sound stopped the man for a second, before he tore open his coat and forced Amber's hand into his groin. Underneath the coat, he wore a sweatshirt and nothing else. Zahra's pitch went up.

"Oi!"

On the opposite bank, a man's blond head appeared over a

garden wall. Ferret-man jumped, released Amber and ran back in the direction of Green Lanes. The blond man climbed over the wall, shouting to people behind him. Amber collapsed, sobbing, cradling her arm, but holding her hand at a distance.

Zahra was still screaming.

Chapter 9

As she slammed the front door, Beatrice heard Adrian's voice coming from his flat.

"About time! I was beginning to think you'd forgotten. Now I hope you haven't eaten, because I've done chicken cacciatore and opened a red to die for." He appeared in the doorway, wearing a Breton-style striped top with black jeans. He rested his hands on his hips and noticed her expression. "Oh Lord. What's happened now?"

"Some bastard nicked my laptop."

Adrian clapped his palms to his cheeks and his jaw dropped. All he needed was a bit of white panstick and he could have passed for a French mime.

"Not the one with the photos on it?"

"I only have one laptop. And it's police property. The infuriating thing is that whoever stole it cannot possibly use it. It has a security lockdown and will destroy all the data before allowing unauthorised entry."

"But if all you wanted was to get rid of any images that might be on there, that fact wouldn't bother you. This cannot be coincidence, Beatrice. Someone wanted to make sure any trace of those pictures disappeared."

"Yes, I had actually realised that much."

"See, we should have looked at them last night. We've lost them now." His voice was reproachful.

"Wrong. I told you I'd put them on a memory stick to bring down with me tonight. Which I did. I'll go and fetch it. I'll be a few minutes, mind, I have to call Matthew to check he's OK."

The chicken was sublime. Rich tomato sauce with garlic and oregano, a generous splash of wine and green peppers at the crunchy stage blended perfectly with the delicate meat. Accompanied by a glass of Portuguese Dão, the meal and the company combined to make Beatrice's noxious mood recede.

"Whoever stole the laptop was determined to destroy those images, you know. Therefore you should count yourself lucky it was just taken from the pub." Adrian pointed at her with his fork.

"Yes, you're right. But it's so bloody embarrassing, on top of everything else."

"At least he's convinced that he's got the pictures now. So he'll leave you alone." He topped up her glass.

"Don't make gender assumptions. Lazy police work. But what I don't understand is how they knew those photos were on my machine. I can see how they might get my address – all the identification I possess was in my handbag. God knows, they could have taken impressions of my keys and all sorts. Copied my driving licence, noted my address. I must change the locks and use the safety chain. But how did they know I'd already downloaded the pictures?"

"The only person you've seen so far was male, so there's nothing lazy about that assumption. If he was watching the house, waiting for you to go to bed, he could have seen you. It's the countryside. You can creep up to a house and even from quite a distance, you'd see if someone was looking at a screen." Adrian shuddered.

Beatrice rolled her eyes. "And he followed me all the way to London, to work and to the pub to get those photographs?"

"Looks that way. Is Matthew all right?"

"I don't know. He wasn't home. I'll call again in a minute."

She put down her cutlery, her stomach acidic. She felt a powerful urge to go upstairs, to be alone, but couldn't be so rude.

"Let's check the pictures."

As Adrian set up the program, Beatrice looked out of the window and worried. It really was time Matthew got himself a mobile. Stubborn old Luddite. It was no longer charmingly eccentric, it was a bloody nuisance. She would talk to his daughters; Tanya and Marianne could be forcefully persuasive.

"Beatrice? Most of these photos are of some child."

"That's Luke, Matthew's grandson. The beach ones will be at the end."

"Thank you, I worked that out for myself. But there are only two of you on the beach."

Beatrice felt a guilty twinge. "I deleted a few. I didn't look my best."

"Those were also on the beach?"

"Yes, exactly like the others. I didn't move, just let Matthew snap away."

"The only thing in the background is cliff."

Her mobile rang. Matthew. She sighed into the handset. "Good timing. I called you about half an hour ago and I was just starting to worry. Did you work late?"

"No. Marianne and I attended an exhibition. Queerest thing. This artist friend of hers has some sort of disease and makes pictures out of her own dead skin."

"How disturbing. Is everything else all right?"

"Absolutely. How's your hip?" His voice sounded relaxed and believable. But she knew he was practised at disguising his concerns when he didn't want to worry her.

"Fine. Itches like buggery, which is a sure sign it's healing. So no problems at your end?" Beatrice was ashamed of her unsubtle probing.

"Nothing to speak of. I just called your flat. Why aren't you at home? And how was your first day with the Man-Eater?"

"Productive. She's an interesting individual, but still a

complete carnivore. I'm downstairs having dinner with Adrian. Chicken cacciatore with a spectacular Portuguese red."

"I'm furiously jealous. Mainly because of the wine. Did you thank him for that Toro Termes? What's his view on the Amarone?"

"Yes, I did. I haven't asked yet. But all is calm at home?"

"Of course. Why wouldn't it be? Are you all right, Old Thing? You sound a bit off. And you don't normally call on consecutive nights."

"No, but neither do we normally get mugged and robbed in one weekend. I'm perfectly well. Just checking up on you. Right, I'd better neglect my host no longer. I shall call you again tomorrow, whether you like it or not."

"I like it. It's unusual for you to make a fuss. I adore the attention. Give my best to Adrian and wish him luck with Saturday's Cowboy Camp. Have a good week, my love."

"You too. Bye-bye."

Adrian did not look up from the screen as she joined him.

"Matthew said to thank you for the Spanish red. We had it with marinated kebabs."

"My pleasure. And when you next speak, do thank him for the Alsace Pinot Blanc. He was right about the asparagus. I'm saving the Amarone for the right occasion."

"Whilst we're on the subject, you two can stop sending each other bottles via me. I feel like a wine mule. Have we found anything yet?"

"I'm still refining." He hesitated. "Beatrice, this is none of my business, but I'd say there was an omission in that conversation."

"You're quite right. It is absolutely none of your business."

"If someone I loved was robbed, especially for the third time in a week, I'd want to know about it."

Stress levels and insecurities unnaturally high, Beatrice was in no mood to be lectured. Her patience snapped. "Firstly, that's how *you* feel. It has no bearing here. Secondly, Matthew lives in Devon. The only thing he can do at that distance is worry. Thirdly, I will tell him next weekend, when I can look him in the eyes and reassure him. And explain to him how, thanks to my protective, concerned and slightly interfering downstairs neighbour, I feel safe as trousers."

Adrian clicked the mouse and turned to face her. "It's finished. I'm sorry. Seriously, I am. I really should keep my nose out and I apologise. I think we just had our first row. Perhaps we should have a toast?"

"Hardly a row. Yes, we probably should. Cheers. I'm very grateful to you."

"Cheers. I'm happy to help. Makes me feel useful. Shall we look?"

Nothing.

In the background: rocks, cliff, and sand.

In the foreground: Beatrice, looking every bit as grim as she remembered. She replayed the beach scene in her mind. Sunrise, seagulls, rushing waves, sandy toes, wind and wild hair. She shook her head and looked at Adrian.

"I'm being particularly dense. Of course it's not on the camera. I took a couple of pictures of him from the opposite direction, on my phone."

Adrian's eyes widened and he rubbed his hands together. "Come, detective, we have work to do."

"Yes, you're right. But do you think we could do all the refining business tomorrow? I'm awfully tired and there's really no rush."

"Up to you. At least let me download the pictures so I can make a start."

Beatrice fetched her handbag. "You see, there's no way I can deal with this while working the London Transport thing. I need to get back to the Met. What I have to do is get upstairs, boot up my old computer and write a report which will get me off this flasher. Maybe then I can concentrate on suspicious happenings on a Welsh beach. Tomorrow is going to be another difficult day."

"And tomorrow is going to be another exciting evening. I'll have everything ready for you and by bedtime we'll have hammered out a theory. I'll cook."

"No, you won't. And nor will I. But I'll pick up something suitably sophisticated for us on the way home."

Adrian raised his eyebrows. "I know your definition of sophisticated. But what the hell, it's been ages since I had fish and chips. Please may I have your mobile now?"

Beatrice sighed and handed it over. "You have all the qualities of an excellent police officer. Tenacity, enthusiasm and bloody-mindedness. Have you never thought about joining the force?"

Adrian was busy umbilically attaching the phone to the computer, but gave her a superior smile.

"I know it's a gay cliché to fancy men in uniform, but it's just not me. The outfit puts me right off, especially with all those accessories. Do you want to check there are no embarrassing shots before I download?"

"No, go ahead. When taking embarrassing shots, I prefer a camera. What do you mean by accessories?"

"Hmm? Oh, you know, handcuffs, truncheons, great ugly walkie-talkies. I couldn't be seen in public dressed like that. Imagine if someone saw me! I'd feel like a low-rent strip-o-gram and never go out again. There! All done."

Shaking her head and smiling, Beatrice took her phone, thanked him for dinner and trudged up the stairs, humming *Dedicated Follower of Fashion*. As she unlocked the front door, her mobile rang.

"Hello Virginia?"

"Hi Beatrice, sorry to disturb you so late, but I thought you'd like to know. He's done it again."

Adrian sipped at his Dão and brought the screen back to life with a touch of the mouse. Matthew's hair looked absurd. But much more importantly, the background contained more than beach, cliffs and gulls. A boat.

He zoomed in. Despite the poor definition, he could determine that the boat was dark blue, and the two figures heading up the beach were dressed in black. Both carried some sort of package. It reminded him of something. He zoomed again, but the quality was too poor to make anything out. He clicked on the second shot.

The detail behind Matthew's clownish coiffure revealed the two disembarkers heading towards a solitary figure, standing up the beach. The wind had messed with her hair too, whipping it into a streamer behind her. No features were discernible, but it was unquestionably a female. This was evidence!

Adrian clasped his hands together and glanced at the phone. Beatrice had been fidgety, stressed and tense all evening. Instinct told him she would not be pleased to have him disturb her now, while she was working and he was full of excitement. It could wait till tomorrow night.

He studied the photographs again. No doubt about it. Something was definitely going on and Beatrice had visual proof. He wondered if they would ever have noticed the backdrop to Matthew's comedy hair pictures if these shady characters hadn't been so hell-bent on getting rid of the images. He sat back with a satisfied smile. Fabulous! Detecting was so much more fun than watching *Grand Designs*.

Chapter 10

"Stubbs, you are deliberately wasting my time. This is not a football match in which I can substitute players at will." Hamilton's frown deepened to such an extent one could have played noughts and crosses on his forehead. "I cannot change personnel one day and reverse my decision the next without making either or both of us appear a total arse."

"My point, sir, is an extension of your decision. You sent a senior detective to assess the importance of the case. I delivered a report to you, indicating my view. Which is ..."

"I heard you the first time. And I've read your report. My answer remains unchanged. I thought I had made it clear at your first briefing – this case is about much more than getting a dirty old man off the streets. It's vital proactive police cooperation to promote a positive image of the force, in the face of media hostility. Following up claims of harassment is insufficient. Taking rape victims seriously is not enough. The IPCC's accusation of sustained failure regarding serial sex offenders can only be countered by an exercise such as this."

"But if someone else investigates the indecent exposures, such as Detective Sergeant Reynolds, we can achieve a double media coup with knife crime. All I am asking ..."

"We're failing women, Stubbs. And if you, as one of the party, will not stump up by putting personal concerns aside, my belief is beggared. Frankly, after yesterday's events, rather than trying to persuade me to send someone junior, you need to change up a gear with your sexual harasser."

"Sir, if I can simply explain my reasoning ..."

"I have heard more than enough. And can I remind you, this is supposed to be a preventative exercise, *id est*, catching the man before he goes too far. As far as I am concerned, what he did to those little girls yesterday means he already has. Pull your finger out, Stubbs. Have your phone routed to BTP HQ and make sure the loss of your machine is properly reported. Data protection, and so on. Good day to you."

Kicking cabinets in the ladies' toilet at Transport for London did little to calm Beatrice's anger, and merely hurt her foot. She leant against the sink and steamed, cursing Hamilton with every malign expression she could conjure. The door opened.

"Back already? I thought we wouldn't see you till coffee break." Virginia wore a pale blue dress, modestly cut below the knee, with a matching jacket. The duck-egg shade accentuated the colour of her eyes. Her heels were low and her legs were tanned and bare. She looked lovely, which irritated Beatrice still further.

"I overestimated my reporting time back at Scotland Yard. But I'm here now. Do you want to get some coffee and discuss the latest incident?"

"We can do better than that. I've spoken to the Family Centre and got permission to observe the interviews with those two girls this morning. Facilitators are going to chat to them and elicit statements, while we watch and see if we can glean anything from their stories. If we get over there now, we can brief the facilitators first. Are you fit? Or do you want a bit more time to abuse the furniture?"

Beatrice spotted the dark smudges against the cupboard door. "Come on, let's go. But I'd better come back later. I'm not leaving that for the cleaners."

Virginia gave an understanding smile. "Believe me, it won't be the first time they've removed shoe leather from those cabinets. I once fractured a toe."

The Family Centre on Piccadilly reminded Beatrice of a doctor's surgery. Cheerful, welcoming entrance, all pastel colours, pine and glass. After announcing themselves at reception, they waited in the vestibule. Neither of them wished to join the pale faces and hollow eyes in the waiting-room. A woman strode towards them, with tumbling red hair, jeans and an outstretched hand. A face familiar with smiles.

"Hello, I'm Doctor Maggie Howard, sorry to keep you. Who's low?"

Beatrice stared. "Sorry?"

The redhead gurgled with laughter.

"That didn't come out right. I'm meeting a Detective Stubbs and a Detective Lowe. I just wondered which was which."

Virginia offered her hand. "I'm Virginia Lowe, of British Transport Police. My colleague is Beatrice Stubbs, from the Met. Pleased to meet you, Doctor Howard."

Beatrice noted Virginia's use of first names and the fact she didn't correct the doctor's omission of the word 'inspector' in their titles. She understood. In such an environment, a friendly atmosphere took precedence over protocol. The doctor shook their hands. Her grip was firm, but her skin was soft and she smelt vaguely of aniseed. "Likewise. And please call me Maggie. We have time for a chat before our interviewees arrive. Can I get you a cup of tea?"

Beatrice chose to observe the interview with Zahra Esfahani, while Virginia opted to watch Amber Clarke, who had suffered the physical assault. Sitting in the darkness, behind the one-way mirror, Beatrice had the impression she was almost in the room with Maggie and Zahra. They sat in two adjacent armchairs, as if it were a cosy lounge, thus lessening the pressure of eye contact.

Magazines, toys and games were scattered over the coffee table in front of them. The girl had the typical coltish proportions of a thirteen-year-old. Skinny denim-clad legs, a purple T-shirt with a Pineapple Dance logo across the front and white leather ballet flats. She wore her hair in a high ponytail. Her bone structure would serve her well in the future, as would her large black-brown eyes, which she occasionally flicked upward from the floor.

Maggie Howard's technique was awe-inspiring. She managed to create an atmosphere of near-complicity in their first few exchanges, like a favourite aunt. Fascinated by the delicate process of gaining reliable testimony from a child, Beatrice noted the pattern. Closed question, open question, sympathetic comment, closed question, subjective question, positive reinforcement, expression of validation.

"So you were coming home from rehearsals. Do you rehearse every evening, Zahra?"

"Yeah. For our performance."

"Yes, your performance. What's the show about?"

"It's, like, modern dance? Ensemble and solo pieces on the theme of 'The Elements'. It opens Friday night."

"I'll bet you're getting butterflies! I would be!"

A shy smile. "I am a bit."

"You and Amber live close to each other, don't you?"

"Same street. So we always walk home together."

"When you walked home yesterday, what was different to usual?"

She thought for a moment and shrugged. "Nothing. Amber was moaning, as usual. The river was dirty, as usual. The only different thing was that perve on the path." The girl's voice darkened and her fingers fiddled with the woven bracelet on her left wrist.

"OK. That's great. You're doing very well, Zahra. I have a feeling you could be a very helpful witness."

Despite her invisibility, Beatrice nodded in agreement. In

the first thirty seconds, she'd already decided the teenager was bright and reliable.

As if Maggie sensed her approval, she continued. "The whole police force is so pleased that you and Amber came forward. Without people like you, we'd have a much harder job to catch him. But with your testimonies, I think we've got a better chance."

The girl looked down, but tried to smile.

Maggie got to the point. "Now, can you tell me, in your own words, exactly what happened from the moment you first saw the man? Take your time, and I'd like you to use these rag dolls to demonstrate. Just to help me understand who was where and so on."

Beatrice found herself nodding again. By using the harmless-looking dolls, Zahra could avoid using words that might embarrass her. Showing was easier than telling, and Maggie made it sound as if it were for her own benefit. Zahra's shaky but coherent description of the encounter made Beatrice thoroughly uncomfortable, building a sense of dread. Maggie asked frequent open questions on his accent and appearance, encouraging the girl to make comparisons to celebrities Beatrice had never heard of. When Zahra manipulated the dolls to show exactly what he'd done to Amber, a nauseous disgust washed over Beatrice. Followed by a swell of anger. Her toes and fists clenched, and for the first time, she really wanted this filthy bastard off the streets. Zahra put down the dolls and seemed to curl into herself.

Beatrice wanted to give the child a hug, but Maggie made no move to touch her. Of course not. Exactly the wrong thing under the circumstances. Beatrice's admiration for Maggie's professionalism rose still higher. It must be the most distressing work, dealing with these frightened victims of assault and abuse, coaxing details from damaged young people. Although Beatrice knew she could never do such a job, she was grateful for people who could. Softening her voice, Maggie began asking questions about Zahra's role and costumes for her show. Gradually, she pulled it around to a description of their assailant.

"Sounds gorgeous. I can almost see that dress. You're very good on details, Zahra, I'll say that. Something else I meant to ask: you mentioned the man's 'skanky trainers'. Can you give me any more details about the sports shoes he was wearing?"

Zahra's enthusiasm faded, but she gave a nod of comprehension. "They were just old, you know. Grey and skanky-looking. I couldn't see any logo. I *thought* it was weird, wearing a big coat and trainers with no socks."

"No socks?"

"I couldn't see any. But I didn't look at him for long, you know."

"No, of course you didn't. I always find it amazing, though, how people can take in the smallest details in a quick glance. The human mind is incredible. Younger people tend to have even better recollection, in my experience. OK, Zahra, you spotted the fact that his trainers were old and he wasn't wearing socks. What about his sweatshirt, can you picture the colour?"

The girl flushed and shook her head. No, that was natural. When he opened his coat, her eyes would be drawn down, not up.

"Fair enough, I understand. Now, last thing, you said he wore a baseball cap. I don't suppose you'd remember the colour."

The girl cocked her head to one side, thoughtful. "It was dark, maybe black or navy blue, and it had writing on the peak. Well, not writing you can read, but ..." She tailed off.

"Not writing you can read. Maybe it was in another language?"

"No, not another language, but more like symbols." She closed her eyes and thought. "Like three stripes horizontal, three vertical and so on. A bit like a floor, you know?"

"Hmm. If you saw this man again, Zahra, do you think you'd recognise him?"

"Too right. Weird eyes." Her face paled. "I won't have to, will I? You won't make us identify him in a line-up or something?"

"No. As I explained on the way in, you don't have to do anything. We asked for your help and you've given it. When we get this man under arrest, we may ask you to confirm from a photograph. That's all. Now, I think we should get something to drink and see if Amber has finished. While I pop out, would you do me a favour and see if you can draw those baseball cap symbols for me? Coke, juice, water ...?"

"Water, please."

Seconds after Maggie closed the door behind her, she entered Beatrice's observation room with a quick smile.

"She's good, isn't she? Just wanted to check before I wrap it up – anything else you need me to ask?"

"I don't think so. You've covered age, accent, physical description and clothes. I just wondered, could you ask her to go further on the 'weird eyes'?"

"No problem."

Maggie ducked out and Beatrice stood up to peer at what Zahra was drawing. She could see what the girl meant. It looked like parquet flooring; tiles of three grooves, one horizontal, the next vertical. She went on to sketch the baseball cap, thereby indicating exactly where the symbols were, and made a note on colour, before Maggie returned with two tumblers.

"That's fantastic, Zahra, thanks. Here's your water. What happens next is I'm going to write up our chat from the recording. Then I'd like you to check it, make sure I didn't get anything wrong, before we give it to the police. Now, do you have any questions you'd like to ask about all this?"

Zahra didn't drink but lifted her eyes to Maggie. "Do you think they'll catch him soon? The papers say he often comes back again."

"That's an exaggeration. You know what the papers are like. Plus we've asked your area community officers and neighbourhood watch to be particularly attentive for the next few weeks. The police will catch him, yes, and it won't be long. I can't make you any promises, but believe me when I say everyone wants to stop him as fast as possible. And you've given us a lot to go on."

The girl nodded. She didn't look entirely reassured, but it was clear she trusted Maggie to tell her the truth.

"Before we finish up, Zahra, can I ask you one more thing? You said the man on the path had 'weird eyes'. How do you mean?"

Zahra picked at her bracelet. "I don't know. Weird. Like, really black, sort of shining. Scary."

"Right. I see. You've been a great help. Thank you. I'd like to talk to your mum and dad now, so shall we go find them?"

Zé's came out top as the preferred lunch venue. By the time Beatrice paid for her soup and sandwich, Virginia had already plonked her tray outside in the sunshine, slipped off her jacket and was making eye contact with the suit sitting on the adjacent table. Beatrice joined her, with a sigh of release. The tension of the past two hours, extreme concentration and no natural light had affected her mood. She sat back and tilted her face to the sun. Tourists and office workers swarmed along the street, enjoying lunch alfresco.

"The only trouble with this place is they lay the mayo on so thick." Virginia scraped white goo from her baguette onto a napkin.

"How odd. That's one of the reasons I like it." Beatrice heard the chair behind her scrape back and watched Virginia's eyes follow the departing suit. She caught Beatrice's scrutiny and went on the offensive.

"Good. He's gone. So now we can talk. I'm not sure whether that Clarke girl was any use, to be honest. Little drama queen. Half the time I wasn't sure if she was acting or seriously distressed." Virginia took a bite of her undressed sandwich.

"Seeing as she was sexually assaulted yesterday afternoon, I'd lean to the latter," said Beatrice.

Virginia stopped chewing. "OK. That probably sounded

unfair. But the facilitator agreed with me. Plenty of theatrics. I'm guessing your Esfahani was more genuine."

"Yes. What she witnessed left Zahra deeply shaken. And hearing about it did something to me, too." Beatrice stirred her soup.

"Aha. I think I can guess what." Virginia put down her sandwich and wiped her fingers. "She's the first victim you've met. This case became personal for me after interviewing the French girl. You know what I felt? Shame. I was embarrassed and ashamed that this lovely girl couldn't stay here, learn our language and quietly earn her living without some dirty deviant putting the fear of London into her. And that's why when I see a 'performance' of traumatised, compared to the real thing, it gets on my tits."

"Fair enough. I didn't meet Amber Clarke. But as a matter of fact, you're right. I was going through the motions before, if I'm honest. Now, I want to grab this ugly little bastard and put him away."

Virginia nodded with enthusiasm. "I want this fucker so badly I'm losing sleep. He's already preparing his next victim, Beatrice. If he gets that far, we've let her down. For all kinds of reasons; professional, political and just from the gender standpoint, we've got to nail him. And I reckon we'll be more efficient if we're on the same side."

Her cool blue eyes were intense. Beatrice put down her spoon and held out her hand.

"We're on the same side."

They shook, exchanged a smile and returned to their lunch.

Virginia took a sip of juice. "I thought we could prepare tomorrow's briefing when we get back. I really want to whack them with how important this is. I'm bringing in that psychological profiler."

"Good idea, but I have a medical appointment at two, so I may not be back till around four." Beatrice kept her expression open.

"Oh. Sorry to hear that. Nothing serious, I hope?"

"No, no. Just a check-up. Shall we say four o'clock and bash out a plan?"

"Fine. I'll add the data from the girls' interviews and crosscheck. Did yours give us much?"

Beatrice felt a dual pull of relief and guilt at Virginia's blithe acceptance, but pressed on. Mind on the job.

"Zahra said he had 'weird eyes; black, shining and scary'. I'm thinking drugs."

Virginia tore off a piece of baguette and considered. "Could be. But in my experience, drug users are sloppy. This guy seems meticulous. I suppose it could be poppers, to elevate the sexual high."

"Did you get anything useful from Amber at all?"

"Not exactly. She said he smelt. Bad B.O. apparently. But as for description, useless."

Beatrice tilted her head. "That's got potential. We should put that in the profile mix. I got lots of detail on appearance and a picture of a logo he had on his hat." Beatrice reached into her pocket for Zahra's drawing. Since the robbery at The Speaker, she kept things close.

Virginia pursed her lips. "Don't recognise it. But we can run some checks. How's your soup?"

"Cold," Beatrice said, taking a spoonful.

"Sorry. We should eat first and talk later."

"No, it's supposed to be."

"Cold soup?"

"Gazpacho."

"Bless you!"

Beatrice let out a belly-laugh, attracting amused attention from passers-by. Despite all her best efforts, she rather liked Virginia Lowe.

Chapter 11

"James, I'm sorry I'm late. Bloody hold-up on the Piccadilly line."

"No need for apologies. That is London transport. But we will still have to finish on time, I hope you understand?"

"Of course." Beatrice flopped into the armchair and dragged a bottle of water from her bag." I don't think we'll need the full hour today, anyway. Not much to tell."

"Well, let's wait and see. Shall we begin with practicalities, or is there a particular issue you would like to work on?"

He gave a faint smile, as James often did, lulling one into a feeling of unconditional support. His short grey hair shone blond in the sunlight and his skin had a post-holiday glow. White gauze curtains softened the view of the opposite office block, the parquet floor and cream rugs gave an impression of cleanliness and peace. The room's air-conditioned coolness and calm atmosphere began working on Beatrice instantly.

"No, there's nothing ... Well, I'm lying to Matthew." It blurted its way out before she had even formulated the thought.

James's head lifted in enquiry.

"Not lying exactly. Just being economical with the truth. My laptop got stolen and I haven't told him. The thing is ..."

It looked like they would need the full hour after all. James sat absolutely still, listening to her complex explanation.

"So I want to investigate this, without Hamilton, without

Matthew and without that inverted snob Howells. I want to show them this is not hysteria, or paranoia or even a whole new dementia. There is something untoward going on in Wales and I want to prove it. Hamilton thinks it's personal, Matthew thinks I should stay home and concentrate on what I'm good at and Howells thinks I'm trying to teach him to suck eggs."

"You seem very sure of what all these people are thinking. I'm going to ask some questions and I want you to answer honestly. If you'd rather think about it before doing so, that's fine. Is it possible that you're building a wall of hostile men from a series of disconnected resentments?"

"I don't know what you mean by that."

James paused to look at his notes. "Might each man have his own agenda, unrelated to personal perceptions of you?"

"That is exactly my point. They're trying to keep my in my place, slap me down, hold me back. The little woman who belongs in the kitchen, but not in the workplace. Well, not Matthew so much, but he doesn't want me to rock the boat either. He'd rather I did découpage than detective work. They all want to chain me to my own little groove and stick to the script."

"Your tone seems unusually defensive. And, if I may observe, full of 1970's feminist rhetoric and mixed metaphors. What chance is there that your own insecurities in each case are projected onto these individuals?"

"James, you know perfectly well how hard I fight to be taken seriously in the professional sphere."

"Fight? I think I could accept 'fought', but I ask myself how that is relevant. I also wonder if you're feeling a little victimised for no reason."

Beatrice felt a flare of annoyance at James's deliberate deflation of her righteousness. Fanned by the awareness that he had a point.

"Howells may well have rubbed me up the wrong way, that's true."

"And perhaps vice versa?"

James was exactly like a dentist of the mind, invariably prodding at the painful bits.

"Fair point. But Hamilton still regards me as a loose cannon and Matthew clearly wants me to settle for an easy life, calm down and stop looking for trouble."

"Let's deal with one thing at a time. Hamilton. Entrusting a person with a vital case for the force's image is not where most people place a loose cannon."

Beatrice huffed through her nostrils, but James didn't push it. He didn't have to, the seed was planted.

"So you're saying I shouldn't feel it's a conspiracy to undermine me. That each man has belittled me and made me feel inadequate for the sake of their own egos."

"You began this session by telling me you were lying to Matthew. So in your view, which of the two of you is showing least respect for the other?"

Beatrice looked at the floor, her mind whirling back forty years to the headmaster's study, to the day she was carpeted for starting a fight in the cloakrooms.

James wasn't going to give up drilling. "Howells, you claim, is defensive and resistant to what you described as 'interference from the big boys'. Thus your depiction of a patriarchal bully rings hollow. Do you see where I'm going?"

Beatrice rested her forehead on her hands. "Yes. I think so. I've painted black hats onto the good guys." She inhaled deeply. "As a victim without a perpetrator, I feel frustrated. I'm laying blame so I can feel hard done by."

James's voice softened. "You know yourself very well, Beatrice. Now let's return to your original worry. If you intend to tell Matthew about the loss of your computer soon, what exactly is your reason for feeling guilty? Waiting for the right time to tell someone is not the same as lying. And you've stated that you're going to tell him at the weekend."

"Yes, I have. And I will." She shifted awkwardly in her seat, unable to envisage that conversation.

"Beatrice, forgive my pushing, but I wonder if there could be another reason for your feelings of guilt, or disloyalty."

"No, there's nothing more than that, really."

"When you have found someone you trust, like Matthew, that trust becomes precious. As time goes by, if you are truthful, open and believe in each other's honesty, a bond grows. A precious bond, like a gold chain. It's strong, forged from two people's love and loyalty. It can withstand immense external onslaughts. Almost nothing can break it, except for a moment of dishonesty from within. Being deceptive, in any form, has the potential to crack a link of that chain. The relationship between you and Matthew is based on truth."

"Which is ironic considering its origins."

"Its origins, if you really want to revisit that topic, can be discussed in our next session. However, they are immaterial in the context of this discussion. Look at it for what it is now. It is and always has been a relationship based on truth. You have a responsibility to that."

"I know." Beatrice's eyes stung and her voice sounded small.

"Another relationship based on truth is the one between you and me. So if I think you are not being entirely honest with me, I feel I have a responsibility to find out why."

Her nose was running. She reached for the box of tissues with such familiarity, this could have been her own bedroom.

"Yes, okay, okay. You're bloody right, as usual. I justified not telling him for all those reasons, but in fact, I want to keep this thing to myself. There's no way I can get it taken on as a case; Hamilton won't have it, so I'll have to do this in my spare time. Howells is being deliberately obstructive, so I'll just go behind his back. And I can't tell Matthew, because he will fret for me, or want to help me, or try to stop me. And I don't need any of that."

"Are you planning to do this alone?"

"Not exactly. I have a neighbour who's helping."

"A neighbour. Who presumably knows Matthew?"

"Yes. A neighbour who knows him well and who's mad keen to become Clouseau of the East End. I'm trying to rein him in, but it's like trying to rationalise with a spring lamb." She released an enormous sigh. "I have to tell Matthew, don't I?"

"I can't tell you what to do. I just want you to make decisions that are both right for now and for later. I have no doubt you know what the best thing is."

"Yes. I do. James, I'm sorry for being so bloody awkward."

James looked up from his notes with a frown.

"Beatrice Stubbs, if you break the terms of our contract one more time, you will be fined. We agreed, and you have had more verbal warnings than I care to count, that you need never apologise for yourself. Not in this room. Now look, we have five minutes left. So to practicalities."

"Practicalities, yes. The mood balancers seem to be working and I take one daily. As for the diary, well, I've been busy, so I can't say I'm up to date."

"When do you take your medication, Beatrice?"

"Last thing at night."

"The perfect time. Keep a notebook under your pill box. As you take the tablet, make a note of the day's moods. Even if you write only one line, that will help us chart your emotional movements. Will you try?"

"Fair enough, I can manage that. Look James, thank you. You have phenomenal patience. You knew we'd need the whole hour, didn't you?"

"Mostly when people announce there's nothing to say, the opposite tends to be true. Please take care of yourself, Beatrice. See you in a fortnight?"

"I'll look forward to it. Goodbye."

It was true. Whenever she left James's office, she couldn't wait to return. As so often after one of his sessions, she felt like a power hose had cleaned the inside of her skull and she wanted to skip all the way back to the office. But she knew from experience such enthusiasm would be short-lived. Two weeks later and she would resent the trip to Islington. Dreading the illumination of dark and dusty emotional corners and anticipating her embarrassment at how, in only fourteen days, she had allowed her mind to get into such an appalling mess.

Chapter 12

Only three stops and they were already south of the river. Beatrice and Adrian came out of the Tube at London Bridge and walked through Borough Market, thankfully closed, otherwise Beatrice would never have dragged him away from the food stalls. He could waste an entire morning sniffing chanterelles and tasting goat's cheese. She always insisted on taking this particular route when they had their Tate Nights. Walking along the South Bank, full of atmosphere both ancient and modern, was part of the whole soothing experience.

They dodged another cluster of guidebook-reading Nordic sorts and walked under the shadow of Southwark Cathedral. Beatrice waited till they had turned the corner before firing a question at her companion.

"How many people were in that group of tourists we just passed?"

Adrian faltered and made as if to turn but Beatrice wagged a finger.

"Just approximately. And if you can hazard a guess as to nationality, I'll give you another point."

"Six, I think. And they were all adults. As for nationality? British, possibly from Newcastle, judging by the accents."

Beatrice sighed in mock despair. "Eight. Grandparents, parents and four children. Scandinavian, certainly, but I could have been no more specific than that until I saw the Swedish flag on the teenager's backpack."

Adrian didn't seem particularly impressed. They passed The Golden Hinde and circumnavigated the queue outside The Clink before he spoke.

"I think you're cheating. If I were actively detecting, right now, I'd keep my eyes open for anything relating to my case. Not wasting brain space with lots of irrelevant detail about Swiss tourists."

"Swedish. How do you know exactly what is relevant to your case?"

"Here, probably nothing." Passing Vinopolis, they stopped for a moment to admire Banksy's artwork on the bridge. "But if I were in Wales, I'd be looking very carefully at anyone wearing boaty gear."

"Boaty gear. I see the logic. Anything else? Which other angles would you use for such enquiries?" Beatrice increased the pressure.

Adrian rose to the challenge. "Apart from checking out boat people, I'd find out when the tide comes in, so I'd know when to wait for boats arriving in the dark."

"Very astute." The laughter and chat from the crowd outside The Anchor flowed over them as Adrian's head flicked left and right, overtly taking in every detail. He expected another test, so Beatrice changed tack.

"It's natural that men are less aware of their surroundings. You have a different kind of focus. Single-minded. Whereas women, from our hunting and gathering days, developed far better peripheral vision."

"Beatrice, please don't tell me you buy into all that hard-wired gender traits crap. You are an intelligent woman. Surely you cannot believe we have evolved so little from the days of the woolly mammoth."

She laughed. "No, I don't. No more than I believe in behaviour dictated by signs of the Zodiac. But I knew it would get your shackles up."

It was Adrian's turn to laugh. "Get my shackles up? That's a Bea-line I've not heard before. As a matter of fact, I share far more typical characteristics with fellow Sagittarians than I do with cavemen. Oh, look at The Globe. I do love it when it's all lit up."

Beatrice stood beside him to admire the theatre, listening to the rush of the Thames at her back. The warm evening, the feeling of people making the most of their city, the anticipation of a couple of happy hours at the Tate Modern, followed by dinner at their favourite Thai, filled Beatrice with optimism. She bunted Adrian with a shoulder and they walked on towards the Millennium Bridge.

"So, which play was on at The Globe tonight?" asked Beatrice.

"Is that pertinent to a case involving criminal activity on a Welsh beach?"

"It's pertinent to your powers of observation. You stared at the poster for several minutes so you must remember some of the detail. I'll give you a clue. It's a play by Marlowe and the title is just one word."

Adrian's face was a study of concentration as they approached the art gallery along gravel paths. Beatrice looked up at the immense edifice, crowned by its monolithic chimney, with a sense of admiration for its functionality, past and present.

"I remember! *Cymbeline!*" Adrian's expression was triumphant.

"Tsk. That's Shakespeare. It was *Tamburlaine*, twerp. Come on."

"*Tamburlaine Twerp* is two words."

After nosing around the Turbine Hall, they made their way upstairs.

"Can we start on Level Three?" asked Adrian, leading the way to the escalator. "I want to feed my Surrealist urges."

"You're becoming fixated with weird types and I'm not at all sure it's healthy. Yes, let's start there but I do want to see some Impressionists this evening. I've had a hankering since Wales." She held onto the handrail. How refreshing to just stop and stand still on an escalator rather than barging up on the left, tutting at tourists.

"Talking of Wales, have I convinced you yet?" He looked down at her from the step above as they travelled up two floors. The olive-green shirt looked most elegant against his tan. Summer suited him.

Beatrice decided it was time to be honest.

"I am most grateful for the photographs you managed to print from my phone, don't get me wrong. And as I told you before, you have many of the right qualities I look for in a detective. Unfortunately, you lack training, experience and an understanding of protocols. So while I am happy to bend the rules by sharing information with you, I can't possibly sanction your taking on a potential crime investigation. Not on your own."

He didn't answer, turning to look forwards as they neared the top. He walked ahead to the first room without waiting for her. Beatrice sighed. After all these years of neighbourly harmony, it would be a shame to fall out over such a situation. She wandered through various rooms and found him standing in front of Paul Klee's *Walpurgisnacht*. The strange, scratched canvas of blue straw-like figures evoked bats and rituals and owls and paganism. It appealed to her in a way she couldn't explain.

"I like it. Very witchy."

Adrian smiled. "I hear the New York Times art critic said exactly the same."

They moved on to Edward Wadsworth, Yves Tanguy and David Smith. Adrian seemed drawn to these juxtaposed angles, odd assemblages and curious compositions, in the style of de Chirico.

"They like sticking things together to create bizarre representations, don't they? Sort of artistic Lego."

Adrian shot her a sly look. "Perhaps it's a male thing."

Beatrice drifted away to Franz Roh's *Total Panic II*, involving a rather well-drawn elephant scene, incorporating an apparently random bat and snail. Adrian joined her.

"Makes you want to hear the whole story, doesn't it?"

She nodded. "Yes. Funny how these things can work on our emotions, despite not having a clue as to their true meaning."

"Do you want to go stare at some pastels now?" he asked.

"When you're ready. I have no wish to exacerbate your sulk."

"I am ready, after our usual stop for *Metamorphosis of Narcissus*, and it's not a sulk. I just feel a little disappointed that you don't trust me."

Beatrice frowned at him. "I do trust you. With all my secrets. Well, most of them. But I'm not prepared to put you in harm's way. It's lovely of you to offer to help, and I'm touched. The fact of the matter is, I can't investigate, because I have to throw all my energies into catching this twisted sex offender. And if I can't, you can't either. It's too dangerous. We have no idea what we're dealing with."

They stopped and gazed at the Dalí. Disregarding her lack of enthusiasm for Surrealism, she admired the wonderful use of light, echoes and reflection, the rich colours of the sky, and the always intriguing background detail. She never minded pausing for Narcissus.

Adrian sighed. "It does seem a real shame to let these thefts go unpunished. There could be something far worse behind the pictures. And all because you can't get away from the Finsbury Park Flasher."

"Yes, but when I've got him where he can do no further harm, I'll insist on chasing any leads myself. And the evidence hasn't been abandoned. Don't forget, the Welsh police have all the facts, including your photos, and are still making enquiries."

"You said yourself you had no faith in Inspector Howells."

Beatrice acknowledged the truth of that. Perhaps she should share a little less with her nosy neighbour who forgot nothing, so long as it interested him.

"Well, never mind that now. At the moment, there's nothing you or I can do about it. Just as soon as I am free to look into things myself, I'd be happy for you to join me. Does that pacify you?"

"A bit. OK, I've had my Surreal fix. Let's go and see some Old Lady Art."

Beatrice swiped at him with the back of her hand but he was already out of reach.

Chapter 13

Trouble with these girls is they think too much.

Rick rolled up the shutter without checking the window display. No need. Sign says 'Sex Shop' in pink and blue neon. A few vids, pair of handcuffs, crotchless drawers and your punter knows what he's getting. Yeah, it looks tired, a bit sleazy, but who cares? When he finds the next shop girl, she can do a bit of dusting. Or not. Shiny shop front or shabby faded velvet, they'll come. *Heh, heh. They'll always come.* Maybe dirty makes them feel at home.

He'd not expected Caz to lose her bottle. Well disappointing. She was a cynic from the start; tats, studs and a tongue-lash he'd not heard the like of since Madam D. She understood money and sex. Or at least Rick thought she did. One of the few girls he trusted to handle herself without security. Saved him a packet. And now she'd quit. Bad news.

The door opened and the bell pinged as the first one arrived. Rick nodded at him and looked back to the computer. He never judged them. Not to their faces. These losers were his bread and butter. But how sad are you if you need wank-fodder at ten past nine? Geezer went straight in the back for the DVDs. Rick sighed as the door opened again.

Jason. Another wanker.

"Alright Rick?"

"Jase."

Jason stood beside the soft-porn mag rack as if he was comfortable, but Rick saw his eyes flickering over the opposite wall. He was staring at nurse costumes, rubber gimp suits and lubricants with a giggly compulsion.

"I said I'd call you if I needed any deliveries, didn't I?"

"Yeah, deffo. Just thought I'd pop in and see if you needed a hand, now Caz has pissed off."

Rick didn't look up from the screen. Jason was desperate to manage the shop. Desperate. And therefore the worst possible person to leave in charge. Like letting an alkie run your Ibizan beach bar.

"Nah, you're alright, Jase. I got it sorted. I'll give you a bell if I need anything."

Another bloke came in, greeted them and made straight for the back room. Obviously a regular. The shop was doing decent trade, so all Rick needed to do was find a decent manager. Jase was still hanging about.

"Jase, I got work to do."

"Yeah, sure, got it. I'm off then. Listen, why did Caz leave?"

Rick shook his head. "Dunno, mate. Maybe she's got a bloke? Just said she'd had enough, is all."

The phone started ringing and Jason finally pissed off out of it. Rick dealt with a coy query about lesbian films and a professional sales geezer trying to flog paperbacks of Mommy Porn. Could help the first, no chance with the second. Randy housewives don't go to sex shops. Try Mothercare.

By lunchtime, he'd sold sixteen DVDs, a chocolate lubricant, a gold cock ring, thirteen mags for differing tastes and two Rabbits. Busy morning. He planned to close up over lunch and go to The Blue Posts for a pie and a pint. Five to one, the bell pinged and another punter turned up. Rick looked up to acknowledge the guy but he kept his head down. Classic. Baseball cap, shifty behaviour, no eye contact, just standing there looking at restraints. Rick waited for the bloke to decide and thought about Caz.

He missed her. Simple as. Always timed it so as he was here around eleven, brought her cakes and coffee and they had a laugh. Why would she up sticks and walk? He'd always treated her right and never tried it on. Not his type, anyway. And he had a funny feeling he wasn't hers either. But she was a great laugh and a damn good manager. Shit. He knew she wouldn't come back, not even for a raise. She'd gone for good. He'd probably never see her again.

He was hungry, he needed a pint and there was a right pong in the air. This punter was giving off a chronic stink. Rick closed down the till and picked up his keys. The bloke carried on staring at the handcuffs. Rick recalled Caz's voice. *Sometimes, you look into someone's eyes and you just know. No matter how much they spend, you don't want any part of that world.*

The stink was getting worse.

"Right then, sunshine. I'm off on my lunch break. Back about two. Unless you've already decided?"

The foul-smelling git looked over his shoulder, back at the display and slunk out the door, the bell signalling his departure. Rick shook his head. Not known for civilised small talk, your average pervert. He locked the door and bent under the counter to find the Febreze.

Chapter 14

"Classics Department, Professor Bailey?"

"Matthew, hello. This is Adrian speaking. I hope I'm not disturbing you?"

"Hello Adrian. No, not at all, it's nice to hear from you."

"I called you at home, at first. I thought one of the perks of university lecturing was a massive summer holiday. So I was surprised when your cleaner said you were in your campus office."

"Not so much of a cleaner, more of an untidier. That was Tanya, my youngest. She's using the library, hence my banishment. Er, is everything all right?"

"Oh yes. Beatrice is fine, don't worry. We had dinner the other night, as you know. No, the reason for calling was simply to thank you for that heavenly Amarone."

"Ah. The Tommaso Bussola. What did you think?"

"Dense. Both colour and nose and the palate goes on forever. Spices from entry to finish, but so well balanced."

Adrian could hear Matthew smiling. "Quite. It's powerful, impressively so, but has real elegance. Did you try it with duck?"

"No, I gave the wine centre stage. Supporting acts were some organic bresaola, parmigiano reggiano with a drop of balsamic vinegar and fresh crusty ciabatta. It was absolutely sublime. So much so that I couldn't have shared it. I can't thank you enough."

"You're more than welcome. Your appreciation is my reward. Are you well?"

"In rude health, thank you. And you?"

"Almost normal, apart from a certain frustration at a loss of research data. Beatrice told you of our mishap in Pembrokeshire, I presume? When my camera was stolen, I lost a fair few images which were important to my work. I should learn from Beatrice's example and always make a back-up."

"Yes, she did tell me. To be truthful, Matthew, that's my other reason for calling. I hope you won't mind, but I've tried talking to Beatrice about this a couple of times. She's so absorbed in chasing her flasher, she seems to have lost all interest in this case."

"Which case would that be?"

Adrian explained the photographs, taking care not to mention the stolen laptop, outlined his theory and stressed his conviction that someone, somewhere really should investigate. Matthew was silent for a long time.

"It's decent of you to be concerned, but I'm not really sure how I can help. Chasing the Welsh police is likely to be counter-productive. The local inspector has already told Beatrice to keep her beak out."

"I agree. Which is why I thought you and I might be able to lend a hand."

"Taking on the role of the Hardy Boys while Nancy Drew is occupied?" he asked.

"Well …" Adrian didn't want to admit it, but he was thinking more along the lines of Poirot and Hastings.

"Despite the fact that Beatrice has access to all the necessary resources, possesses years of expertise and experience, and bearing in mind this may not even be in her jurisdiction, you think we should poke about and ask questions, possibly jeopardising any official investigation?"

Adrian found Matthew's tone patronising. "My angle was

more as support. Matthew, Beatrice has no time to apply all her resources and etcetera. All her time and energy is dedicated to this dirty raincoat. And rightly so. But she's frustrated by the fact she hasn't got time to make enquiries. She told me she couldn't allow me to investigate alone. The way I see it, there's nothing stopping the two of us doing some helpful groundwork, asking casual questions, making enquiries in a subtle fashion and then handing over our findings when she's got time to take it seriously."

"That sounds reasonable. But I don't think she'll be keen."

"Nor do I. She'd probably issue a three-line whip. Which is why I called you, to see if we can't manage something discreet and supportive, but keep it to ourselves. A sort of gentleman's investigation."

Matthew laughed. "A gentleman's investigation. Well, that's certainly an idea. It could liven up my summer holiday no end. Why don't you tell me what you have in mind?"

"Great! It would be better to do that face to face. Who's doing the travelling this weekend? Is she coming to you?"

"No, she's staying in London and I've been given the choice. She will have to work part of the time, so if I can promise to amuse myself, I am allowed to come for a visit. That fits in rather well with our potential scheme, I'd say."

Adrian smiled. "It most certainly does. And I'm free all weekend during the day. I have a dress rehearsal on Friday and my performance is on Saturday night. Oh, I'm so pleased you're up for this. All detectives should have a sidekick, because apart from anything else, it's so boring on your own. So, see you sometime over the weekend? Do you have my mobile number?"

"I do, but I might just pop downstairs and knock on your door, when I get a chance. I wish you all the very best with the show, break a leg and all that. And yes, you're right. All the best detecting tales involve an older, wiser professional supported by a keen young pup. See you on Saturday at some point. Thanks for calling, Adrian, I appreciate your trust."

As Adrian hung up and returned to the computer, he tingled with anticipation. All the fun of detective work with none of the unattractive uniforms, paperwork or politics. He just hoped that Matthew understood the situation. Keen young pup, indeed. No one puts Adrian in the chorus.

Chapter 15

"Morning everybody and thanks for coming. As you all know, this is a special operation and let's just get one thing straight. I've heard more than one person saying, why the fuss, it's *just* a flasher. Well, that stops as of now. There is a far more serious reason for getting this man off the streets." Virginia paused, her eyes scanning the room.

Beatrice did the same, searching for any tell-tale sneers, any significant looks, any evidence of disbelief. Such officers would be either replaced or stuck on paper detail. Both women had agreed they wanted total commitment from all involved. None of the twenty-six faces; British Transport personnel, constables from the Hackney, Islington and Haringey boroughs, Safer Neighbourhood officers and Met Police Volunteers, showed anything but curious interest.

"Right, so I'll hand you over to Doctor Simon Rosenbaum, our specialist profiler."

The presence of the profiler increased attention from the assembly. Beatrice noted shifts in seats and a few slouchers straightening up. Rosenbaum's appearance was unremarkable. His fair hair was thinning, his eyes were grey and his clothes – a striped shirt with no tie, jeans and deck shoes – reminded Beatrice of Sundays in Greenwich Park.

"Good morning folks. DI Lowe has asked me to explain the reasoning behind this case, as it is largely due to my concerns that you're all here. I work with a team of psychologists and behavioural experts at University College, London. We've collaborated over the past six years with nine other European universities, all of which have strong links with their local police forces. Our research, compiled from six years of data on sex offenders, shows a pattern.

"The vast majority of those who indecently expose themselves are no cause for concern. Exhibitionism, drunkenness, a momentary misjudgement ..."

"A wardrobe malfunction," added Ty Grant, to general laughter. Virginia joined in. Beatrice, hiding her irritation at the interruption, smiled briefly. Rosenbaum handled it well.

"Precisely. That can happen too. But these are people that do it once, and with a different set of objectives. When someone exposes himself, and it is usually a male, with the intent to intimidate, frighten or shock the recipient, we class that as a sexual offence. Now, those who repeat the offence are the ones we need to watch. Point one: repeat exposers frequently demonstrate other kinds of anti-social behaviour, which is often an indication of some social maladjustment. Point two: the offences generally become more serious. In these cases, we have found that the offender is likely to assault, even rape and on some occasions, kill. We are working with forces all over Europe to try and encourage greater awareness of this phenomenon and thereby prevent serious sexual assaults."

His message provoked sober nods and thoughtful expressions.

"Our Finsbury Park man is following the behavioural sequence exactly. Just from the cases we know about, the incidents are increasing in frequency; he started off roughly once a fortnight. In the last three weeks, we've received three reports, and this week he's struck twice. Not only that, but at first it was one woman, usually in the small hours. The last two incidents: two foreign students leaving a friend's flat at around 10.30pm. The friend was an earlier victim. Any alarm bells ringing yet?

"Then he waited for two girls, aged thirteen, and encouraged one to put her hand in his pocket. When she refused, he opened his coat and pressed the girl's hand to his genitals. He was interrupted, fortunately, or it might have gone further.

"I cannot stress highly enough how urgent this is. My team and I believe he will commit a serious sexual assault in the next few days. Your job is to stop that happening."

Rosenbaum sat down, and Beatrice could see how the atmosphere was galvanised by a sense of collective responsibility. Good job, Doctor Rosenbaum.

Virginia gave it a second before she got to her feet. Her sleeveless scarlet polo-neck, paired with pedal pushers, gave her the air of Jeanne Moreau. "We're grateful to you and your team, Dr Rosenbaum. Right, this is how it's going to work. The guy's victims have nothing more in common than their gender and the fact they all use Finsbury Park Tube. He selects them, follows them, understands their habits and chooses his moment. He's very aware of cameras. He hasn't yet been recorded. We believe he learns their routine and follows them from the Underground.

"We run two parallel plans of attack. First, surveillance teams in pairs stationed in and around the Tube station. In your briefing pack, page nine, you'll find your partners and your locations on the map, specifically chosen to be in the gaps between cameras. You watch, you wait. In shifts from six till six. We're looking for a man acting suspiciously, wearing the gear described on page thirteen. Or a woman alone, especially the more vulnerable. He's picked on a train cleaner, a primary schoolteacher, a foreign student, a barista, a new immigrant, two contract cleaners, those students and now these teenage girls. That we know of. Now I'll ask DI Stubbs to describe procedure."

Heads lifted toward Beatrice. Her skirt suit and flats gave her the air of Miss Marple.

"Hello everyone. Priority number one is to get this man into custody. If you're suspicious, follow him. Do not let him know you're there. Do not attempt to apprehend unless you are sure of success. If we scare this man and lose him, he will run. He may wait a few weeks, he may change his patch, but he won't stop. We are not advertising our presence, we're not a deterrent, we want him where he cannot terrorise any more women. This activity will be called Operation Robert, and Robert will be your codeword to alert other teams that you are following a suspect."

Grant was grinning. "Operation Robert? Shouldn't it be Operation John Thomas?"

At least some of the meathead's colleagues found him distasteful, judging by the mixture of subdued sniggers and disgusted glares.

Beatrice fixed her gaze on Grant's ruddy, self-satisfied face. "The reason we decided on Operation Robert was in acknowledgement of Robert Peel, founder of the Metropolitan Police Force as we know it. As I'm sure you're aware, this is why police officers used to be described as 'Peelers.' Also, Robert is an innocuous name which is unlikely to attract attention in an awkward situation. The reason we decided against Operation John Thomas was that, unlike you, Sergeant, we find nothing amusing about sexual assault. Does anyone have any more pertinent questions?"

Grant looked at Virginia in confusion. After a second's discomfort, a female officer raised a hand. "The girls, on Wednesday. That's quite a distance from Finsbury Park Tube."

Beatrice nodded. "They go to a dance school in Arsenal. They catch the Tube and the twenty-nine bus back to Green Lanes, then walk along the riverbank. It's quite a journey. Recently they've been doing it every night, at exactly the same time."

The officer wrinkled her nose. "He followed them all that way? Stalker."

"Exactly. Which leads me to the second plan. DI Lowe?"

Virginia shot her a look. If that was intended as some kind of disapproval regarding her remark to Grant, they would have words. That man was an oaf.

Virginia took Beatrice's place in front of their team.

"Honey trap. Sergeant Grant and Sergeant de Freitas will be hovering at Finsbury Park Tube Control Centre. They'll be watching all the exits and entrances, all the in and outs."

Grant gave Virginia a sly smile.

"Meanwhile, Constable Harrison of BTP is our decoy. She'll be leaving early and returning late. We're hoping our man will spot her and make her a target. She'll have a team of three officers nearby at all times, watching her, and watching anyone who's watching her. Harrison, you want to introduce yourself?"

Harrison raised her index finger to identify her presence. With a jerk of her head, Virginia indicated she should stand. Reluctantly, the constable pushed out of her chair, and glanced around the judgemental faces. Everyone was thinking the same thing: is the lure attractive enough?

Her short blonde hair was cropped close to her head, framing a milky complexion now reddened with embarrassment. Her uniform did not flatter her skinny frame. She wore no make-up, but her eyes seemed bright and lively.

Virginia continued. "Harrison will be playing Party Girl. Well, obviously we'll dress her up a bit, pile on the slap and she'll pass. The plan is for her to act like she's spent the whole night on the alco-pops and is off her head."

"Should be a doddle for you, Karen." Grant just couldn't keep his mouth shut. This whole briefing drove Beatrice to distraction. She had never experienced such sloppy attitudes and poor discipline. Hamilton would have had a fit.

She turned with a frown to stare at Big Mouth and even Virginia adopted a warning tone, saying, "Ty."

He merely grinned back as the constable sat and lowered her head.

"Read your packs carefully, and get some sleep tomorrow, because you're all going on twelve-hour shifts. Any questions, DI Stubbs and I will be happy to answer them. Thanks all and best of luck."

On the grim march back to Virginia's office, both women strode side-by-side, breathing through their noses, keeping an ostentatious hold on their tempers. Beatrice pictured a pair of livid chickens, on their way to a hen fight.

She'd barely closed the door before Virginia began. Standing behind her chair, she slammed the heel of her hand onto the desk.

"What in the name of God do you think you're playing at? Do you want to poison this whole team against us before we start? Ty Grant is probably one of the most popular men on this op and you start by making him look an insensitive fool!"

Virginia had taken the high position, on her feet, taller, louder and demonstrably angry. Although she'd rather not, Beatrice could play status games. She pulled out the chair opposite, sat and kept her voice and expression calm.

"He didn't need my help for that. And he's not the only one. Insensitivity? How do you think Karen Harrison felt during that briefing? You exposed her and basically said, 'OK, so she looks bloody awful now, but we can sort that out'. Then you allow Grant his little pot shot at discrediting her ..."

"For fuck's sake, Beatrice, can't you take a joke? He was trying to lighten the atmosphere. He works, and has always worked, as the team glue. Keeping morale high, voicing many people's unspoken thoughts, he's solid gold."

"I see it differently. First he attempts to demean and belittle this op with his suggestion of a better name. Then he makes a slur against a colleague, albeit couched in humour. This is exactly the sort of behaviour we agreed not to tolerate. But now you seem to have changed your mind. Why is that? Is it personal, Virginia?"

In Gibraltar one year, Beatrice and Matthew spent many happy hours watching the monkeys. One could learn much from watching the interactions of a bunch of apes. Beatrice had noted one particular expression, which remained with her. When crossed, one of these primates' frowns would clear as it pulled up its scalp. The effect was to reveal the whites of the eyes, she supposed. Whatever the reason, it signalled danger. Virginia did something very similar. Her face went blank and hard, as if a line had been crossed.

"Are you calling my judgement into question, Beatrice?"

"Frankly, yes. I'm sorry to say this, but your treatment and tolerance of the men on your team is very different to the way you handle the women. As far as your department is concerned, that's your own affair. But as Operation Robert is a joint effort, I cannot allow a case like this to bear any tones of sexism. We are going to have to find a compromise."

"I knew it. Just when I thought we were making progress, you have to score petty points. I presume this is down to Dawn Whittaker? You are determined to punish me for that three-minute indiscretion and just waited for the right moment to raise sexual politics. That's bullshit, Beatrice, and you know it!"

"I am not prepared to discuss what happened between you and Ian Whittaker. That has nothing to do with this case. I assure you, had I never heard about that, my reaction today would have been the same. You treat certain team members differently and it's counter-productive. The atmosphere you created today encourages the nudge, snigger and snort attitude to a situation that apparently disturbs your sleep. I think you need to nail your colours to the flagpole. If you take this seriously, so will your team."

Virginia glared at her and then turned to the white board, apparently studying the data gathered so far. Silence echoed around the room, the change in tempo as unnerving as the shouting.

Virginia spoke. "What are you doing this afternoon?"

"Talking to victims again, with Harrison. You?"

"Calling at Finsbury Park Tube station, talking to security."

"Good. Shall we debrief tomorrow unless something major occurs?" Beatrice stood.

"Sure. Have a good afternoon."

"You too." As she left the office, Beatrice sensed something. A feeling of freshly tilled ground, of ashes and earth, of potential.

Chapter 16

Ray whacked the doors shut and banged home the deadbolts. Jules relaxed. Gorgeous sound. On his way back to the bar, Ray unplugged the fruit machine. Jules switched off the stereo and silence rushed into the space. Even more gorgeous. She loved the peace. Maybe she was getting too old for this game. Ray lined up the remaining empties on the bar and Jules set to stacking them in the glass washer. Neither of them said a word. While that cycle went through, she took the wheelie-bin of empties down the slope to the cellar, rinsing it out and trying to shake the unsettled feeling that hung on her like damp clothes. She'd made a lot of mistakes tonight. Tiredness, partly, but also that staring bloke at the bar. Made her uncomfortable, being watched like that, made her clumsy. He'd gone, eventually. But if he ever came back and did that again, she'd ask him if he wanted a photo.

Ray was restacking the machine when she got upstairs. "Want a drink, Jules? I reckon you earned it tonight."

"Cheers, Ray. But I'm dead on my feet and I got to be back here at eleven tomorrow. How about we have one tomorrow night? I don't have to get up so early on a Sunday."

"Won't say no to that. I'm knackered and all. Listen, how you getting home?"

"Same way as always. Night bus. I got another fifteen minutes, so you want me to mop behind the bar, or what?"

Ray scratched his scalp through its scanty covering of grey

hair.

"Tell you what, I want to get some chips for Pam and me, so why don't I give you a lift? You go check the ladies' for me and I'll tell the missus what's going on."

"You sure? It's out of your way." Jules could have kissed his grey-stubbled cheek.

"Yeah, no bother. All the talk about that pervert round the station, you shouldn't be out at this time of night, not on your own. Go on, sort out the bogs and we'll be off."

The ladies' toilet was on the first floor, and it was quite normal for the queue to stretch right across the landing to the top of the stairs at the weekends. Only two cubicles and one was always out of order. Dragging a bin bag from the wall cupboard, Jules pulled on rubber gloves and steeled herself.

After she shoved open the door, she observed the usual shambles. Overflowing bin, wet toilet roll all over the floor, a smell of urine and vomit and a pair of tights left in the sink. Goodnight, ladies. Hauling the worst of the mess into the bag, she nudged open the cubicle doors. More soggy toilet roll and a discarded lip gloss. Not half bad for a Friday night. Some of the things she'd found in there you wouldn't believe. Used condoms, soiled knickers, a bag of courgettes and on one memorable occasion, an unconscious anorexic from Stoke Newington.

"Jules? You done, love?" Ray called up the stairs.

"Just about. It's not too bad tonight." She pulled off the gloves and closed the landing window. Focused on the stubborn catch, her eyes registered the movement on the street just a second too late. Something had retreated into the darkness of the dry cleaner's doorway. She turned off the light and peered out. It was pitch black in that recess. Nothing moved. She gave up and carried the bag downstairs.

"Listen sweetheart, Pam don't want chips, after all. But I'll walk you to the night bus. Like I say, I feel better if I know you're safe, innit?"

His face relaxed into the well-worn grooves of an easy smile. "You don't have to do that, Ray." But she hoped he would.

"Yeah, yeah. Come on, Droopy Drawers, shake a leg. Pam's doing me a toasted sandwich."

They left through the back door and as they exited the alley onto Adolphus Road, Jules tucked her arm into Ray's and resisted the urge to look at the dry cleaner's doorway. Ray was still enthusing about his Breville.

"And then I discovered ham, cheese and pineapple. Never looked back. Ray's Hawaiian, I call it. You got a top toastie filling, Jules?"

"I don't really eat them. Bit fatty for me."

"That's half your trouble, innit? If you was to eat a toastie now and then, there might be a bit more of you. You women, always counting the calories, you want to live a little."

As they turned onto Alexandra Grove, a shadow in Jules's peripheral vision caused her to stop. She snapped her head around and stared, convinced she'd seen the peak of a baseball cap ducking into the dark.

Ray stopped. "What?"

"Nothing. Sorry." They resumed walking.

"Jules, love, you can't let yourself get too jumpy. Just keep safe, girl, and don't take no risks. But don't go leaping at your own shadow, eh?"

"Yeah. I know. Just all this stuff makes you a bit ... you know. Oh shit, there's the bus. Cheers, Ray, see you in the morning."

Her jazz pumps were useful behind the bar, but essential when running for the bus. She could never have shot across Seven Sisters Road like that in heels. Turned out she didn't need to; there was a small queue which took a while to board. She sat halfway back on the bottom deck, looking ahead at her reflection in the glass. Under the brutal lights, her image was unappealing. Tired, drawn and thin as a rake. How come size eight looked good in magazines, but haggard on her? She turned her attention out the window to see if Ray had gone. No sign of his cardigan-clad shape. The bus closed its doors, before opening them again for one final passenger. Jules almost didn't see him, still gazing down Alexandra Grove after dear old Ray, but as he approached, her skin cooled and she raised her eyes. She looked away instantly, tasting the sour metal of fear. He passed her without a glance and sat somewhere further back.

The baseball cap. She recognised it straight away. The Starer. All night, she'd felt his eyes on her. Not that you could see much of his eyes, with that cap pulled down low. He'd positioned himself on the corner of the bar, so the pillar hid him from sight. But she'd worked there for over a year so she knew where the mirrors were. Reaching up to an optic, she saw him lean so as he could see her. Handing over change for the fruit machine, he watched. Now when some bloke watches you all evening, but leaves without even saying goodnight, it's a bit peculiar. Sometimes they want to ask you out, but can't pluck up the guts. She could understand that. But when someone watches you all night and follows you from outside the pub? She could understand that too. And it frightened her to death.

He was behind her, somewhere. She didn't need to turn; she could feel that cold observation. *Just keep safe, girl.* She was safe on public transport, full of the public. Only when she got off would she be in any danger. She had to make a plan. The glass behind the driver reflected an indistinct image. She saw herself, pressed against the window. Directly behind her, a young Chinese guy, whose earphones emitted repetitive treble tones, sat in his own little world. And two seats back, staring at the back of her neck, him.

Don't get too jumpy. She wasn't. That guy was following her. No question about it. And when she got off, he would follow her home. No way. She wasn't going to show him where she lived. Leave one stop early, but get someone to come and meet her. Slipping her hand into her bag, she located her mobile. No point calling John, he'd be out cold by now. Who, then? Most people were in bed. Quick, Jules, think. You've got seven stops to work something out. Aaron? He'd still be up, but God knows where and who with. Or she could just walk up the front there and tell the driver that she was being stalked. He could take her to the police station.

Her eyes lifted to the reflection in the glass ahead. His cap was pulled down, so all she could see was his chin, and his mouth. She had no idea if he was looking at the glass or at the back of her neck. Neither was good. The Chinese guy rang the bell and stood up, ready to leave at the next stop. Her stalker stood up too. Jules's surprise switched to panic as she watched him slide into the Chinese bloke's spot. Right behind her. She could smell him. He was rank. Her shoulders stiffened and her pulse picked up.

The tune to *Sex in the City* bursting into life almost made her lose her grip on the handset. Aaron. Why the hell was that little bugger calling at quarter to one?

"Aaron? Where are you?"

"All right, Mum? You aren't home."

"No shit, Sherlock. Where the hell are you?"

There was a pause. She never normally spoke to him like that, but fear made her sharp.

"Still at the Snooker Club. Thing is, Mum, I've sort of run out of cash. I thought, maybe if you were home, you could jump in the car and come up here to give me a lift."

The Snooker Club. Two stops further on, so they could get the bus back home together. Thank God. Relief and outrage combined to hone her tongue.

"Oh you did, did you? After I've been on my feet from six till twelve, earning some cash to keep us afloat, while you piss it away with your mates. Then you spend everything you've got, can't get home and expect your mother to sort it out. When are you going to learn to wipe your own arse, Aaron? I am so sick of this selfish, ignorant bloody attitude. Nineteen years on and I am still carrying you, you little shit!"

"Mum!"

"I'll be there in under ten minutes and you had better be outside, waiting. Because if I have to come in there, Aaron Michael, you are going to fucking well regret it. I am NOT in the mood for this!" Her teeth were clenched, aware that her speech was directed as much behind her as into the mouthpiece.

"All right, Mum. Jesus! I'll go and stand outside now, OK? And I'm sorry, I really am."

"Talk to the hand, Aaron." She ended the call and clenched her hands to stop them from shaking. She wasn't exactly sure what 'talk to the hand' actually meant, but the way Aaron used it was the equivalent of sticking your fingers in your ears and going, 'Ner ner ner ner'. Pretty much how she felt right now.

The bell tinged, requesting a stop. Her eyes flicked back to the glass. Stalker moved to the door. Jules held her breath, facing forward.

The doors opened, his long coat swung out into the night and he was gone. Jules watched him walk off, just in case. The bus pulled away. He'd gone. He left her alone. Thank God. Thank Aaron.

She was three stops away from her son.

Aaron. Her accidental saviour. And as soon as she saw him, she was going to kick his arse.

Chapter 17

Insomnia isn't always a bad thing, Beatrice thought. Something about the combination of Matthew's company, which inevitably involved fine dining on a Friday night, and a feeling of officially sanctioned disengagement tended to bestow a sense of release, relief and indulgence at the weekend. She always slept far better on Friday and Saturday nights. So what the hell was she doing poring over spreadsheets at five o'clock on Saturday morning?

This guy's following the pattern as if he's read the manual.
Patterns.

She skimmed the skin off her coffee with a teaspoon, took a sip and ran the program again. Dates, times and locations formed an unmistakeable link. And an ugly one at that. Even when the coffee was cool, the results were the same. Beatrice ran it again. One more time, she tried to prove herself wrong.

"Beatrice? What's wrong?"

"Hello, Virginia. I'm sorry to call so early, but I need to ask you a question. Who operates the CCTV cameras at Finsbury Park Tube?"

"The cameras? I don't know. Shit, Beatrice, it's ten to seven. On Saturday. And you want names of the camera operators right now?"

"Not names, although I suspect that will be necessary in time. What I want to know is which organisation is responsible for observing the daily footage of all the British Transport Police cameras in the Finsbury Park area."

"Well, that would be the London Underground and DLR. We share footage with the Met or City of London police when required, but everyday surveillance is carried out by our own people. Why?"

"I see. That's both good and bad news. Look, Virginia, I think I've found something rather disturbing. But I don't want to spoil your weekend lie-in. I can call back later this morning, if you like?"

"How much sleep do you think I'm likely to get after your telling me you've 'found something rather disturbing'? Come on, I'm awake now."

"Very well. I don't suppose you have the case files to hand?"

"Of course I do. They're right here, under my pillow." Virginia's voice was tetchy.

"Sorry. It is a bit early, I suppose. Well, I'm sitting here in front of my computer and I've spotted a pattern ..."

Ninety minutes later, Beatrice allowed herself a small celebration. Exotic fruit, miso soup or a salmon bagel may well do wonders for the mind, but on certain occasions, nothing in the world can beat a bacon sandwich. Large streaky rashers curling and spitting away in the pan. Two thick white slices warming in the toaster, a bottle of HP and the papers waiting on the table. *The Independent* for her, *The Times* for him. The espresso machine gurgled and hissed on the hob. The sunshine, their imminent breakfast and the thought of Matthew still crumpled under the sheets had already elevated Beatrice's mood. But the real reason for optimism was the revelation which had struck her in the wee small hours. They were closing in. She began to whistle.

"Good morning. And thank you." Matthew's hair resembled an unkempt guinea pig, and both pyjamas and slippers were candidates for the bin.

"Good morning." She kissed him lightly and returned to the

coffee. "Are you thanking me for the breakfast, or my angelic dawn chorus? Do you want tomatoes?"

"Always. Tomatoes are the civilised person's brown sauce. And the cumulative effect of bacon, fresh newsprint and my loved one whistling Simon Jeffes would make any man happy to be alive." He drew the papers to him and checked the headlines. "Dare I ask why you are so chirpy?"

Beatrice ladled rashers onto bread, shaking off fat, and transferred mugs and plates to the table.

"I've had an idea. *Bon appétit.*" She gave the sauce bottle a hefty whack, dolloping a brown stain across a Warburton's Thickest Slice.

"*Bon appétit* to you too. An idea about what?" He said, cutting plump beef tomatoes onto his plate.

"The case." She placed the sauced slice atop the bacon and pressed down. "I woke up at four this morning, put together a spreadsheet and proved myself right." She took a large, satisfying bite. A superlative sandwich: classic, comforting and containing all the optimism of a Saturday morning.

Matthew poured a glass of pink grapefruit juice and rubbed a hand over his eyes. "Right about what? Spit it out, woman, I want to eat my breakfast."

Beatrice swallowed and smiled. "The women we interviewed gave us some useful information. But the most interesting was the timing. He does nothing for a week, then he attacks. It's every other week. Now in the early stages, it's just one incident. Recently, he's stepped up his activity. But still only every other week. What does that tell you?"

Matthew thought as he drank his juice. "Build-up, I'd say. The man is compulsive and has to expose himself, for whatever reason. He does so, feels temporarily satisfied, and it takes a few days for the itch to return. Also, for fear of capture, he returns to his lair."

"So why two in the same week? Why not save one for the week after?"

"Extra itchy? I'm clueless, Old Thing. Put me out of my misery."

"He can't. For some reason, he only has the freedom to serve his urges on certain weeks. Shift work."

"Oh, I see. A night worker, perhaps? Used to being awake when others are not, spending a week of boredom, possibly fantasising the time away, until finally he is released. Yet unreleased."

"Matthew, you are the most wonderful man I know. If it weren't for your snobbishness about brown sauce, you would have a fine mind. But let's go one step further. He works every other week in a job which enables him to see these women. He studies their habits, learns their routines and then, when he's free to do so, he goes after them. He's never been seen on a CCTV camera, not arriving, not leaving. Tell me, why would that be?"

He dabbed his mouth with a piece of kitchen roll. "This coffee is simply perfect. Better than anything I've ever had in Italy. Right, his habits indicate a study of his environment. You say the only link is the fact the women use public transport. And they are all working-class women, some on the poverty line. Therefore, so is he. He works shifts in a factory of some sort and thus sees these poor females on his journey to or from work. He follows them, selects the ones that he thinks will cause him the least trouble and picks his moment. Do I get a gold star?"

Beatrice popped the corner of her sandwich into her mouth. Matthew's eyes strayed to the broadsheets. She needed him to pay attention.

"How, Matthew? How does he see them? How can he follow them? Why does he avoid all the CCTV cameras?"

"Because ... because he knows where the cameras are?"

Beatrice's smile spread. "Well done. Gold star. So?"

"We're not finished yet? I thought our tradition was to breakfast silently, digesting fine food and fresh press. This morning feels like a boot camp for my brain. You'll suggest jogging next."

"He works shifts, he watches cameras, he plans his attacks.

Matthew, I am in no doubt. He works for the British Transport Police. He's one of ours."

His sandwich returned to the plate. "That is a most unpleasant thought."

"Unpleasant. But correct."

"What do you intend to do about it?"

"Last week, he attacked twice. So this week, he's back at work. We have to identify him and set a trap. I spoke to Virginia about an hour ago and we're meeting at ten. I'm sorry, Matthew, but I did warn you. We have seven days to stop him, we can't afford not to."

"I understand. Please don't concern yourself about me. I thought I might say hello to Adrian, see if he fancies a trip to The Wine Academy. They have a course on perfect accompaniments for cheese today."

"Good idea. That'll give you both something to pontificate about for weeks."

Satisfied, Beatrice picked up the other half of her sandwich and opened *The Independent*. Matthew gave a theatrical sigh of relief and started on his breakfast.

Eager to get to work, Beatrice arrived at quarter to ten. Virginia was already waiting, in jodhpur-style trousers with loafers and a flimsy white shirt. She indicated a paper bag on the desk.

"Muffins and cappuccinos. I thought we deserved it. Hope you haven't had breakfast?"

Beatrice inhaled the aromas of coffee and cake. "No one could call one bacon sandwich breakfast. And as I was up with the dark, this is practically elevenses. Have you had thoughts?"

Virginia smiled as she unpacked the breakfast bag. "Yes, a few. First, we need a photo of every man on last week's day shift, to try for a positive ID."

"I agree. And when we know who it is, we have to make him believe we're looking the wrong way. He'll be on nights this week."

"Blueberry or double chocolate?"

"Do you really need to ask?"

"Here." Virginia passed over the cake and coffee. "When you say, 'looking the wrong way', you mean make him think we're following false leads?"

"Exactly. So I think we keep the surveillance pairs, and make some, if not all of them, common knowledge. He knows where they are, and will therefore avoid them. That way we can keep certain routes safe. But the Harrison honey trap stays confidential."

Virginia took a swig of coffee. "Mmm. Good thinking. And if Harrison's route is well away from the surveillance pairs, it will encourage him to ..."

"... to target her. I have a feeling we're closing in. I also have a feeling this is skimmed milk. You didn't ask for skinny cappuccinos, did you?"

"Says the woman with a mouthful of double chocolate muffin. Yes, I did. I also order a Diet Coke with my Big Mac and fries. Don't you?"

Beatrice scowled. "I'm happy to say I have never eaten any such thing. Yes, he's bound to go for Harrison. We must ensure top quality personnel are stationed at Finsbury Park Control Centre. Who's there now?"

Virginia wrapped the uneaten half of her muffin in a tissue and popped it back in the bag. "Ty Grant. I know you're not his greatest fan, but he's actually very sharp. I'd prefer to leave him in place."

"If you have faith in the man, so shall I. But our problem lies in the control room. Can we plant a presence without arousing suspicion? Can we watch the watchers?"

"I'm not sure, but I doubt it. Would you stalk while someone's watching? We need to liaise with senior officers there. This is going to be even more complicated because Finsbury Park is literally on the junction of three policing boroughs. But Hackney is the place to start. That's where most of the incidents have occurred.

I'll organise a briefing for key personnel this afternoon."

"Right. And then we should head to Hackney. I'd better make some calls. Thank you for breakfast. But next time, proper milk, please."

Virginia shot her a sidelong look. "Next time, you can get it. Just remember, I cut calories wherever I can."

"Killjoy." Beatrice dialled Finsbury Park Underground Station.

With five BTP staff and one Met officer, including Beatrice and Virginia, personal space became an issue in the London Underground Surveillance Centre. Inspector Kalpana Joshi sat in front of the bank of images, a touch screen at her fingertips. The first BTP officer worked with a headset, answering calls; the other operated the replay suite, reviewing footage. Ty stood behind him, asking occasional questions. Beatrice and Virginia devoted their attention to the Inspector's brusque presentation.

"Right then, from this room, we observe the borough via a hundred and seventy cameras. As you can see, we have five control joystick panels to monitor the Petard cameras. We've also three control panels for fixed views, known as Molynx. The supervisor operates everything via this touch screen, pulling whichever image they need from any one of these forty-four monitors onto the main viewer." She demonstrated by scanning the plethora of images, selecting an angle of the underpass, and dragging it to the enormous display. The clarity startled Beatrice; the size and level of detail was impressive.

"If there's cause for concern, we've got a variety of options. In circumstances such as graffiti artists and wilful damage, reckless behaviour, smoking or mild harassment, we mostly use a 'message from God' – the customer service intercom. Alternatively, we might deploy station staff, especially for drunks or vagrants."

Beatrice asked the obvious question. "What if it's something worse?"

"If we see the incident as more serious, we can deploy officers instantly, or for something such as suspected terrorist activity, we share these images immediately with MICC."

Beatrice glanced at Virginia. "Management Information Control Centre – in our building. These places are the eyes and ears, MICC is the brain."

Beatrice nodded. "Thank you. Do you share your recordings with anyone else, Inspector Joshi?"

She twisted in her seat to face Beatrice, nut-brown eyes raised under dark lashes. "Kalpana, please. Yeah, we got two dedicated computers for communication with other agencies. For example, in an accident scenario, we can share our live footage directly with the emergency services, or traffic management. Law enforcement takes precedence, so if a camera's being used to monitor traffic transgressions, we override that to follow a suspect."

Beatrice leant her head to one side. "I'd like to go back. You mention you have moveable cameras?"

"Correct. Petards."

"Wonderful name. *Pétard* is French for 'joint', but I expect you already know that."

"As in knees and elbows?" asked Virginia.

Beatrice and Kalpana spoke simultaneously. "No, spliffs."

The inspector met Beatrice's eyes and exhaled a sharp snort of laughter. "You ever think you've been in the job too long?"

"Daily. But in my case, it's probably true. Now these Petards are presumably in and just outside the station itself?

"Yeah. Mostly on the concourse and platforms, they can pan right and left, tilt up and down, rotate three hundred and sixty degrees and, crucially, zoom in on detail, such as passing of packages."

"So you have an officer watching these, and another on the fixed cameras?"

"Depends on the time of day. During peak periods, we got one on each. But from two a.m. to six a.m., there's only one. Four people in here during rush hour. Two on these cameras, one on replay, and one on calls."

Virginia looked at the bank of monitors to their right, where Ty bent over the desk. "This replay function – checking for activity around the time of an incident?"

"Amongst other things. Sometimes we need to check footage for Data Protection reasons before releasing it. But much of it is surveillance – who was where at a certain time. We also use it to monitor patterns, especially on football Saturdays. Comes in handy."

"I can imagine," Beatrice said. "And this other chap is taking calls from where?"

"He's operating the hotline. People calling to report incidents, passengers having problems and pressing the help buttons on the platform, not to mention plenty of lazy gits asking for the next bus to Crouch End. A great deal of patience is needed for this task."

"And I bet you get lots of emergency calls which are in fact requests for help?"

Virginia's question made Kalpana smile. "Yeah, course. Dealing with the public. Drives you to tears, doesn't it?"

Beatrice laughed. "Both of desperation and admiration. But it's always bloody hard work. Do you have a quiet room somewhere so the three of us might discuss how best to proceed?"

"Sure. My office. Would your sergeant like to see how this works? Jacek, show the Met sergeant how to use it, would you?"

"Ty, you want to take over now?" Virginia asked.

He nodded and took Kalpana's place at the observation monitors, as the three women made for the door.

Ty grinned. "Mmm, you warmed the seat for me."

Kalpana replied without looking back. "Don't speak to me like that, Sergeant. I find it disrespectful."

Beatrice followed the slight figure from the room, biting her lip and memorising both line and tone.

Chapter 18

Adrian had only popped out to buy stamps, but somehow, he'd purchased a pair of African violets. As he was walking home, deliberating where best to display them, his mobile rang.

"Hello Beatrice. I'm just coming past the Co-op. Do you need something?"

"Actually, Adrian, this is Matthew. I'm calling you on your mobile phone due to the fact that I got no response when knocking at your door."

Adrian dropped his voice. "Matthew! I was wondering when you'd make contact. Has she gone to work?"

"I can barely hear you. What is all that noise?"

"Old Street on a Saturday morning. I'll be back in five minutes. Tea or coffee?"

"Tea, please. I've drunk far too much coffee and feel a little nervous."

"Tea it is. Me too, I can't wait! See you in a bitch."

Hugs seemed inappropriate, so Adrian chose the strong handshake and pat on shoulder routine. Matthew wore his own version of casual. A faded denim shirt, which had the air of real as opposed to faux-faded, paired with downmarket chinos. Fortunately, he'd opted for espadrilles. Adrian approved. Ill-kempt feet were one of summer's horrors, along with flies and cycling shorts.

"Come in! I've made tea and taken it into the office. We may as well get down to business. I thought we'd start by showing you the progress I've made."

"Sounds good to me. When you say progress ...?"

"Come this way and all will be revealed. You'll be surprised by what a knack I have for this sort of thing."

Matthew's fingers drummed on the desk as he studied the screen with a frown.

"One hesitates to jump to the obvious assumption, but does this strike you as possible drug-dealing?"

"Exactly my thoughts." Adrian pulled out a folder with printouts of the two enlarged photographs. "Two men, I'd say, carrying bags. The first is older and you can see his face. That means he was looking in your direction. The second, with the ponytail, is side-on, looking up the beach. The person waiting to meet them is female, you can tell by her clothes. But there's no chance of seeing her face, her hair's hiding it."

Matthew left the screen with reluctance. But his eyes widened when he saw the photographs. "The ponytail man! That's the burglar, no doubt about it. His hair was unforgettable. This picture is quite startling, I have to say. Much clearer than on the computer. Well done!"

"Well, this level of magnification is down to my knowing the right people. I happen to be friendly with a graphic designer who has sophisticated technology and infinite patience. I'm lucky to have Jared." Adrian sighed. "Now look over here."

He indicated the top left of the picture. The shapes remained in shadow, with an oblique shaft of light hitting the sand in front. Lower, a small rectangle stood out as lighter than the background. Adrian willed him to see the combination for what it was.

"Ever tried the 3D picture books, Matthew? Let your eyes unfocus and then tell me what you see."

"Ah yes. The arrangement of shapes suggests some sort

of vehicle. And this must be the number plate. Impossible to identify it, of course, but it's large, like an off-road vehicle, and obviously black. No wonder we can barely see it. So these two come off a boat, carrying two bags, and meet the driver. We're taking pictures, they spot us and try to get the camera back. Whatever is in those bags, they certainly didn't want it on film."

"Drugs." Adrian poured them both a refill from the pot. "What else would it be?"

"Let me see the second photograph."

Adrian handed it over, trying not to show off. All three heads had turned toward the lens and the woman's hand was raised, as if to shield her eyes, or hold back her flailing hair. Whatever the reason, her gesture made her features indistinguishable. Ponytail's rodent expression and the older man's suspicion were visible. Imperceptibly better light threw a clearer perspective on the trio, their boat and their looming vehicle.

Matthew sat back with a satisfied sigh. "Bravo! That is excellent work, Adrian. We can now connect the man who took Beatrice's bag and the camera thief to this figure on the beach."

"But we still have no proof he was the one who stole her laptop."

"Sorry? Did you say 'stole her laptop'?"

Adrian should have known. Being a double agent meant remembering exactly who knew what. And he'd already forgotten.

Matthew accepted the news without fuss. "My only challenge now is acting surprised when she tells me. One can only hope she's too distracted by her serial flasher to notice my lack of concern."

"The only reason she didn't mention it was out of worry for you. I'll vouch for that. I nagged her. Really. We almost rowed."

"Adrian, it may sound sarcastic, as we're going behind her back, but I do believe she has a genuine friend in you. As for the pictures, I'm most impressed! Congratulations on some very astute detective work."

"Thank you! Although the compliment is due more to my persistence and contacts, but what the hell. Grab glory where you can. And after all, what more is there to detective work than dogged opportunism?"

Matthew inclined his head, as if considering the truth of that statement. Adrian fidgeted. Always save the best till last. He rubbed his hands together and smiled.

"There's more?" asked Matthew.

"There is. With a combination of Jared's skill and my creativity, we have a partial ID of the number plate." Tucking his leg beneath him, Adrian passed Matthew a cropped version of the second photograph. In the centre, seven figures or letters were discernible, but rendering them comprehensible could only be guesswork.

"Now, I know it looks hopeless and I just about gave up. But as I left his studio, Jared said the only other thing he could suggest was trying out templates. Imposing letters and numbers over this image and seeing which came closest. Yesterday, I spent the entire afternoon doing just that, when I should have been doing a stock take of European beers. And through a process of trial and error, I think I have it."

He flipped open the file to reveal a sheet of A4, with one typed line in the centre.

CMG287M

Matthew examined it and shook his head. "I have to commend your persistence, but this car is relatively new. It's not possible that it would have such a plate."

"What do you mean?"

"New cars have two letters, denoting region; two numbers, denoting year; and three random letters. So ..."

"Maybe it's a personalised number plate?"

"Would you pay for a plate which read see-em-gee-two-eight-seven ... hang on."

Matthew bent forward, hands forming a triangular screen over his brow. Adrian gave him a moment and took another sip of tea.

"You may just have something here. CM, if that is correct, is the area code for Cardiff. Possible, given the location. G2, or more likely, 62, to identify its age. This car was registered after the first of September 2012. The final three elements should be letters. 87M could be BZM, or N."

Adrian's pride returned. "So I did get it, after all?"

"You did. Or at least, you've given us something to go on. I wonder how we can find out who owns it?"

"Ask Beatrice."

"Beatrice?"

"Of course. Tell her what I've got so far and see if she can trace it. Play it casual, sound a bit bored by my puppyish enthusiasm, but tell her it's worth a try. You don't need to tell her we're actively working this case."

"That's actually a rather good idea. And I have noted the stage directions. What if she finds it?"

"Perhaps, unless you have plans for next weekend, we could sneak off to Wales?"

Matthew's eyes widened and he flashed a most impressive set of teeth. "Certainly possible. I have a seminar in Rome the end of next week, so may just tell her I'm staying on a few days. She's likely to be so busy, she'll barely notice."

Matthew glanced at the photographs once more and his eyes narrowed.

"What is it?" Adrian leant forward.

Matthew jumped to his feet, looking around Adrian's tiny, but perfectly neat office.

"Something I said?" Adrian followed him into the lounge, watching him pace up and down with the pictures.

"The bags they're carrying. Why would you carry something

that way? Would you happen to have a holdall? Anything with a handle?"

Adrian considered a moment and retrieved his Tod's leather sports bag from the hall. Matthew took it, with a nod.

"So here I am, leaping off a boat at dawn, with my bag." He jumped onto the cowskin rug. "Now, most folk would carry it thus, arm straight, bag hanging from their hand. However, these two," he jabbed a finger at the pictures, "have their elbows bent, holding the bags higher off the ground. Why is that?"

Recumbent, arms folded, Adrian was unimpressed. "Drugs, yo. Can't afford to get that shit wet, know what I'm saying?"

Matthew eyed him with some bemusement. "Hmm. On the beach? It could be, I suppose. It reminds me of cricketers, or tennis players. How they hold their kitbags, as if they are precious."

"Several kilos of heroin would be pretty precious. And disastrous to get it wet. It's drugs, Matthew. Stop looking for the obscure explanation when the obvious is biting you on the buttock."

"You're right. I wonder where they're coming from? A larger boat out in the bay, perhaps?"

"Bound to be. And with any luck, we'll soon have the details of their dealer. What are your plans for the day?"

"Nothing particular. Pottering over to Persephone's for a browse, organise something for dinner ..."

"Do that first. Then come back here and I'll take you to one of my favourites in old Spitalfields market for lunch. It's my treat and the wine list is an absolute joy. You won't feel like shopping afterwards, I warn you."

"That's an offer I cannot refuse. But is it wise to indulge when you have to be on optimum form for this evening's performance?"

"Believe me, Matthew, a glass or two of Chateau Plince has only ever improved my rendition of *The Surrey with the Fringe on Top*."

"I trust your judgement. Very well. Meet you back here at twelve?" Matthew made his way to the door.

"Perfect. And I'll start packing for next weekend."

Matthew turned. "Adrian, you have a full week ahead of you. Why would you start packing already?"

"The sooner the better. I need to plan the perfect capsule wardrobe, with all the appropriate accessories. Now I've done *Roman Holiday, Death in Venice* and *Leaving Las Vegas*, but I have never done Detecting Drug Dealers in Devon. So it will require some thought."

"It's Wales, not Devon."

"Even better. I'll need to buy a phrasebook and everything. See you later."

Wales. September. He would start with his panama. He rarely wore it in London, not with his linen suit, because the ensemble suggested Hannibal Lecter. But in Wales, that would hardly matter.

Chapter 19

"And she replied, 'Don't speak to me like that, Sergeant. I find it disrespectful'. Didn't even look round. Nor did I, but I'd love to have seen his face."

Dawn shook her head and picked up another piece of sashimi. "He sounds like a total baboon. He and Virginia Lowe deserve each other."

Beatrice couldn't quite agree. "The man is an utter ape, which is why I can't understand her attitude to him. She may be a lot of things, but she's not stupid. It was a glorious moment, though. That BTP Inspector, barely forty, a wisp of a little thing, slapping him down like an impertinent school boy. I could hardly contain myself."

"I can imagine. What about the case? You any closer to nobbling Jack Flash? This tuna smells a bit off, I don't think I'll eat it. Check yours before you ... Beatrice, what is it?"

Her expression had given her away. She marshalled her thoughts.

"It's hard to put into words, but the ... trivialisation of this case is at the heart of the problem. I know you mean nothing by it, but we are talking about a potential rapist, an assaulter of teenage girls. Calling him Jack Flash, or a dirty old man, or in any way diluting the threat of this individual is what allows him to get away with it for so long. Dawn, I'm sorry. I don't mean to get at you, of all people. I suppose I'm just articulating my own change in attitude."

Dawn raised her brows, but looked away. Beatrice took a slice of pickled ginger between her chopsticks and placed it down again.

She made another attempt at explaining. "The thing is, there have been so many of these casual ..."

"Beatrice, it's fine. Eat your food. I agree with you. Listen, Frances did a university project on inter-racial tensions last year. And one phrase from her dissertation leapt out at me and has kind of stuck. 'Micro-aggressions.' Those daily little put-downs, reminders of your place, flexing of superior muscle, you know what I mean? I've suffered from this myself. So have you. Obviously, Frances used it to talk about race."

"An example?"

"OK. You're at the sandwich counter. 'Where are you from?' you ask the white kid who serves you. 'Leytonstone,' he replies and you say you know it well. The next day, an Asian kid serves you. You ask him where he's from. 'Walthamstow,' he says. 'No, but where are you really from?' Subtext: I belong, you don't. It struck me as applicable to so many other situations."

Beatrice chewed over both *maki-zushi* and concept.

"What I'm saying, Beatrice, is that I agree. You can belittle a person, a fear, even a crime by the language you use. The message came across louder still when I worked with abused women. Expressions like: 'a little shake', 'only the back of my hand', and my favourite, 'an affectionate slap'. So I do get it and I'm sorry for being so tactless. I can't even blame the *sake*, as I haven't drunk it yet."

"Well, it's time you did. I apologise for getting snippy with you and I'm glad you appreciate my point. How do you say 'Cheers' in Japanese?"

"No idea. But *Sayonara* means 'goodbye' so that'll do. *Sayonara!*"

Beatrice raised her glass but was interrupted by a loud tut of disapproval. The counter worker continued his rapid chopping, but glanced up at them under his white hat.

"Sort it out, ladies. If you're saying goodbye, fair dos." His accent was pure Gravesend. "But when raising a glass, in Japanese you say, '*Kampai!*' Awright?"

Beatrice gave a respectful semi-bow. "Thank you. *Kampai*, Dawn."

"And *Kampai* to you too." They slugged the *sake*, the warmth hitting Beatrice's cheeks seconds later.

Dawn's complexion rose at the same pace as her smile.

"It works, this stuff, doesn't it?" Beatrice asked.

"No doubt. *Kampai*, I must remember that one. I have to say, this place is an unexpected find. An oasis amid the madness. You should bring Matthew here next weekend –does he like sushi?"

"Most definitely. Even makes it himself. He is a passionate Japanese fan. But next weekend would have been my turn to do Devon." An odd sense of unease slithered down Beatrice's spine, an unpleasant sensation, all the more so for being familiar. She was nurturing a microscopic resentment, prodding it, fanning it and encouraging it to fester.

"Would have been? You have to work?" Dawn asked, with her natural gentle interest.

"I probably will. But he didn't know that. I don't even know myself yet. Nevertheless, he has extended his stay in Rome after the Ostia seminar, 'just to shop and savour the atmosphere of Rome.' And frankly, that whiffs."

"Of what? Having a weekend of self-indulgence? It's his summer holiday, he's entitled. Come on, Beatrice. You must be due some time off. So when you've caught that rotten little shit from Finsbury Park, you can take a break and indulge yourselves together. What's bitten you?"

"Nothing, really. Just being a petulant brat. Tell me about your weekend."

Dawn set her chopsticks on their little china holder and rested her chin on her hand, eyes searching Beatrice's face.

"Leave me alone," muttered Beatrice, staring at her soy sauce.

"I have nothing more to say. It's up to him what he does with his weekends." She picked up some sashimi. "Tuna tastes fine to me, you're just being fussy. Oh for God's sake!" She placed her chopsticks down and glared at her friend.

Dawn shrugged. "You may as well cough it up. And I'm not talking about the fish. Why have you wound yourself into a spin about Matthew having a couple of extra days in Rome?"

"Because it is just not like him. His seminar ends on Friday, but he wants to come back on Sunday. Why? He hates Rome in summer. Too hot, packed with tourists and all the restaurant prices go up. He forgets that when he agreed to present his research, he moaned to me for ages about having to go there at all. Now he wants to stay an extra day. And ... he's got a look in his eye. He's excited about something. Or someone."

Dawn rolled her eyes. "You seriously suspect Matthew of having an affair?"

"Lepers don't change their spots."

"Nor do leopards. And how can you, of all people, make such an accusation? Have you shared these thoughts with your counsellor?"

Beatrice swilled her *sake* around the glass. "Not yet. I suppose I should."

Dawn's face creased into an understanding smile. "Or better still, talk to Matthew."

"Perhaps. I'm just afraid of what I might find out. All right. I'll talk to him. It's not healthy just to hypothesise and fret; I can feel myself getting sucked into it all again. You're very good for me. And for the price of a plate of sushi, much cheaper than a session with James. I'm sorry." Beatrice smiled, before returning her attention to her food.

Dawn picked up her chopsticks with an air of satisfaction. "Actually, I'm happy you told me. Friends rarely share their fears regarding infidelity, suspected or otherwise. They must think the subject too painful for The Betrayed Wife. Ian's indiscretion has come to define me, for most people. But not you."

Beatrice studied Dawn's kind, open face. "That's the half-full perspective. It could be that I'm a self-centred, thoughtless drain, who only cares about her own problems."

"Trust you to spin yourself in a positive light. You didn't eat that tuna, did you? How far are we from the nearest A&E?"

Beatrice reached over and helped herself to Dawn's rejected fish. "If I'm having my stomach pumped, I may as well make it worth their while."

Dawn laughed and pinched an Eskimo roll between chopsticks, popping it into her mouth and turning her gaze out at the street. She shook her head in a disbelieving gesture.

"Something wrong?" Beatrice asked.

"No, nothing at all. Good food, great company. Nice little shot of liquor, and yet another amusing haircut for entertainment. Can't complain."

"Nor me. Which haircut?" Beatrice polished off her ginger slices. Somehow orchestral in its refined combination of flavours, one could almost applaud Japanese food.

"This horrible trend toward shaving above your ears, leaving a Davey-Crockett one-length hank from forehead to shoulder blades. You haven't noticed? They're everywhere; men, women and, worst of all, children."

A bell rang in Beatrice's consciousness. Picking up her *sake*, she focused on Dawn. "That night in The Speaker, when I came back from the loo, you said something about haircuts. Do you remember?"

Dawn's smile faded, replaced by a concertina of concentration.

"Oh yes. While you were in there, a guy walked past the window. He spotted me and gave me a wink so I smiled back. He mouthed some words and held his hand like this, you know?" She extended her little finger and thumb and raised her hand to her cheek.

"He wanted your phone number?" Beatrice's incredulity was unmissable.

Dawn didn't seem offended. "Apparently so. I pointed to my ring finger – he couldn't see it from there – and shook my head. He just shrugged and moved on, and I noticed his haircut. Short, dark and almost normal at the front, but at the back, he had a blond ponytail. I'm not keen on ponytailed men at the best of times, but in a different colour? Why would anyone make such a hash of their hair?"

"And do you remember, when you mentioned that, I told you I had a story to tell? More *sake*, or shall we revert to old habits?"

Dawn turned to the counter-chopper. "Do you think we could have two large glasses of dry white wine over here?"

Chapter 20

Onto camera, 7.09 p.m., Blackstock Road. Turquoise mini dress, denim jacket, white heels. Chewing gum. As she waits to cross the street, she pulls her dress further down her thighs, and pushes her hair up at the temples.

Above her, a camera tilts and zooms. Her progress through the station is slick; she's done this before. Oyster card, no hesitation, trotting down the tunnel and onto the escalator. She keeps walking and arrives on the southbound platform just as a Piccadilly line to Uxbridge thunders in. She looks pretty and fresh and expectant. And a bit nervous. Ticks all the right boxes.

In the surveillance van parked at the end of Station Place, Virginia and Beatrice watched the replay of PC Karen Harrison's movements. Current footage from Finsbury Park's Control Centre still streamed onto their system, yet their attention was on images recorded three hours ago.

Five cameras covered each stage of Harrison's route, but the main object of interest was the central screen, which reflected whatever was on the main console at BTP. When the officer in the control room dragged an image onto his main screen, the same pictures popped up in the discreet black van down the street. Watching whatever the watcher watched.

"Girl done good." The officer turned round with a grin.

"She did, Fitch. Some very nice little touches there," Virginia agreed.

"And he watched her from Blackstock Road to the platform. Got a close-up and everything." His face was lit, both by monitors and enthusiasm.

Beatrice smiled back at Fitch. She understood. There were few finer feelings than the first nibble on the bait.

Virginia seemed satisfied. "Check the record sheet for timings and find out exactly who was on the console. Double check there were no last-minute changes to the rota. And I want you to do the same after her return journey. Good work, PC Fitzgerald."

"Don't thank me, ma'am. It's Harrison wants thanking." His smile remained in place while he replaced his earphones and returned his attention to the screens.

"Should we get into position, Beatrice? It's ten to eleven. She'll be on her way back soon."

Somerfield Road, a residential street of Victorian terraces, remained quiet although it was just gone chucking-out time. Their unmarked BMW, with tinted windows, fitted in perfectly with its surroundings. Listening to the updates on the police radio, the two women sat in attentive silence, until confirmation came – Harrison had boarded a northbound train from Leicester Square. Her job was to give the impression of someone who'd spent the evening dancing and drinking an excess of Smirnoff Ice.

In reality, the girl's evening had been slightly more pedestrian. On arrival in Leicester Square, she had entered All Bar One, met a second officer in the toilets, changed her clothes and trudged down to Charing Cross Police Station, where she had spent three hours watching TV and drinking coffee. The reality of police work. Waiting. Watching and waiting and trying not to fall asleep. Dull diligence.

Virginia let her head fall backwards. "So we've got around half an hour before we're likely to get a visual. God, I wish I still smoked."

"No, you don't. Concentrate on staying alert for Harrison, picking up every detail and in about an hour, we can go home to our beds."

"Yes. Hold that thought. Bed, duvet, cat. I am exhausted. What have I done today? Push papers. But now, on the street, in the middle of the action, I'm knackered and I want to go home."

Beatrice could sympathise. This week had been stressful for all of them, and as the weekend approached, signs of strain affected the whole team. Time was ticking away. In two more days, their man would become active again. She rubbed her face; her eyes were drooping. Small wonder: she'd been awake since four. Best thing would be conversation.

"It's because you know nothing will happen tonight. He's at work, so he can't do anything. But we have to be wide awake, just in case. What's your cat's name?"

"Tallulah. A bad-tempered Burmese. You have creatures?"

"No. But the lack of four-legged, or even two-legged creatures makes my bed no less appealing. In some ways, it makes it more so."

Neither spoke, matching words with impressions.

The radio continued its chatter and Grant's voice confirmed all was calm at BTP Control Centre, everyone working their designated shift.

"From what I hear, we're in a similar position," Virginia said, folding her arms.

"In what way?"

"The men way. We both have a permanent partner, who is absent for most of the time. Or have I been misinformed?"

Beatrice considered how much she wanted to share. As a rule, she kept her private life ring-fenced and off limits.

"Yes, I suppose you're right. Although I would express it differently. My partner and I spend weeks apart, and weekends together. 'Absent' smacks of neglect. Our arrangement is very much a mutual choice."

"You're lucky. Our arrangement is very much a mutual 'no choice'. My husband works for BAE Systems and he's based in Dubai. When we married, we both assumed the other one would give up the job. I thought a London lad, with a wife and home here, would be desperate to come back. He couldn't see why I would want to continue working when I could live the luxury life of the expat housewife. He doesn't want to stop working. Nor do I. So we see each other for two weeks every quarter. Plus the odd holiday and occasional weekend."

"Hence the cat."

"Tallulah and I were together long before I met Stewart." Virginia turned to Beatrice with a laugh. "He's a dog person."

"Oh dear."

"No, it's actually fine. It's just ... on paper, we shouldn't work. He's younger, by nine years. He's serious, hard-working and loves being alone. I'm frivolous, feckless and can't be without company. He likes white, I like red; I fancy beefcake, he has a concave chest; he's attracted to large breasts, I'm a 32A. But the thing is, with him, I'm totally relaxed. He makes me laugh, in person, on screen, on the phone, and I miss him all the bloody time."

"Well, that *is* a surprise," Beatrice responded. "I'd have put you at 34B easily."

Virginia snorted with laughter and gave her a sideways glance. "Well, that's me in the spotlight. Your turn."

"Would you feel terribly short-changed if I didn't volunteer my bra size?"

Virginia made a mock-disappointed face.

"My story is simple and rather dull. Matthew and I have been together over twenty years and prefer to live apart. He has two daughters from a previous marriage, and one grandson. I've never been married, have no offspring and no regrets about it. Our relationship is based on room for independence, not to mention trust. And it has always worked terrifically well."

The radio crackled, and Beatrice checked the time. Harrison

should be approaching the Tube station now.

"I sense a 'so far' in that statement?"

Beatrice could go no further without a lesson in her personal history. "It's complicated. Can I ask a question?"

"On your behalf, or Dawn Whittaker's?"

Her defensive tone surprised Beatrice. Seemed like events at the award ceremony had left a bitter taste in several mouths.

"Mine. I'm curious. Where does Ty Grant fit into the picture?"

Virginia's face hardened and she looked ahead. "He doesn't."

"I see." Beatrice faced front. "Fair enough."

Virginia slid her fingers up her face, dropping her forehead into her palms.

"Look, it's the opposite of complicated. A bit of a flirtation, harmless way of passing the time. I'm not interested in Ty. I just get ... bored, you know?"

"Does Ty see it as a harmless pastime too?"

Virginia's head swivelled. "He hasn't said anything, has he?"

"To me? Good God, no. I just wondered if both sets of expectations were equally innocent."

Virginia checked her watch and sighed. "No, Ty is trying to push it further. And I really like the guy. He's exactly my type, but ..."

The radio hissed and distorted, before informing them they were about to get a visual on Harrison.

The street was silent as the poor girl maintained her persona right to the door of 'her flat'. Stopping, swaying, almost tripping over, she looked like someone whose judgement was suspect, whose coordination was clumsy and whose radar was down. An excellent performance. Once inside, she could change, rest and enjoy the weekend. Because the following week she'd be doing it all over again, with every expectation of being followed by a pervert. She made it without mishap, and staggered inside. A faint round of applause came from the watching teams over the airwaves.

Virginia turned the ignition. "I'll drop you home."

The usual stop-start journey though London became slightly smoother once on Green Lanes. Beatrice picked up the handset, announced the end of the evening's activities, wished the team a good weekend and switched the radio to its usual frequency. Virginia drove without a word. As the BMW approached Newington Green, Beatrice chose to speak.

"Virginia, I believe our earlier conversation was one-sided. I'm sorry if I offended you and I didn't mean to interfere in your private life."

"Yes, you did. But it's all right. I often think we're hard-wired to winkle out the truth. We're trained detectives, but much more significantly, women. Look, I was doing exactly the same thing, asking you if your relationship had worked well 'so far'. Your interview technique was better, that's all."

"Thank you. And you were right, in fact. I've always been wholly truthful with Matthew, about everything, good and bad. Now, for the first time in years, I find myself tempted to ... how can I put it?"

"Stray?" Virginia's focus remained on the street.

"No. Not to stray. To exclude him. I want to do something, chase something, and I should tell him about it. It could be a risk, but that is precisely why I want to keep it to myself. And, well, I suppose a small part of me wants to show him that I'm not quite past it yet." The truth had a habit of sneaking up on her recently.

"I get that. A small part of me wants to prove the same thing. Although I know I'd rather be with Stu than anyone else."

Beatrice took a deep breath. "Forgive me for speaking out of turn. Let's ignore the fact that you're Ty's boss, that no police romance ever stays hidden, that you're married, that any encounter would cover him in laddish glory while seriously jeopardising your career. None of that is relevant. However, listening to you talk about your husband, I'd say you've been lucky enough to marry your best friend. The risk of losing that could never be worth a mess of porridge."

Virginia remained silent.

Along Balls Pond Road, the atmosphere relaxed. Beatrice looked out at shuttered shops, bright kebab joints, cabbies yelling and the usual flow of humanity kissing, cursing, laughing, pissing, crying, swearing, hugging and fighting. A wave of dismay crashed over her.

That's all any of us have: each other. And what a shifting, unreliable, inconstant place to bury the treasure of your hopes. Of your love. You'll probably never find it again. Some bugger will dig it up and nick it.

Virginia's voice shook her from her spiral. "And you? Chucking away twenty years of bliss for some self-determined goal? I suppose you'll go all gnomic on me if I ask you what it is. What dragon you're trying to slay, all on your own?"

Beatrice sat up. "Where are we?"

"Kingsland Road. Why, is it a long story?"

"No. But it should keep you entertained till we hit Old Street."

"Right then. I'm sitting comfortably. You may begin."

Chapter 21

Adrian met Matthew at Paddington Station with nothing more than eager anticipation and a perfectly packed Tod's holdall. It was only one day, after all. London could manage without him. Armed with Beatrice's email, they were following up a concrete lead.

Well done on the registration. You were only one letter out. DVLA confirmed it's a car hire company in Cardiff. Details below. So looks like the SUV might be a dead-end. Thanks anyway. B x

No such thing as dead ends. On the phone to Williams Car Hire, Matthew did an excellent impression of Beatrice's boss. And the rest was like taking candy from a baby. Williams Car Hire provided the name Marie Fisher as the renter of the Jeep Grand Cherokee with those plates over the Bank Holiday weekend. Fifteen minutes of research on the Internet gave them Ms Fisher's address, phone number and employer – Bevan and Gough Property Management, 56 City Road. Adrian and detective work really did seem to be a match made in Heaven.

Both men had agreed. The train was by far the most relaxing option. Matthew loathed driving anywhere more crowded than Much-Middling-in-the-Marsh, or wherever it was he lived. And Adrian, blissfully, had no licence. Not forgetting the lack of stress, the buffet car and the opportunity to discuss interrogation techniques. Matthew had treated them to First Class tickets and

Adrian found himself whistling the *Poirot* theme tune as they located their seats. He stopped as soon as he realised. Apart from the lack of subtlety, whistling was second only to smoking for causing wrinkles on the upper lip. First Class proved to be an excellent choice. They enjoyed a table to themselves and the carriage was practically empty, apart from two businessy sorts absorbed in the Financial Times. Both wore suits and ties and frowns.

"Two hours. What say you to a nice read of the paper, get some breakfast and then knuckle down to making some decisions on technique?" asked Matthew.

"Very well, my friend. Can't expect the little grey cells to function on an empty stomach," Adrian replied. Matthew gave him a baffled look, but unfolded *The Times* with a nod.

On arrival at Cardiff Central Station, the two men were ready to stretch their legs, so chose to walk to their destination. Their route took them right through the city centre.

Cardiff intrigued Adrian. Gorgeous arcades, a proper castle smack in the middle, pedestrianised shopping streets, outdoor cafés and every kind of store you'd find in a half-decent London suburb. But so much more space. Wide streets and lots of sunshine. He might well consider coming back here. Two hours on the train. It was time Jared saw something more of Britain than London's East End and Old Compton Street.

Bevan and Gough's premises looked more like a car showroom than an estate agent. Double windows displaying photographs and hyped descriptions of local property obscured the interior, where presumably welcoming faces waited behind desks. The prices came as a real surprise to Adrian. Directly to his left was a beautiful Docklands flat, with a divine view, kitchen/diner and no less than two bedrooms for something approaching affordable. It wasn't beyond the realms of possibility that he could get a transfer to Wales. Downshifting. Living in a smaller city, he'd buy a bike and even get a dog. Jared could set up his own business in one of those glorious arcades, and on Saturday mornings they could shop for organic Welsh produce with their black schnauzer, called ....

"Adrian?"

Matthew gestured for him to go first and they entered the shop.

A heavily made-up blonde looked up. "Morning, gentlemen. Seen something you like?"

Adrian gawped at the Max Factor mask in front of them, while Matthew responded with his effortless grey gravitas. "Good morning. Unfortunately, we're not interested in property. We're from Williams Car Hire, Head Office. Looking for a Marie Fisher?"

Adrian caught the head to his right pop up. Dark, medium-length hair, sharp features. She might easily be the woman from the beach.

The blonde's interest waned. "Marie? Some blokes to see you from the car hire place." She returned to her computer screen. Adrian could swear he saw playing cards reflected in her glasses.

Marie approached them, hand extended, eyes suspicious. Adrian made constant mental notes on body language, hair, shoes and mannerisms. 'Every detail matters.' Beatrice had drummed that in more times than she'd cooked him hot dinners. So, Marie Fisher – thirtyish, crows' feet and hints of a growing-out dye-job. Expensive nails, good shoes, and those earrings weren't cheap. She put herself together well.

Matthew shook her hand with a reassuring smile. "Ms Fisher. My name is Michael Bryant, and this is my colleague, Andrew Ramos."

Adrian smiled, more at the thrill of hearing his new alias than social convention, and shook her hand. Matthew continued, offering his business card, which Adrian had designed and printed two nights ago.

"We work for Williams Car Hire, Head Office. Andrew and I

investigate any problems resulting from our rentals, the objective being to sort it ourselves. Pembrokeshire police contacted us, regarding an incident near Porthgain a few weeks back. We generally prefer to make direct enquiries about incidents involving our vehicles and avoid adding to the police burden, if we can. Is there somewhere we could talk?"

"Oh I see. Right so, follow me. We've a staff area out back."

She'd swallowed it. He restrained a temptation to nudge Matthew.

Marie was Irish. No doubt at all. Adrian's skill with accents was legendary and this woman was watered-down Irish. Very interesting. The back yard contained two cars, half a dozen white plastic chairs and a dirty table with a pockmarked ashtray advertising Brains Bitter. Marie placed coffee cups in front of them. Adrian took one sip and held back a grimace. She dug in her bag for cigarettes, before politely offering the packet. They both refused.

"So you said this incident happened in Pembrokeshire?" she asked, lighting up.

Matthew opened his file, keeping it tilted to him. Very smart. Adrian watched Marie's eyes focus on the back of the folder.

"Correct. On the twenty-seventh of August, a couple of holidaymakers were involved in an early morning bag-snatching incident on the cliffs near Porthgain. They reported the theft to the police and gave them the possible number plate of a utility vehicle they believe was involved. The police traced the vehicle to us and asked us to confirm the identity of the renter. The couple involved were older and not sure they recalled the number plate correctly. We grabbed the chance of running our own investigation. You know, find out if there's any substance, before handing over the details. We're not keen on being involved in any criminal proceedings as you can imagine, so if we can prove it was not one of our vehicles, so much the better for all of us."

Adrian piped up. "Our files tell us you hired the black Jeep

Cherokee with those plates from the twenty-seventh to the thirty-first."

Marie's eyes slid from Matthew to Adrian and back again. "I see. So you want to know where I went that weekend. It was the Bank Holiday, wasn't it? Looks like I can help you out. I did hire a car that weekend, for a trip to Snowdonia. A group of us met up on Friday and headed to the mountains for some camping, climbing and a bit of off-roading. The weather was grand and I drove us back down on the Monday evening. Returned the Jeep on Tuesday. When exactly was the accident in West Wales?"

"Saturday morning, very early. Just after sunrise."

"When I was still curled up in my sleeping-bag in Dolgellau. There has to be a mistake, Mr Bryant. Could the elderly couple have misremembered the car at all?"

Matthew nodded and turned to Adrian with a smile. "That's what we were hoping to hear. It's bad for business, our cars being used in illicit activities. So if this Jeep wasn't involved, that's good news for all of us. Do you have a name of the campsite, or anyone who can confirm that you were there, Ms Fisher?"

"Now there's a question. I can't recall the name of the site, but several people will tell you I was there. Would you like me to email you their names and contact details?"

"You couldn't just write them down for us now?" asked Adrian.

Her frown twitched. "I've already taken ten minutes away from my desk to answer your questions. Now I'll need a while to check my diary. I'm keen to help, but as you can see, I'm at work. I'll send you anything relevant, but it might be tomorrow."

Adrian squinted at her, quite deliberately. Her behaviour seemed very defensive for a person with nothing to hide. She returned his look with an enquiring twist of her head. Matthew's voice was soothing.

"That's kind of you, Ms Fisher. It would help us a great deal if you could. Now, we shall keep you no longer. Thank you for your time and the coffee. We'll make our own way out. Have a pleasant day and thank you."

As they exited the shop onto City Road, Adrian let rip.

"What crap! 'Time to check my friends' details?' Total bullshit. Time to set up some fake email accounts, more like. Does she think we were born yesterday?"

Matthew raised a finger for silence. He led the way up the street before shoving open the doors of the first pub they came across. Adrian checked over both shoulders before following him inside. You could never be too careful. While Matthew ordered two glasses of wine, Adrian sat at a quiet table by the window, disgusted by how a person could tell such a blatant lie without shame.

Matthew placed the glasses on the wobbly table. "Adrian, I agree with you. But we're powerless in this situation. We can't challenge her and she knows that. However, we can rattle her a little." He checked his watch and the blackboard above the bar. "Let's drink these and have some lunch here. After that, we'll give her a call. Now for a toast. For our first interview, we did rather well, I think. Cheers!"

Adrian lifted his glass. "Cheers. *You* did rather well. Very smooth, the way you tossed off our pseudonyms. I almost believed you. All I was good for was staring."

"Taking in all the little things, you mean. Your observations will be invaluable, I have no doubt. As Beatrice always says, the devil is in the detail. Tell me what you saw."

Adrian clasped his hands and crossed his legs, rewinding his impressions.

"Marie Fisher is Irish, in her early thirties and very well-groomed. The shoes looked Lanvin to me. The suit was Phillip Lim. No question. Jewellery, hard to pin down. Her watch, did you see? Omega, rose gold. But those earrings ... I can't be sure. Her handbag was Hermès. She takes excellent care of her nails, has quite good skin for a smoker and I'll bet she's got a hair appointment booked in the next week. Her roots need attention.

She also wears a touch too much *Angel* by Thierry Mugler."

Matthew, clearly concentrating hard on Adrian's words, shook his head.

"Adrian, whilst competent in Italian and Greek, I cannot speak Fashion. Could you translate?"

Sitting there in the dusty sunlight, hair overgrown, trousers a few centimetres short, and wearing a jacket rarely seen outside a faculty office, Matthew didn't need to state his lack of street-style to Adrian. It would be such a treat to take him shopping, but he suspected Matthew would rather visit the dentist.

Adrian explained. "She's an estate agent. She earns what, twenty-five, thirty grand a year? Her handbag costs a month's salary. The watch would be more. She dresses like a woman who earns twice as much."

"Good God. You see, I'd never have picked up any of that. All I noticed was she smelt of cake." Matthew tasted the wine. "And she was a bit prickly when you asked for details right there and then."

"That's what I thought. But of course she was bound to get stroppy, because she can't prove she was in Estonia."

"Snowdonia. It's in North Wales."

Adrian shrugged. There was a limit to his enthusiasm for the provinces. A thought arose. "We could call the car hire people and see if she brought the car back all muddy! If not, she was obviously lying!"

Matthew replaced his glass with a nod. "For a standard pub, that's a reasonable Antipodean Chardonnay. Yes, we could try the Williams people again, but two things trouble me about taking that tack. Firstly, do they keep records on exterior conditions of their vehicles on return? Naturally, damage would be noted, but mud? Secondly, this firm have no idea why they keep getting calls from the 'police' regarding one of their vehicles. They may decide to be less helpful if constantly pestered."

Adrian could not help himself. Despite his annoyance at Matthew's lack of enthusiasm, he acknowledged the tactful way he rejected the idea and found himself smiling at his diplomatic associate. His wine glass was slippery with condensation as he raised it to his lips.

"Mmm, actually, you're right. Heavy on the vanilla, but it's an acceptable background wine. How exactly do you plan to rattle her?"

"I thought we might phone her, and ask her if it's convenient to pop back at five o'clock. Put her under a bit of pressure and see how she reacts. We're likely to get no real confirmation from her 'friends'. So we could prod her a little, observe her response. That might give us some idea of whether she's worth watching."

"Good plan! And I'll go and stand on the street, but the other side. No one will notice me and I can observe what she does. I'll be discreet, honestly. I'll even wear my panama."

Matthew sighed. "You're really rather enjoying this, aren't you?"

The other side of City Road was absolutely hopeless. Even without the constant inconvenience of passing traffic, Adrian couldn't see enough of the interior of Bevan & Gough to differentiate individuals. Removing his jacket and drawing down the brim of his hat, he crossed the street and examined the pictures. His eyes refocused from the details of a two-bedroomed terrace in Splott to his own reflection in the glass. His stylish appearance struck him. The white shirt and panama hinted at a youthful Pierce Brosnan, a look he could grow to like. He concentrated and casually gazed beyond the photographs, deeper into the shop, locating Marie Fisher's desk. It was empty. He scanned the room. Five other occupants: two men, the blonde, and an older woman talking to a customer. Marie must be on a break.

The blonde picked up her phone, listened for a second and shook her head. The conversation was brief. She hung up and presumably went back to playing Patience.

Adrian abandoned his post and strode back towards the pub. Matthew wandered outside, looking vague and tapping his thumb against his chin.

"She's not there, is she?"

Matthew's eyes locked onto Adrian's with an intense stare, followed by a smile.

"No, she's not. Gone out for lunch. So I announced myself as Williams Car Hire, and the young lady was positively rude and told me to stop pestering Marie. Apparently Ms Fisher has already cancelled the rental she'd booked for next weekend, as she was dissatisfied with our service. She's already arranged a vehicle from another company."

His stare bored into Adrian, as if he was trying to communicate a hidden message. Adrian thought.

"But that means ... she's ... if she was ..."

Matthew's smile broadened. "Our timing seems rather fortuitous. On the last Bank Holiday weekend, I think she drove to Pembrokeshire. I think she met some people on the beach in the early hours of Saturday morning. I think one of them used her car to try and retrieve our camera. And I have a very strong suspicion that her destination next weekend will be the same."

Hairs stood up all along Adrian's forearms. "My God! This could actually be it! We should go. Get to that beach, hide, wait, and see what happens! Oh my God!"

"My thoughts precisely. I'm glad you have such a sense of adventure, Adrian. We'll have to come up with a reason for our absence on two successive weekends, but I believe we are onto a lead. Now, what do you think? Ought we to head back to London? I had plans to visit an ex-student of mine in Chelsea this evening and arrive on Sunday as arranged. But it occurs to me that we could hire ourselves a vehicle and poke about a bit in Pembrokeshire instead. What say you?"

"Poking, no question. But you know I can't drive."

"No matter. I'll get behind the wheel, you can navigate. Where might we find a copy of the Yellow Pages, do you think?"

"You can locate the nearest car hire company on your phone."

Matthew's expression was dour. "I don't have a mobile phone. I telephoned Ms Fisher from the call box in the pub."

Adrian shook his head in disbelief. The Man That Time Forgot. He snatched an opportunity.

"Right. I'll find us a car and after that, we're going shopping. If we're planning a stakeout next weekend, we'll need the appropriate gear. Trust me, I'm good at this sort of thing."

As he turned his attention to his screen, he caught Matthew's expression of alarm. A twinge of worry nagged at him, too. Nothing to do with finding something stylish in black, but more to do with their planning a trip to a remote Welsh beach to spy on drug traffickers. For the first time since the investigation began, Adrian missed Beatrice; her presence, her good sense and her natural caution. And worse, this was his first free Saturday night in ages. What the hell was he going to tell Jared?

Chapter 22

The dread of a bleak and cheerless weekend had built up for days. Beatrice knew she would be unable to stop working herself into a state. Worried about Hamilton's scrutiny of her performance, fearful of more women suffering sexual harassment, afraid of having missed something vital in her casework, haunted by imaginings of what Matthew might be doing and with whom, and feeling generally lonely, negative and neglected. Even Adrian had plans for a weekend away with his boyfriend and she couldn't face calling James. Dismal.

Instead, she leapt out of bed at seven o'clock. She should have been exhausted. She'd stayed up till half past one, drinking red wine, batting around ideas with Virginia. It was all most out of character. But her colleague's enthusiasm, intelligent analysis and voluntary assistance last night had buoyed Beatrice enormously. To such an extent that this morning she belted out some Carole King in the shower.

At ten o'clock, Virginia would pick her up and they would drive to Wales, to investigate something which could be nothing. She had to be back by Sunday afternoon, as Matthew would return to spend the week in London. Compensation for missing the weekend. And she would find time for a conversation with him, a truthful conversation in which she voiced her fears. A little break and a change of scenery would do her good. Cardiff and Pembrokeshire on a sunny weekend. Beatrice's spirits were fairly bubbling.

Passing the exit for Chippenham, the Volvo XC60 overtook a National Express coach at 80mph, before returning to the left hand lane and slowing to the speed limit. Driving with smooth skill, Virginia made cheerful conversation, proposing theories and picking holes in them, offering opinions on music, news items and other people's driving. Far nicer than the train, it had to be said. No one could call it an attractive vehicle, but the inside was undoubtedly comfy. From her elevated position in the passenger seat, Beatrice could observe the scenery and other road users, yet her attention kept returning to the same cyclical worry loop.

If Matthew found out what she was up to, he would be hurt and disappointed. Adrian might be even worse, particularly as he was the one who had discovered the number plate. And she'd also lied to her counsellor. James asked her if she planned to tell Matthew, and with blithe confidence, she'd assured him she would. It was foolhardy, rushing off to Pembrokeshire on a whim. She should be at home, or in Finsbury Park Control Centre, protecting the public. She released a heavy sigh. Nothing was going to happen. She had Virginia with her and all they intended to do was take a look around. Their sex offender could do no harm either, as his shift would be working over the weekend. Until Monday, women of North London were safe. From him, at least. Another huge sigh escaped her.

Virginia glanced across at her. "What do you say, should we stop at Leigh Delamere? Or press on a bit?"

"I'd prefer to get over the bridge before stopping. I'm keen to get to Wales. Perhaps we could stop in Cardiff? Have some lunch and do the car hire firm today?"

"We could do, but I think it might work better the other way round. Pembrokeshire first and the car hire firm on Sunday. Everything will be open in the holiday village today, so we can ask around the shops and cafés. But everything will be shut on

Sunday. Whereas the car hire people will be busy and resent our intrusion on a Saturday. If we leave it till tomorrow, it'll be staffed by a couple of bored teenagers, who'll fall over themselves to give us any information we want. What do you think?"

"Good thinking. So Pembrokeshire first. In that case, you should take a break when you're ready. You're the driver."

"Oh, I'm fine. I love driving, always have. I passed my Advanced Driver's Test before I even joined the force. That's how much I enjoy being behind the wheel."

Beatrice twisted to look directly at her. "I wondered about doing that test. Hamilton offered me ADT training, but I turned it down. Seems it's not all about car chases, so I confess it looked rather dull."

"Not at all. It increases your awareness of potential hazards, teaches you more about vehicle handling and there is a small element of managing high-speed pursuit. But you learn to be more interested in bins than flashing blue lights."

"Bins? Is that some sort of euphemism?"

Virginia laughed. "No, I mean rubbish bins. For example, you're following a suspect through Chiswick. It's a residential area, you're trying to keep your target in sight, but you need to be aware of what else is going on. Tunnel vision is your enemy. So you notice that there are wheelie bins on the pavement. And you make the connection. If there are bins, there will be a bin lorry. You are prepared to come round the corner and find a bin lorry blocking your path, or oncoming vehicles overtaking it. You heighten your sensitivity to your environment. You do drive, Beatrice?"

"Rarely. I live in London."

"What about if you move from London?"

"If that were to happen, I'd start driving again, I suppose. Or more likely leave it to Matthew. Sorry, Virginia, I know I keep reverting to the same subject and I'm even boring myself. I've just got a real bean in my bonnet about lying to him."

Virginia switched off the radio and one of Beatrice's low-level irritations ceased instantly. God, she was getting old, but really, was there anything more annoying than radio phone-ins? Wasps, perhaps.

Checking the mirror, Virginia indicated and pulled out past a horse-box. "So tell him. Play it down, you're just looking around, no cause for concern, but you've been honest."

"I think I just might. He's due back from Rome tomorrow, so I'll drop it casually into conversation while he's telling me about the seminar. No big deal."

"Good timing." Virginia nodded. "His head will be full of whatever it is Roman scholars talk about at such events. Now you and I can concentrate on digging around West Wales with a clear conscience. Blending in with the tourists and looking normal."

The chances of that were slender, as Virginia's black sleeveless dress and white blonde hair made for a dramatic image. Such a striking woman would always turn heads. All blending would be down to Beatrice.

Porthgain's tiny population was swollen with tourists, so it came as a relief to strike out on the coastal path towards the beach. Having inspected the spot where the photographs were taken, the pair made their way along the sands to the opposite end.

The beach could not have looked more innocent. Families picnicked behind striped wind-breaks, children splashed in the surf, and further up the beach, a group of teenagers posed and smoked on the rocks. Beatrice, shoes in hand, allowed ripples of surf to wash over her toes, feeling the shifting grains beneath her feet. Virginia handed over her bag and sandals, hitched up the hem of her dress and waded out to thigh level.

"There is a sudden drop a bit further out," said Virginia, splashing her way back. "Ideal for bringing a boat as close as possible to the beach. All you have to do is moor it, jump off and walk up to meet your mate with the wheels."

"How would you moor it? There's only sand here."

By way of response, Virginia pulled her dress up over her head. Underneath, she wore a black one-piece swimsuit. No gold embellishments, no halter neck fastening, no cutaway peepholes. For Virginia, it was surprisingly functional.

"That's what I was wondering." She rummaged in her canvas shopper, bringing out goggles and a towel. "I'll go and have a closer look."

She handed Beatrice the towel, adjusted her goggles and plunged without hesitation into the Welsh waves. Beatrice, dressed and dry in midday sunshine, gave a sympathetic shiver. She walked in the opposite direction and compared the overgrown access lane to the photograph in her hand. It must have been built for launching boats. Less used nowadays, but awfully convenient. She turned back to the sparkling surf, glad of her sunglasses.

Hair sleek as a peroxide seal, Virginia walked back up the beach, dripping wet. Beatrice proffered the towel and an enquiring look.

"Thanks." She rubbed her face and wound the towel around her body. "There's a concrete block out there. It's lying on the bottom, with an iron ring embedded. There's a rope, too. One end tied to the ring, the other tied to a plastic bottle, which floats on the surface, so you can find it easily. It seems our friends use this spot pretty often. Did you see anything up there?"

"Not much. There's a hard standing at the bottom of the lane, presumably for vehicles to unload boats. That's where the driver must have parked. It would be useful to walk up the lane and see where it comes out. When you've finished, Little Mermaid."

"I've finished. And The Little Mermaid has red hair and a far larger chest. Jessica Rabbit with a tail."

Beatrice suppressed her amusement at Virginia's choice of imagery. "Should we head back to the car?"

"Let's walk while I dry off. Then we should find somewhere to eat."

"Good idea. I suggest we head for The Clipper Inn. Firstly,

because we can make discreet enquiries about ponytail man. And secondly, because they do excellent fish. Sea air gives me a terrific appetite, you know."

Virginia towelled her hair and picked up her shoes. She turned to scan the sea. "So it looks like they sail in here, transfer the stash in the dark and sail back to wherever they came from. What we need here is regular surveillance." Her eyes ranged over the cliff top.

Beatrice followed her gaze. "My point precisely. But can I get the local force to listen?"

"To be fair, they may not have the resources. You'd need a pair of officers on open-ended night shifts."

Beatrice remained unconvinced. "Hmm. Perhaps." They picked their way up the lane, heat shimmers suggesting tarmac at the top. Beatrice stopped. "Hang on, if that block was put there for the boat people's convenience, how can they be sure no one would find the plastic bottle and the rope?"

"Look." Virginia indicated the strand stretching away from them. Most people had congregated near the central section, where the shore dropped away gradually, where there were fewer rocks and no shade. In contrast, the shadow of the cliff loomed over their end of the beach, clusters of seaweed littered the sand and the water crashed against outcrops of stone.

"It's not the most appealing part of the beach for holidaymakers, but it's certainly convenient if you want to land some light cargo. That plastic bottle is far enough out not to attract attention from rock-poolers. And this is not what I'd call a popular beach. What was that noise?"

"Possibly my stomach rumbling. Come on. I want fish and chips. I'm starving."

Virginia slipped her feet into her sandals. "Me too. Well, fish and salad, at least."

The long, hot walk from the beach was bad enough. But the increasingly frustrating wait for a table and the delay in service due to the number of tourists put Beatrice into such a foul temper, she felt the weekend would be irrecoverable. However, after they were eventually seated, her bonhomie was restored by a large plate of battered haddock, perfectly cooked chips and fresh garden peas, accompanied by a dry German white. The crowds thinned as they ate, and by the time the waitress cleared their plates, the pub had returned to a small, friendly local. Beatrice spotted the landlord sitting at the bar, chef's tunic unbuttoned, with a newspaper and pint of ale, and seized her moment.

"Sorry to bother you, especially after such a hectic session. I just wanted to extend my compliments. The food was excellent. Does it get this crowded every weekend?"

A stained T-shirt and old jeans suggested youth. But although he could be no older than forty, his face was lined and tired. He ran a hand through ragged, greying curls, and gave her a weary smile. "Thanks. In summer, yes it does. Today was especially mad; there's some event up at the fort. Did you go?"

"No, we've been revisiting spots from our previous visit. We stayed in the Dan-y-Coed cottages over the last Bank Holiday. You were kind enough to recommend the restaurant over the road, which we plan to try this evening."

"Oh right. Dan-y-Coed cottages? You weren't the woman who had trouble with an intruder?"

"News travels fast. My name is Detective Inspector Beatrice Stubbs and I work for the Metropolitan Police."

He folded up the paper and gave her his full attention. "Gary Powell. So, whoever it was broke into a copper's cottage. What a berk. And now you're back to investigate?"

"Let's call it research. We had a couple of mishaps that Bank Holiday weekend. The thing is, I'm keen to locate a certain young man, just to eliminate him from our enquiries. I wondered if you could point me in the right direction. He's quite distinctive, you see, and this is a small enough village for him to stand out. He's mid-twenties with short brown hair but he has a blond ponytail."

The landlord scrunched up his eyes and nodded. "That rings a bell. Hang on. Lyndon? C'mere."

The young barman approached. How marvellous to be bestowed with such thick, dark curls. And glorious bones. An Eastern European perhaps?

"Lyndon, this lady's from the police. You ever seen a guy around who has brown hair but a blond ponytail? Youngish. I have a feeling he's been in here, but ..."

"Yeah, I know who you mean. Drinks lager. He's not a regular, like, but he comes in every few weeks. Very thin, with a pointy nose. He's always with another bloke, older. Miserable-looking git." No trace of Poland in that accent, but could have been Pontypool.

Beatrice cautiously withdrew one of the blown-up photos. It showed nothing of the bags, the beach and the car, but exposed the two men's faces. "This one?"

The lad nodded with definite emphasis. "Yes, exactly. That's them. They come in once in a while, on a Saturday night, have a few pints and leave at shut tap. I thought they must be fishermen; the clothes, the occasional visits, but I don't know for certain."

"I see. That's very helpful, thank you. And of course, neither of you would know his name, I suppose?"

Both pairs of eyes flicked up and right as they searched their memories. Both heads shook slowly.

"Thank you both very much. Kind of you to give me your time. Mr Powell, I'll leave my card in case anything else occurs to you. And I'd be grateful if you could keep this to yourselves."

"No worries. Best of luck with your research." Gary offered his hand.

Beatrice shook it, smiled at Lyndon and returned to her monochrome companion.

She tapped the photo. "According to the staff, those two come in here on occasion, always together on a Saturday evening. The barman said they might be fishermen, but that is mere supposition."

Virginia leant forward, chin resting on hands. "So they bring their stuff here on Saturday morning, hand it over to the contact in the SUV, come in here for a few beers, and sail back to wherever they came from on Saturday night."

"Sounds about right to me," Beatrice agreed. "But what are they bringing and where from? If we could find out when they come in here, we might uncover a pattern. And if we knew their timetable, we could ..."

"Excuse me? Could I have a word?" The barman stood at their table.

"Hello, Lyndon. This is a colleague of mine, so you can speak freely."

"Right. Well, the men in the photo, I think they're Irish. I'm not sure about the younger one, with the ponytail. But the older one told me once if ever I put a head like that on a pint in Cork, they'd throw it back at me. It's not much, I know, but I thought ..."

Beatrice smiled. "That's actually very useful, Lyndon. Can I give you my card, and ask you to let me know the next time this man comes in? This is just between us, of course."

The young man nodded and took the card. "OK. I can do that. Enjoy the rest of your holiday."

He flicked a polite glance at Virginia, who responded with a slow blink and louche smile. He turned and hurried back to the bar. Scared witless, no doubt.

Attractive and charming, with a sharp intelligence, Virginia qualified as one of Beatrice's most useful assets. If only she were a little less memorable.

Chapter 23

Who'd have thought Wales was so much like Ireland? All wild and windswept, green and sheep-covered, full of cute villages and the signs in a foreign language. All Adrian's previous impressions had been of somewhere small, inhospitable and covered in slag-heaps. He just had to bring Jared here, it was too ridiculously romantic.

Jared. Getting a Friday off work had been far less problematic than getting time away from his boyfriend. Tucking his phone back into his jacket, Adrian puzzled over the heated call. Jared's concerns about his detective neighbour were not, obviously, as a sexual threat, but more that she and her problems absorbed so much of Adrian's time. Fair point. But when he also referred to Beatrice as a bad influence, Adrian could only shrug, at a loss as to how to reply. Odd behaviour, but secretly pleasing. Jealousy, in small, non-psychotic doses, was an excellent indicator in a new relationship.

He turned to Matthew, who seemed to have finally adjusted to the gears and braking system of the rented Vauxhall Corsa. Adrian was grateful. Much longer and he suspected his neck might have suffered Repetitive Strain Injury.

"How are you feeling? Tired yet? I mean, it's not like I can take over or anything, but I can sing, tell stories or expose you to more embarrassing personal phone calls to keep you awake."

Matthew's face creased into a smile, although he didn't take his eyes off the country road and his posture remained rigid as a tin soldier.

"I'm fine. We're all but there. And I trust your new man isn't too offended."

"He'll get over it." Adrian could only hope that was the truth. It must seem very dismissive, abandoning their evening to go off amateur detecting. Would Jared understand?

"Without trying to be intrusive, I wondered why you told him you were with Beatrice, rather than the actual facts?"

Adrian looked out at the countryside in the late afternoon. Beautiful stone houses sheltered in dips on a hillock and in the distance, the sea glittered and shone.

"Saying Beatrice just makes it easier. He knows I'm involved and totally enthusiastic about this case. He sort of understands. But if I'd told him I was with a man – despite said man being Beatrice's partner, due for retirement and so far from cutting edge that he doesn't even own a mobile – believe me, things would have been far more complicated."

"Hmm. It's always interesting what people choose to tell their close ones. And what they prefer to hide. Ah! We're very close to Porthgain, but there's a gallery I'd really like to see in the next village. Would you mind stopping for half an hour? After all, we spent over an hour traipsing round the shops."

Evidently still sulking about both the expense and the style. But he'd be grateful later, and Adrian just knew Beatrice would be overjoyed. Matthew looked stunning in black.

"Not at all. Pity we couldn't have put on our new stuff first. That gear would be perfect for posing in galleries."

"It's not that kind of gallery." Matthew's voice bordered on terse.

The whole place just got cuter and cuter. A delightful gallery filled with watercolour landscapes, the B&B with real patchwork quilts that didn't come from Habitat, a friendly landlady and the walk down the lane to the divine little harbour all combined to make Adrian feel childishly excited. After exploring the beach at sunset and finding little in the way of clues but some fabulous pebbles to decorate his bathroom back home, he followed Matthew as they made their way back to the village.

The sun sank out of sight and small lights glowed from the huddle of houses and The Clipper Inn. Stopping at the bend in the path, Adrian turned to face the sunset. Matthew, a few paces ahead, turned back to stand beside him with a satisfied smile. Pewter-coloured sea reflected the riot of pinks, peaches, greys and deepening blue above. The insubstantial clouds scattered in mackerel patterns, ending with an almost artistic whorl. The painter whose gallery they'd visited could not complain of lacking subjects.

A long wall stretched out from the harbour, protection from the elements. A solitary figure stood facing out to sea. Too far to see the gender but whoever it was looked awfully French Lieutenant's Woman.

"It doesn't happen often, Matthew, but I am speechless. What a glorious place! I've already decided, and nothing will shake me, that this will be the location of my next mini-break." Adrian had it all planned. He would bring Jared for a weekend; they could stroll in the surf, chat to the locals and fantasise about living here, before buying some cheese and heading home. "Now, do we try the fish restaurant, or the pub?"

"I'd be keen on either, but if our friends from the beach are likely to use one or the other, I'd lean to the pub."

"Very wise. Sagacious, even. Let's go."

Chapter 24

The visit to Fishguard Police Station was surprisingly pleasant. Convinced of a hostile reception to their turning up unannounced, Beatrice was relieved to learn that Inspector Howells was making an appearance at Cardiff Crown Court. She asked to speak instead to PC Johns, who had taken her original statement. He seemed delighted to see her and positively hypnotised by Virginia. He also proved himself a bright spark by asking some perceptive questions, which they debated on the drive back to the B&B in Porthgain.

"He's right. They couldn't leave the boat out there all day on Saturday. It would attract all sorts of attention," said Virginia.

Beatrice's gaze wandered over the hedgerows. "What I don't understand is why they wait. Once they've dropped the cargo off, why not turn around and go back where they came from?"

"Ireland."

Beatrice tutted. "We don't know that. No making assumptions. All we know is that they stick around for Saturday night. So they must berth the boat somewhere. Very probably Porthgain harbour."

"And sail back to Ireland, or wherever else, overnight on Saturday to Sunday."

Two crows repeatedly attacked a buzzard, creating a graceful dogfight in the sky. Beatrice wondered if it was aggression or protection.

Virginia indicated right at Croesgoch. "But you're right. Why do they wait? Just to have cover of darkness? I don't know why that's necessary if they've got rid of whatever illicit goods they're carrying."

"Perhaps they take something back in the other direction. If only bloody Howells would put some surveillance on them, this could all be cleared up in a matter of days. And he, and his force, would be applauded all over the country for cracking a million-pound drug-smuggling operation."

Virginia glanced at her as she eased the Volvo down the country lane. "Now who's making assumptions?"

"I was exaggerating. That's different."

They fell silent as the vehicle rolled down the slope to the tiny harbour. Beatrice took in the huge sea wall, curving like a immense cradling arm around the moored fishing boats. In brilliant sunshine and calm water, the scale of the edifice seemed excessive, but she could imagine what a haven it must be when a storm hit the coast.

Virginia reversed into a parking space, turned off the engine and stuck a police permit on the dashboard.

"Right, let's find out who registers and records which boats come in and out. We might even turn up a name and address. Then I want a shower before dinner. Are we going to the fish restaurant, or back to the pub? I wouldn't mind another look at that barman."

Beatrice sighed and released her seatbelt. "We are going to the restaurant. Firstly to cover all bases, and secondly, to keep you out of trouble. And how do you expect me to get out now? You've parked right up against this Corsa."

"Not my fault. He's straddling the line whereas I have parked correctly. Come out this side. Whoever he is, that driver must be an arse."

The harbourmaster was of a similar breed to Howells. Unconvinced by Beatrice's credentials, he would only confirm that he did indeed keep records of boats coming in and out of the harbour, but unless compelled by a legal ruling, he was not prepared to share. Virginia tried sugar-coating their request, but it was clear the man's ego was fed by his own power. They gave up and Virginia ranted about little Hitlers all the way back to the B&B.

"Virginia, just forget him. I'll contact PC Johns and get him to turn up in uniform. A local lad might have more success, but it may be a little late to disturb the man now. I'll send him an email."

Beatrice, appalled by her own selfishness, felt the need for solitude. A sense of claustrophobia was exacerbated by the only remaining room available at the B&B being a twin. Her urge for space became as strong as a thirst. She chewed over how to broach the subject as they checked in. Fortunately, she had no need. Virginia let her off the hook.

"So, I'm going to shower and check in with my husband, if that's OK with you? He'll be having breakfast around now."

"Great plan. I think I might just dump my bag and walk awhile. Clear the cobwebs and see if I can see any logic behind all this." Tension lifted from Beatrice's shoulders.

"If you're sure? I'm not chucking you out; it's just that this is the one opportunity ..."

"I was wondering how to put it tactfully, but I too need some thinking time. As an anti-social old trout, this fits in perfectly for me."

Virginia's face softened. "Thank you. I just need a half an hour or so. And for an anti-social old trout, you're very good company. Here, give your bag to me. See you in a bit. Don't forget the restaurant's booked for seven."

She trotted up the stairs with such alacrity, Beatrice could not help but smile. Yet, Virginia's evident eagerness for her husband's voice threw a stark light on her own situation. In one of these moods, Beatrice could find black holes in a rainbow.

The reception room was oppressive. Prettily decorated, with

lace curtains, patchwork cushions and white woodwork. Very twee. She was being unfair. But she felt like being unfair. She shook herself. She needed to walk. To think. To outpace the low growls behind her.

Once out of the low-ceilinged building, she hesitated. She'd intended to go up the cliffs but had an immediate urge to get as close as she could to the sea. The harbour wall drew her. A barrier against the elements and a path into the ocean. A safe place from which to observe the danger. She hitched her handbag over her shoulder and followed her instinct.

The inside of the harbour was all late-afternoon gentleness, slapping ripples and metallic clinks of masts and anchor chains. Oily patches of grime and detritus collected in corners. A rich smell encouraged her to fill her lungs. Half ozone, half diesel, it lifted her somehow and she picked up speed. When she reached the bend, the furthermost point of the wall, she stopped to watch the waves pounding the bricks beneath. As always, she stared in awe. *The elements have that hold over humanity; that ceaseless fascination. We believe we own earth and air, but find out soon enough the opposite is true. Yet with fire and water, we recognise our visceral urge for mastery is outclassed.* Beatrice watched the constant rhythms of the sea attack her foundations, and acknowledged its superior power.

The sea. We describe it as raging, cruel, beautiful, uncontrollable and endlessly changing, but it simply is. All we can do is strengthen our walls, be eternally prepared. It will never go away. We just have to learn to live with it.

Chapter 25

Luck had always favoured Adrian. A Sagittarian with Libra rising, he often found his heart's desires falling into his lap. Tonight was no exception. The menu offered homemade fisherman's pie, the wine list had surprising potential and the barman, with Rufus Sewell curls and cheese-grater cheekbones, was sending him certain signals. A good detective had to use every means at his disposal.

"I think I'll have the steak and ale pie," announced Matthew. "And this Australian red might be worth a punt. What do you think?"

Adrian checked the description. "Looks just the thing. And we're on holiday, sort of. We ought to indulge ourselves. I am going to try a glass of the Chenin Blanc as an accompaniment to fisherman's pie. We have to order at the bar. Now, I insist on getting this, for two reasons. First, you got the train. Secondly, I'd like to take the opportunity to chat up the barman. Purely in the interest of investigative thoroughness, of course."

"Thank you, that's very kind. He is undoubtedly a striking-looking chap. Tell him I'm your uncle or something, and I shall sit here quietly and do the crossword. Could you ask for a side order of chips? As you say, we are on holiday. And Adrian, remember to pay in cash."

On seeing Adrian approach, 'Rufus' slid past the barmaid so he happened to be ideally placed to serve him. Slick.

Adrian gave him The Look. *I'm checking you out. I'm hard to please, but so far, I like what I see.*

"Hi. Could I order some food?"

"Sure. Where are you sitting?"

As if you didn't know. You haven't taken your eyes off me since I walked in.

Adrian pointed at their table, where Matthew was peering unsubtly over the top of the paper. "Next to the fireplace. For drinks, one large glass of Stormy Bay Shiraz and one of Chenin Blanc. I'll have fisherman's pie and my uncle would like the steak and ale pie, with a side order of chips."

"What about you? You fancy anything on the side?" His head still bent over the till, he lifted his eyes to Adrian.

"Don't tempt me. I like to leave room for afters."

Eye contact, secretive smiles and deal sealed. Adrian handed over a fifty-pound note. As the barman counted out the change, he asked casually, "On holiday, is it?"

"Sort of. Doing a tour of Wales, trying to find my cousin." Adrian dropped his voice. "He got in a bit of trouble and did a midnight flit. All we know is he was heading to Wales. I agreed to help my uncle search for him."

"Wales is a big place, plenty of room to hide. Got a name?"

A name? Good point.

"Better than a name, we have a photograph." Adrian removed the picture from his bag and placed it on the bar, just as a man in kitchen whites emerged from the kitchen. While the barman studied the picture, the chef surveyed the pub.

"Lyndon, will you collect some glasses, please?"

Lyndon? Oh yes, it suits him. Just as romantic as Rufus if not more so.

"In a minute. Gary, come over by here. This man is looking for someone. He's got a photo." He turned back to Adrian. "Gary's the landlord."

Gary nodded a greeting to Adrian and picked up the

photograph. He threw a sharp look at Lyndon and glanced back at Adrian immediately.

"And you are ...?"

"Andrew Ramos. This man's my cousin."

"Is your cousin in some sort of trouble?" The landlord's eyes were suspicious.

Adrian affected a laugh and indicated Matthew with an inclination of his head. "Only with his father. There was a family argument, and ... Tim flew the nest. We just want to find him and persuade him to come home."

"I see. Well, we've never seen him round here, but if he does turn up, we'll let you know. Could you leave a number?"

Odd how he spoke for both of them.

Lyndon's eyes met his, but his look contained no flirtation. More of an apology. Adrian scribbled his false name and real number on an order pad and thanked them for their help.

Matthew, annoyingly, seemed unconcerned by the landlord's behaviour, devoting all his attention to his pie. Adrian was convinced there was something suspicious behind their reactions, so explained it again.

Matthew mopped up some gravy with the last of his chips. "I think you're reading too much into it. The pub's getting busy. The boss saw a staff member dallying too long with one customer and chose to chivvy him a bit. He didn't recognise the man and wanted to get rid of you so his staff would concentrate on their jobs. Nothing sinister to it. How was your food?"

"Sublime. The thing is, Matthew, you didn't see his face when I showed him the picture. He barely glanced at it, but looked at me like a stunned mullet. I swear he's hiding something."

"And the barman?"

"Lyndon. He looked guilty, and didn't even give me a chance to ask any questions. Plus, he's been conspicuously absent all evening ..."

Matthew placed his knife and fork together. "Rushed off his feet, more like. It's only just starting to calm down now. That pie was a triumph. However, beer would have been a wiser accompaniment. The Shiraz was all but overwhelmed. Adrian, have you considered they might even know Ponytail Man? Perhaps they went to school with him, or he's the son of a local sheep farmer. And here you are, inventing a new identity and saying he's run away from home?"

That hadn't occurred to Adrian and the thought bothered him. "If that were the case, their reactions would make sense, I suppose," he admitted. "And now Lyndon thinks I'm some kind of loon, which is why he's avoiding me. How would you have done it?"

"I don't know. Pretended I was a private investigator, maybe? Which is, in effect, what we are. What do you say to a harbour stroll before we head back to the B&B? I feel the need to stretch my legs."

Adrian finished his wine with a last look at the bar. No sign of Lyndon. Shame, really. That one had potential. He hurried after Matthew.

As they stepped into the cool air of the night, Adrian's mobile rang. He didn't recognise the number.

"Hello?"

"Mr Ramos? This is Lyndon, the barman. I wanted a quick word before you leave. About the photo."

"Oh, right. I'll come back in."

"No, I'll come out. Two secs."

Matthew discreetly continued to the lane and wandered on down towards the harbour. Adrian sat on the low wall, waiting and listening to the murmurs of conversation from the outdoor tables. Lyndon appeared from behind the pub and beckoned Adrian to follow him round the back.

Amid the large refuse containers, Lyndon sat on an upturned beer crate and lit a cigarette, watching Adrian.

"I only have a few minutes for a fag break. But I wanted to catch you to explain. A police detective was here today, asking about the same bloke. There were two of them and they had exactly the same photograph. That's why Gary freaked. The detective said to keep it quiet, but now someone else turns up."

"A police detective? Did he say why he was looking for this guy? Tim, I mean?"

"It was a she. No, not that I know of. She might have said something to Gary, but she only asked me if I'd seen him before. Which I had. Like I told her, they come in about once a month, two of them and I think they're Irish. Only ever seen them on a Saturday night. You wouldn't forget a ponytail like that, would you?"

"Did the detective give you her name?"

"She gave me her card." He stood, retrieved his wallet from his back pocket and extracted the card.

Detective Inspector Beatrice Stubbs, Metropolitan Police.

Despite knowing what it would say, Adrian shivered as he read the words. He handed the card back.

"Two detectives, you said? Did you get the other one's name?"

"No. But I can give you her description. Tall, peroxide blonde and right rampant, she was. Tried to pull me. But she's not my type."

Adrian picked up his cue.

"Why are you telling me all this?"

Lyndon stubbed out his cigarette and stood up. "Because you are exactly my type. Is that bloke really your uncle?"

"No, but something very similar. Listen, we have to leave tomorrow, but I may well be back in the next couple of weeks. Can I take your number? Just in case."

"Here, I'll write it on the back of her card. Call me, OK?"

Matthew turned with a smile as he heard Adrian approach.

"I planned to give you another two minutes before beating a subtle retreat. Were you successful? I don't need details."

"Yes, but wait till you hear this. It seems we're not the only ones being devious. The police were here today, asking about the same guy, using the same photograph. The detective left her card." He held it under the street lamp.

Matthew's eyes boggled. "Good God! So much for, 'I have to work, I'll be busy all weekend'. Of all the bare-faced subterfuge! That wretched female never ceases to amaze me."

"Nor me. But if there was anything here to find, she got in first. Let's get some sleep. And I suggest we head back to London first thing in the morning. This trail is cold."

"Absolutely." Matthew shook his head as they made their way back towards their lodgings. "The most infuriating thing is ..."

Adrian finished his sentence. "... we can't complain that she lied to us. I know. But I still can't believe she did that."

"She takes the biscuit, she really does. The only advantage we hold is she has no idea we've been here. However, we know all about her duplicitous double-cross. Information is power."

Adrian's mind whirred. *Power, yes. But how to use it?*

Upstairs at The Clipper Inn, Gary Powell reached into his tunic. The copper's card was a bit greasy and smelt of onions. He picked up the phone. Half eleven on Saturday; no one was likely to answer, but he could leave her a voicemail message. He had a feeling she'd like to know.

Chapter 26

Shells tinkled a light melody along the beach and the sun sank, turning clouds rosé. Inch by inch, Matthew unzipped her wetsuit, shaking his head with regret. Her dread swelled like a jellyfish in her throat, but she did nothing to stop him. Finally, he yanked open the two edges and stared in horror at what he saw.

"How long have you had that?" he exclaimed, his expression aghast. She tried to open her mouth but her tongue had died of shame.

He shook her by her shoulders. "How long? How long!"

"Beatrice! Beatrice!"

She shot upright in bed, eyes wide and pulse pounding. There was no wetsuit. Her tartan pyjamas were warm, dry and buttoned-up. The sound of waves was coming through the B&B window and Matthew looked like Virginia Lowe. Beatrice closed her eyes and opened them again.

Virginia perched on Beatrice's bed, grey light washing her complexion to nothing. Without make-up and wearing a long white T-shirt, she could frighten a weak-hearted individual into an early grave. She placed a reassuring hand on Beatrice's shoulder.

"Beatrice? Look, I'm sorry to wake you."

"What is it? Was I snoring?"

"No, no. But we have to go. Did you not hear your phone?"

"My phone? What time is it? What's wrong?"

"It's almost half eight. We've got to get back to London now. Our man's just done another one."

Beatrice's mind accelerated and changed gear. "No! He couldn't have! He was at work, we made sure of that."

"Looks like he did this girl on his way home."

Beatrice threw back the duvet, but something in Virginia's voice made her teeth clench.

"What does 'did this girl' mean?"

"She's sixteen, doing work experience at the newsagent's in the station. She left home about an hour ago and that filthy bastard was waiting for her in the back lane. He put his penis into her mouth."

Beatrice grimaced and couldn't conceal the wobble in her voice. "Oh my God. The disgusting, vile ... is the girl all right? Stupid question." She threw back the quilt. "Right, I'll be ready in less than ten minutes. If we leave now, we can be back by lunchtime."

Virginia didn't move, but continued her glazed stare at the buttons on Beatrice's pyjamas.

"What? Virginia? What is it?" She hunched to peer at Virginia's face.

Virginia looked up, her eyes flooded and she bit her bottom lip.

"Beatrice, the girl's autistic. And that sick fucker knew."

Every muscle in Beatrice's body went limp.

Chapter 27

Their previous encounter at the Family Centre gave Beatrice the impression that Maggie Howard was in permanent control. Sensitive, thoughtful, professional and positive. So when Maggie entered the BTP office on Sunday afternoon, it shook Beatrice to see her puffy eyes and tight mouth.

A veteran weeper herself, Beatrice offered tissues and a gentle squeeze on the shoulder, as she closed the door to Virginia's office. She poured them both a glass of water.

"Thanks for coming, Maggie. I appreciate it. Virginia is still interviewing the newsagent, but will join us when she can. I'd like to hear what you managed to find out from the victim this morning. Is she ... is she all right?"

Maggie shook her head and clenched her jaw tighter. Beatrice feared something might break. She breathed deeply.

"Right, I think I'm ready to start. Look, Beatrice ..."

"Don't. If the next thing to come out of your mouth is an apology, just don't. There's no need and we're only human. I gather this morning was hellish."

Maggie's make-up was smudged and her hair disobedient. She looked like a rock star the morning after.

"I've heard some nasty stuff in this job; some really twisted thinking. This goes straight into the top five of the Shit Parade. Cherry James is sixteen and has PDD-NOS. Yeah, I know. Wait till you hear what it stands for. Pervasive Development Disorder

Not Otherwise Specified. Not quite Asperger's Syndrome, not quite autism, but displays many similar behavioural patterns. All these disorders fall under the umbrella of Autism Spectrum Disorder."

"I've heard of Asperger's and autism, but confess my ignorance as to what either really means. I have some vague memories of *Rain Man*?"

"That's potentially helpful, actually. The clue's in the name. It's a neurological developmental disorder. People with this condition don't behave the way we expect them to, don't acknowledge social codes and can often be obsessive."

"About people?"

"Oddly, that's the least likely target. PDD-NOS sufferers tend to be solitary, absorbed in their own interests. And those interests often become compulsive. Dinosaurs, planets, internal combustion engines, toys, video games, anything. Cherry's into sharks. Films, toys, models, pictures and books, so many books about sharks. Which is how this despicable scumbag bastard found a way in."

"Via sharks?"

"He groomed her, Beatrice. He spotted Cherry, working her summer job at the station's newsagent, doing menial tasks but earning her own wage. It seems she loved the job, and became a favourite with some of the locals. She has some communication difficulties, but more social than verbal. She has problems reading emotions and signals, so extends a simple 'Good morning, how are you?' into a lecture on the physiology of hammerheads."

"And one of the people she lectured ..."

"... saw an opportunity. He gave her little presents, pictures he'd downloaded. Never in the shop, she says. Sometimes on her way to the shop or on her way home. Her memory is amazing on some points and entirely absent on others. She knows exactly which images he gave her but couldn't even give us a halfway coherent description of the guy. She just doesn't notice. And yes, the pictures are already being finger-printed. He chatted to her and learned her routines, her timetable. Not difficult, as it's another of her obsessions."

Maggie's voice remained steady, calm and analytical, betraying no hint of her former distress.

"When did this start?" Beatrice's skin cooled.

"We can't be sure – her time awareness is imprecise – but more than a month ago. This is classic grooming. He prepared this girl. And this morning, as she left home, he met her and offered her a deal. He must have thought it would be easy, but like many people on the autistic disorder spectrum, she hates to be touched. Even by those she clearly loves."

"In that case, how did he manage to do what he did?"

Maggie's eyes squeezed closed for a second, as if she'd rather not see. When she spoke, her voice sounded less even.

"He traded. A set of shark tattoo transfers for her, a little favour for him. She had no idea what to do, so apparently he talked her through it. First, he put one of the transfers on her skin. Clever. These kids generally hate to be touched. But she let him, for the sharks. Then he explained what he wanted in return. She's good at following explicit instructions. But that stupid fucking perverted arsehole tried to touch her head. You just can't do that with a kid like her. She reacted violently; screaming, lashing out and rocking, which frightened him off."

"Oh dear God. Did she go home or did someone find her?"

Maggie frowned and rubbed at the bridge of her nose. "No. And this is another shitty thing. He met her as she was coming out of her own back gate. They didn't go far. Just up the back lane. Her mother heard the screams." She inhaled deeply and blew out a long breath.

Beatrice attempted to empathise with Cherry's mother, but decided to close the door on that emotion. It wouldn't do for her to get distressed as well.

Maggie looked up, eyes weary, lines deeper. "Catch him. Do it soon. And when you do, let me into his cell one night. I'll show him justice."

Tired from the tense drive, overflowing with sympathy for Cherry, her mother and for Maggie, and wretched in the knowledge that she had been pursuing her own agenda, Beatrice sensed a chasm below.

She swallowed. "Fair enough. I'll hold him down."

Maggie pulled cleansing wipes from her bag and started to repair her make-up. "While I cut off his dick and make *him* eat it."

To Beatrice, that sounded reasonable.

On entering the meeting room at Finsbury Park Control Centre, Inspector Kalpana Joshi's face gave everything away. She nodded to Beatrice and Virginia, but could not even force a smile.

Virginia began. "Thanks for coming in on a Sunday, Kalpana. We've talked to most staff members, and with at least two victims making a positive ID, we think we need to make a move."

Kalpana did not react, but stared at the opposite wall.

Virginia threw a worried frown at Beatrice.

Beatrice spoke gently. "Kalpana?"

"You ever experienced something like this? Where a member of your law enforcement team uses the advantages of his position to abuse and assault?" Despite her soft pitch, Kalpana's voice sounded harsh and sore, as if she'd been shouting. Her beautiful burnished skin had an underlying redness. Beatrice wished she could give her a hug.

Instead she answered the question. "Not a member of my team, no. But someone I regarded as an ally, someone I trusted, turned out to have my worst interests at heart. It shakes your faith."

"Yeah. That's it. My faith is shaken to its foundations. So how must Cherry James's family feel?"

The three women sat in silence for a moment.

Virginia tried another tack. "Kalpana, he's out there, now. Maybe at this minute, he's on the street with his list of women. He's making plans for the next one. It could even be today. We need to dig into the backgrounds of a couple of suspects."

Kalpana's chocolate eyes turned to them and all her softness dissolved.

"A *couple* of suspects? I thought you got positive IDs from two of the victims?"

Beatrice twisted her mouth to an apologetic smile. "We did. Of two different men."

"Right, let's check their work records, personal details, track record, anything we can find." Kalpana shrugged off her jacket and unpacked her laptop. "You got people keeping an eye on them, just in case?"

"Of course," Beatrice assured her. "They're watching; we're thinking."

Virginia opened the first file. "Nathan Bennett has worked the shift patterns that fit with our man. He's the right age, build and lives in Crouch End. Practically a local."

Tapping commands onto the keyboard, Kalpana shook her head. "Can't see Bennett doing this. He's ambitious, focused on the career ladder."

Beatrice rested her chin on her hand and her gaze on Kalpana. "Can you see any one of your team doing this?"

Kalpana's fingers froze and she angled her head to Beatrice. Her eyes flicked down in thought and she shook her head. "You're right. Let's stick to facts.

"Nathan Bennett, joined the BTP in 2009, and has been raking in praise from superiors, colleagues and instructors. Came over here in May 2010. Looking for promotion. Married, no kids. Wife works as a personal trainer."

"Our profiler saw this man as single," Virginia said. "Not to say the profile is perfect, but ..."

"No, but I know what you mean. The wedding was Christmas 2011, we went to the evening party. It has to be one godawful car crash of a marriage if he's flashing strangers less than a year later. Who's the other one?" Kalpana looked at Beatrice.

"Paul Avery."

Something happened to Kalpana's face. Barely registering as an expression, her nostrils twitched and her eyes dropped to the right. She entered the details without comment, but Beatrice's curiosity was piqued.

"I asked before if you could see any one of your team doing this. Your reaction to this name makes me wonder if you are still as convinced."

Kalpana sat back, lifting her chin to Beatrice and Virginia. "I dislike Paul Avery, I admit. He lacks social skills, he can be over-zealous and his personal hygiene has earned him an informal warning. I had a feeling certain fingers might point in his direction. He's a geek, but a harmless one. I stand by what I said. I can't see any member of my team as a potential sexual offender. Not even this one."

Virginia's narrowed eyes met Beatrice's stare. Virginia asked the question.

"Personal hygiene? Does he have a problem with body odour?"

"No. Halitosis. His breath stinks."

Scotland Yard was eerily calm on a Sunday afternoon. Beatrice stood outside Hamilton's office and sighed. She was prepared to take her verbal thrashing; it was no more than she deserved and she knew it was inevitable. Although she was surprised to receive her summons so soon. Obviously Hamilton couldn't wait till Monday.

She knocked, waited for Hamilton's curt bark of permission and opened the door, expecting an incandescent Norse warrior to unleash bolts of fury.

The late afternoon sun caught his hooked nose, the grooves of his constant frown, and lit a halo behind his grey hair. Yet his eyes, as he lifted them to hers, seemed to contain no anger. His forehead motioned to the chair. She sat.

"You have a suspect."

"Yes, sir. Two, in fact, but one looks like our man."

"Plan of action?"

"A team tailing him every minute of the day. Harrison, our lure, remains in place. He will try something, without a doubt, and when he does, we'll be waiting."

"Your case is not strong enough to take to the CPS as is?"

"Sir, we need concrete evidence. As yet, everything is circumstantial. But we're onto him. He's going to step right into our trap, I'm sure of it. Really, sir, we won't fail."

"As far as I'm concerned, you already have. Cherry James."

Dark wing-beats hovered over Beatrice. She met Hamilton's eyes and waited.

"I understand you were in Wales. With DI Lowe." He forestalled any explanation with a dismissive hand. "I am not interested. Multi-tasking is a marvellous skill around the house. But you are at work. Focus, Stubbs. On your job. Should this man assault or expose himself to anyone else, I will replace you with someone more effective. Thank you for your time."

Beatrice left Scotland Yard with a heavy tread. Fatigued, miserable and dragging a weighty sense of guilt behind her, all she needed was home and bed. But she hauled herself up the road to Transport for London HQ. She owed it to Cherry James.

Ty Grant's usual expression of sardonic amusement was absent. He scrambled to his feet and snatched a file from his desk, meeting her halfway to Virginia's office.

"She's gone home. I'm pretty sure you want to do the same, but could I just have two minutes?"

"If it's relevant to nailing our pervert, you can have two hours. Let's go."

Ty spread the photographs across the table. Eight by fours, both colour and black and white, of Paul Avery. Leaving the newsagent's, smoking outside the launderette, unlocking his front door, emerging in the early evening wearing a baseball cap, boarding a bus, pulling open the door of The Coach and Horses.

"Everything we've recorded today fits the profile. He's single, lives alone, drinks alone and at the paper shop he bought fags and a porn mag. It's him."

A powerful conviction filled her and Beatrice pointed to the cap.

"Remember the logo that thirteen-year-old drew for us? This is a pretty close match. Any ideas?"

Ty shook his head. "Not yet. I'm working on it. I'll find it, if it takes me all night."

His determination surprised her. "Good. Your commitment is ... appreciated."

Ty pulled down the corners of his mouth. "Yeah, well, some things get to you. As you know. Get some rest, DI Stubbs. And don't worry. If he so much as farts, we'll hear it."

She watched him head back to his desk as if he were preparing for a scrum. Time to leave. A blinking light drew her attention to her phone. Six new messages. On a Sunday? Maybe one of them was relevant. She really should listen to them before she left. She sat still, pondering Grant's comment.

As you know. Was her breakdown that well publicised, or was she being paranoid? She shook her head and gave herself an angry reminder. Concentrate on getting this man off the streets. For Paul Avery, there must be no next time.

Messages, home, bed. She rested her head on the back of the chair and pressed *Play*.

Chapter 28

The First Class compartment of the 11.15 from Cardiff Central on Sunday morning was almost empty. Perfect for reading the papers. On his way back from the toilet, Adrian stopped at the door of the carriage to admire his styling expertise. Matthew had actually chosen to wear the black outfit they'd purchased, without any cajoling on Adrian's part. And he looked superb. Black canvas trousers and a black silk shirt. Very gentleman burglar. If only he could be persuaded to cut his hair.

Adrian was smiling as he retook his seat. Matthew cleared away some of the Sunday supplements to make space.

"Your mobile telephone just rang. I'm not sure how to use these things so didn't meddle."

Voicemail message received. Beatrice. He listened once, checked he would not disturb any other passengers, then played it again on speakerphone.

"*Hello Adrian. Beatrice here. It's midday on Sunday, and it looks like I'll be at work some time. It's all kicked off again. But Matthew is due back from Rome this afternoon, so I wonder if you'd mind lending him your key so he can get into my flat. Please call me when you get this. Bye-bye.*"

Matthew shook his head in disbelief. "And what do you suppose that means? 'It's all kicked off at work'. She must still be in Wales. Why else would she ask you to let me in? She must have found something."

Adrian nodded, with a knowing smile. "More than likely. So you'll have to pump her for information, in that Matthew way you have. As if you'd rather be reading a book about Hellenic myths, but you're showing polite interest."

Matthew's eyebrows rose and he blinked repeatedly. "Is it that obvious?"

"Sometimes. And next weekend, armed with any info you get, we go back to Pembrokeshire, catch these smugglers *in flagrante* and hand everything over to the police."

Matthew dunked his teabag in and out of his cup, gazing out at the rushing scenery.

"Might there be a point where we include Beatrice, do you think?"

Adrian scratched his chin. He needed a shave. "There have already been several. Matthew, the only reason I contacted you was because Beatrice showed no interest. I only wanted to help, to find out what was behind this series of accidents. She didn't want to know. Too busy, she said. Now, it appears she's more than interested, she's used my groundwork, but excluded both of us and gone off on her own."

"That much is true. Well, two can play at that game."

Adrian smiled at the stubborn set of Matthew's jaw. "You'll need to be careful, she won't give much away."

"She may be more forthcoming if I take the 'Come, come, dear, you're over-reacting' approach. It infuriates her and she displays proof and evidence and theories and everything."

Adrian laughed. Trust Matthew to know which buttons to press. "I knew you'd have your technique all worked out. As you should. You two have you been together forever. You know, she's never told me how you two met."

"Yes, that is one advantage of a long-term partnership. It also acts as a disadvantage on occasion, because she knows me equally well. Now, my turn to use the facilities. When I return, I may need your assistance with the crossword. Excuse me a moment."

Full of grace and tact, typically Matthew. But unmistakeably a 'No Comment'. Adrian was developing a nose for this sort of thing. And his nose told him there was a story there.

The only positive to dashing back from Wales early on a Sunday morning, having told everyone he would be unavailable, was a full afternoon to get on with his chores. *Distortion* by The Magnetic Fields on the CD, his failsafe mood-lifter, windows open and rubber gloves on, Adrian began by dusting, sweeping and cleaning the bathroom. He chose not to hoover, as Matthew would be resting upstairs. He unpacked his weekend bag, put the laundry on, ironed everything in the wicker basket, then he showered and shaved. He changed into jeans and a cheesecloth shirt, then strolled down to Old Street to buy flowers and the ingredients for Welsh rarebit, to maintain the Celtic theme. He'd buy enough for three, in case Beatrice was hungry when she got home.

At seven, Matthew knocked on the front door.

"Hello. Still no sign of her? Come in, come in." Adrian wafted his hand inwards.

"She's just called to say she's on her way home. So I popped out and bought some bits and bobs from the delicatessen. Thought you'd like to join us for a snack. Two bottles of Franciacorta chilling in the fridge, an array of Mediterranean treats and an opportunity to combine forces. What do you say?"

With a gratified thrill, Adrian noticed Matthew hadn't changed his clothes. He must have recognised how they suited him and wanted to show off. From frump to fox in just two days. Adrian had worked his magic. But he knew better than to offer a compliment.

"Wonderful. For my part, I can contribute cheese and spring onions. Have we got our story straight?"

"I feel confident. And you?"

"Let's go and face the woman. United we stand."

When the downstairs door finally slammed, Adrian jumped, spilling his drink as Matthew scrambled to his feet. Adrian called on all his performance training, leant back on the sofa and flicked through a Sunday supplement.

Beatrice looked awful. Tired, grey and pissed off. Perhaps the impromptu gathering was not such a great idea.

"Hello, Old Thing! Adrian and I got some snacks for you. We thought you might be hungry. Was your day appalling?"

Beatrice placed her bag on the chair. "Hello Matthew, and hello Adrian. Give me a minute, would you?" She disappeared into the bathroom.

Adrian re-read the same page of an article on Corsica four times and still had no idea what it was about. Matthew picked up a bottle and was twisting the cork when they heard the sound of the shower start. He stopped and cast a worried glance at Adrian.

"She's just got back from a long drive. She's bound to be tired," Adrian reassured him in a whisper. "But if she's still crabby afterwards, I may leave you to it."

Finally Beatrice emerged, hair combed back and wearing a deep blue bathrobe with matching towelling slippers. She offered them both a smile.

"Sorry I'm late. Hellish day. Ooh, this spread looks lovely. I tell you, this is just what I needed. What are we drinking? Franciacorta? Fresh from Rome, I suppose. How was the seminar? And what about you, Adrian, did you and Jared have a lovely weekend?" She picked up a stuffed pimento and bit off the end.

Adrian's sensors twitched. Beatrice was furious. Brightly, cheerfully hiding it, but ready to blow like a mushroom cloud. It might be better to leave. But she hadn't finished.

"Let me tell you about mine. While pursuing a lead regarding the stolen camera, I received a call summoning me back to Head Office. Our sexual predator, assumed to be safely at work, attacked an autistic child. Everything has escalated and I am in danger of losing my position on this case. But the best was yet to come. Just before I left the office, I discovered my neighbour and my partner have formed an alliance against me, lied to me, and attempted delicate investigative work in great hob-nailed boots. And Matthew seems to have adopted a whole new look. Are you two about to announce your imminent engagement?"

Her voice was harsh and raw as she grabbed one of the glasses Matthew had poured.

"So, to what shall we toast?"

Matthew looked at Adrian and indicated the door with his eyes. Adrian leapt up in relief.

"Beatrice, I'm sorry you had such a horrible day. But we're on your side, both of us. I'll let Matthew explain."

He sidled out the door and returned downstairs. They couldn't have a row. Not those two. He could no more imagine them arguing than he could imagine drinking a 1987 Petrus Pomerol from a box'.

And to add to his discomfort, he'd left his dinner upstairs. Ransacking the kitchen, he found a bottle of Belgian beer, a packet of kettle chips and two Portuguese Salpicão sausages. He placed the assortment on a tray and sat in front of the silent television, listening for sounds from upstairs. No screaming, no slamming of doors, no throwing of crockery. Not really their style. He picked up the remote control and looked miserably at the tray on his lap. Crisps, meat and beer. All he needed now was football and he could be a screaming great straight.

Chapter 29

Five-forty a.m. and she could tell Matthew was awake. His breathing remained deep and regular, but she knew he wasn't sleeping. Same as he must know she was faking. Both listening, both worrying. She performed a mental scan of herself.

Physical state: better. Sleep had helped.

Mood: bad. Dead weights of guilt and mistrust exerting downward pull.

Attitude toward the day ahead: uncertain, troubled.

"Matthew, look, I ... I'm sorry."

Unlike her, he spoke without hesitation, keeping his eyes closed. "So am I. It was foolish and irresponsible to lie to you. For Adrian and me, this was a bit of a game. For you, I think it's something closer to home."

"Of course it's closer to home. Investigation is my job, and your amateur attempts at helping could put the outcome at risk. Sorry. I'm not going to start on that again."

"That's a blessing. You made your point last night and I subsequently apologised. But that wasn't what I meant. I think this is personal. You are trying to protect me, somehow. You think because I suffered a loss, that of my camera, it is in some way your responsibility to make it good. You mistrust Adrian and me because we are not police officers. That is perfectly understandable. Yet you do not have to do this alone." He opened his eyes and turned to her.

In that second, looking into his dark, intelligent eyes, a surge of love surprised her. She couldn't lie.

"If only it were that noble. No, I'm not your avenging angel; I'm trying to prove myself right. I didn't tell you because I wanted to spare you the worry, in the first place. I wanted to round up enough evidence so that Hamilton would open a joint case with the Dyfed-Powys force. As I said last night, I had no plan to investigate this solo. Things just barrelled along. Hamilton refused, Adrian got involved and then I told Virginia. But by that time, yes, it had become personal. I had something to prove."

"That I can believe. You had something to prove to Hamilton. He's the one who suspects you of not being up to the job. Beatrice, Hamilton will never understand your disorder. When it comes to mental health, he's old school; *stuff and nonsense, pull yourself together*. You'll probably end your days still trying to prove yourself to that upper-class arse. On the other hand, I do understand. As much as anyone can who isn't actually bipolar. We both know your job doesn't help your condition; in fact it may even make things worse. But I supported your decision to go back to work. I told you the same thing as I drove you home from that clinic. I know you need a certain ... validation from colleagues."

Impressed and disturbed by how clearly Matthew could see her, Beatrice tried to smile as tears began an assault.

He hadn't finished. "I'm not Hamilton. I've never doubted your competence, your skill or your intelligence. I know how abysmal things must have seemed if you thought ending your life was the only solution. And it tore me into wretched pieces to think I couldn't help you. So we made a choice, as I recall. We chose to manage these black dogs. Together. You have James, you have your stabilisers, you have me, and you have your job. All working together, we can keep this under control. The point is, Old Thing, if you knock one of your supports away, you're going to have less balance."

Nodding and crying and snuffling, she could barely even see

him. She sat up and groped for tissues. He was absolutely right. Why was her life one mindless loop of warnings about fire and sticking her fingers in the flames? She needed help. She had help. So why did she persist in trying to do without?

"I'm sorry. I never seem to get better at this. James will despair of me."

"As James will surely tell you, getting better is not the issue. The only lesson you need to learn is this: allowing yourself to lean on your support structure doesn't make you weak. The effect is precisely the opposite."

She slid back under the duvet, clutching her tissue, and shuffled into Matthew's embrace. He kissed her temple and rested his head on hers.

"I thought you were having an affair," she murmured.

A deep chuckle rumbled through his chest. "With Adrian? Discovering my true sexuality at sixty?"

"No. With some Roman trollop."

"Well, the same thought crossed my mind when I found you'd lied to us."

Beatrice snorted with laughter, then twisted to examine his face.

"You're serious! An affair? Who on earth with?"

"I don't know. Virginia? That macho sergeant you mentioned?"

"Those are my choices? A straight woman or a gorilla?" She relaxed and shook her head. "I know when I'm well off."

Warmth, security and a sense of having had a lucky escape filled her whole body. Yet one part remained hollow and empty.

"Matthew, I know it's terribly early, but I'm hungry."

"Me too. A handful of olives is barely enough to keep body and soul together. Do you have all the ingredients for Eggs Florentine?"

"I do, if you'll accept frozen spinach."

"In that case, I'll make breakfast, on the condition that you promise me something."

"No more half-truths?"

"That, and you allow us to help. I think with your guidance, Adrian and I could prove useful in terms of legwork."

Beatrice thought for a moment. "If you give me a guarantee that you will not improvise, take chances, run risks or do anything without express permission, it's a possibility. I'll be hog-tied to London until we've got that disgusting excuse for a man off the streets, so any Welsh trips are out of the question for me. But you must faithfully promise. And mean it."

He rose and pulled on his dressing-gown. "Understood. I'll pop into Oddbins later and pass on the good news. Shall I invite Adrian to dine with us, so we can discuss how best to proceed? Or perhaps should I say, take instructions?"

"Good idea, I owe him several dinners. Do apologise for my theatrics last night. I wasn't myself. Right, I'll have a quick shower. Oh, Matthew?"

"I know. You want yours fried, not poached."

"Naturally. But what I wanted to say was, I think you're wonderful."

"You're not so bad yourself."

As Beatrice stepped under the cascade of warm water, she felt lighter, almost skittish, and very, very lucky.

Chapter 30

Karen Harrison's nerves showed after the Friday morning presentation. As Beatrice brought up the lights, Karen sat on her hands. Beatrice softened, recalling her own use of the exact same technique to disguise visible trembles. None of the three women spoke for a moment.

Virginia must have also noticed the young officer's tension and began addressing the girl by her first name.

"Karen, you're doing a storming job. It's been a long, tense week for all of us. Not your fault he hasn't bitten yet. But all the signs point to this weekend, which is why we wanted to talk to you again. If there is any aspect of this operation that makes you uncomfortable, or anything that's not wholly clear, I'd like to hear about it. Your safety comes before everything. If you feel in any way vulnerable, it would be useful to let us know. Now."

"No, ma'am, I'm confident." To Beatrice, Harrison sounded anything but. Her pale skin, wide eyes and determined jaw triggered thoughts of teenage Russian gymnasts.

"Good for you," Beatrice chimed in. "All we really want is your perspective. Remember, DI Lowe and I are on the outside. We're guessing, analysing and making predictions from our standpoint. But you? You're in the victims' shoes. Help us, Karen. Are we missing anything? Do you feel there's a vulnerable side?"

"No, I don't think so. Officers ahead, behind, watching on

camera, response units and several vehicles on the route. What could he possibly do?"

Virginia scrunched up her eyes and sucked air through her teeth in exasperation. "Karen, you have to be realistic about the risks. You can't just wander into this like bloody Bambi. He could pull a gun and take you hostage. Or a knife and stab you, slit your throat. It will take any one of our back-up team at least ninety seconds to get to you, and ..."

"I know." Swellings grew beneath her eyes and two blotchy triangles took over her cheeks. "He's not going to do that unless he knows I'm a plant. The thing is, he's going to make a grab at me. I'm ready for any of this, I really am. But I so hate the idea of being *touched* by him."

The clenched fists, the downward flick of her eyes and the miserable moue on Karen Harrison's face stalled Beatrice. In an instant, she understood how this girl could not escape. The police force needed him to get as close as possible, to attempt to assault her, to sexually threaten this fine-boned girl. After they caught him, she would be feted and celebrated and given an award ... but she would still be a victim of assault. *What the hell were they asking of Harrison? What sort of job was this?*

"Karen, we can't guarantee he won't lay a hand on you. But we'll give you every kind of protection we can. Might mess up your outfit, but I'll organise a Kevlar vest for you." Virginia's voice remained even. "I don't know if they do underpants, but I will make sure you're wearing the equivalent. God knows where I'll find some. DI Stubbs?"

"Yes, DI Lowe. It would be a privilege to lend PC Harrison a pair of my reinforced concrete knickers. However, we're clearly different sizes. She may need a pair of braces."

The girl's explosion of laughter was genuine and a convenient chance to release a few tears. Beatrice held onto hers.

It appeared Harrison's sense of dread had also affected Virginia. Her 16.00 team briefing was direct and brutal. Beatrice was grateful the girl herself was absent.

" ... so if any one of you takes your eye off the ball for a second, half a second, Karen Harrison could be sexually assaulted. She's a police officer, but she's also a woman. She'd have to live with that for the rest of her life. And so would we; because we let him get too close. Or she could be wounded. This guy's ready for physical contact now and could be carrying a knife, a gun, who knows. Ladies and gents, the profilers believe that non-consensual penetrative sex is where Paul Avery is heading. And the chances are high that it will be tonight or tomorrow, because he's back at work on Sunday. If we mess this up, one of our colleagues could get raped. And there's another possibility. Maybe he's already sussed us. He knows she's a trap. In which case, Karen stands a realistic chance of being killed.

"Do you understand what Police Constable Harrison is facing? Seriously? Would any one of you want to change places with her tonight? Nope, nor me. So for fuck's sake, don't let her down. We're all she's got. Good luck."

Beatrice followed the team out of the briefing room and headed for the coffee machine. She had no interest in caffeine, but when it came to casual eavesdropping, its location could not be beaten. Pouring a sparkling water and straining to hear a nearby exchange, she was irritated to see Ty Grant's large, florid bulk in front of her face.

"DI Stubbs? Look, sorry. I know you're on a break, but I'd really appreciate a word."

"I've only got about ten minutes before I go out. Can't you talk to DI Lowe?"

His voice dropped. "I'd rather deal with you."

Beatrice picked up a paper napkin to give her time to arrange her expression.

"Come on, then."

The interview room, cool and anonymous, brought Grant into unpleasantly close proximity. Unlike her, he seemed at ease with the atmosphere. After setting the comms to silent, Beatrice raised her gaze to him.

The dam broke. "DI Stubbs, I can't thank you enough for hearing me out. I did try to explain to DI Lowe, but she thought I had ulterior motives and if I'm honest, and I know I'm out of line for saying this, but some things are bigger than others and she should get over herself."

"Grant, you're not ..."

"Making any sense? I know. Sorry. I was in that briefing and I heard what DI Lowe said and it scared the living shit out of me, as it should. But I am a whole fucking shitload more scared because from what I've seen, we're following the wrong man."

Beatrice studied Ty Grant's high colour, keen eyes and nervous tics.

"Be honest with me and I'll take you seriously, Grant. Have you taken any kind of amphetamines?"

"Amphetamines? No! No, I'm totally clean. Apart from a Pro-Plus last night. Look, I know I'm acting manic. That's the point, DI Stubbs. I worked through the night to find any kind of concrete proof on Avery. There's nothing but circumstantials. So we got Karen out there, showing some tit and hoping to reel in Geek Boy. What if it's not him?"

"If not him, who?"

"Nathan Bennett. Listen, his evidence is just as damning. The logo on the baseball cap? Looks like a woodcut. It's a gym in Crouch End, called *CrossTrain*. Paul Avery's a member, we know. But so's Nathan Bennett. Both these guys work on the same BTP shift, and the thing is, we really don't know who's doing what in that control room unless we're physically there. And we're not. We know who's supposed to be doing which task, but from what I've seen, when there's no senior officer in the room, it seems they spend time on phones or screens or recorded data till they get bored and they switch. So that you can't be sure who's on that screen at any given moment." Ty's face gave away genuine concern.

"What about the positive ID? The smell?"

"We got two positive IDs, Avery and Bennett. The Avery positive came from the bridge woman, who admitted she couldn't see his face. A ditzy teen and a kid with mental problems confirmed it was the same guy. Apart from the French girl, who fingered Bennett, none of the others could be sure. The ID is far from solid.

"Smell, I don't know. But he spends a lot of time at the gym. *CrossTrain* provided all but one of his alibis. The manager, Carlos da Silva, showed me printouts to prove he'd swiped in and out. But I poked around on Facebook and found some photos of Bennett's wedding. Carlos da Silva was Bennett's best man."

Beatrice saw the logic. Her blood seemed to sink to her ankles as she considered how easily they had reached the conclusion that Avery was their target. She shook her head.

"If you're right, we need to widen the op. The security around PC Harrison remains unchanged. But we have to get officers watching Bennett."

"Now, DI Stubbs. Get people on him right now. All our guns are pointing at Avery. Nathan Bennett has the freedom of the city."

Beatrice looked into Ty Grant's eyes and saw fear and hopelessness. She recognised the expression. She'd seen it in the mirror.

Chapter 31

A deep-blue Ford Focus sat in a dip on the Pembroke coastal path. Two figures occupied the front seats. One peered into the darkness, head rotating like an owl, while the other slept, curled up under a cashmere rug.

At five am, a mobile phone emitted a gentle Japanese wind-chime effect.

"Adrian, turn it off. Quick!"

Matthew thrust the handset towards him. Adrian took it, killed the alarm and tucked the still bright screen into his jacket, all while waking up. He blinked into the darkness. It was totally pitch black. He couldn't even see Matthew.

"Sorry. Didn't mean to snap. But round here, even such a tiny light is like a beacon."

Adrian nodded, before realising the gesture was pointless. "Of course. Sorry. That didn't occur to me. But how are we going to find our way to the cliff? I can't see enough to find the door handle."

"We'll manage. Your eyes get used to it after a while."

Adrian rubbed a hand over his face. "You've been awake some time then?"

"An hour or so. Shall we go?"

Sleeping in cars was best done as a teenager. Rumpled, dry-mouthed and in need of a fully appointed bathroom, Adrian knew he probably looked like Matthew.

At least it occurred to him to turn off the interior lights before they exited the vehicle. He closed his door silently, bunted it with his hip to close it properly, slung the strap of his camera around his neck and allowed his eyes to adjust. The moon gave limited illumination through thin cloud cover and far across the fields, Adrian could see the friendly glow of a single sodium lamp. He followed Matthew through the scrubby grass, scanning each flank as if he were in *Platoon* until he tripped over a tussock. After that, he kept his eyes on the ground ahead, remaining alert for the glint of binoculars. Although, would binoculars glint if there was no light? He was still pondering this when Matthew held out his hand to stop him. Below them to the right, a vehicle bumped down the track to the beach, using only side-lights. The sight came as a shock and Adrian froze, his pulse pounding with the horrifying realisation that this was real. Actual drug dealers were down there, driving through the dark to an assignation. And he and Matthew, enthusiastic incompetents, were in the right place at the wrong time.

They should leave. Immediately.

Matthew watched the SUV till it disappeared from their sightline and turned back with an appreciative smile. "It must be a great feeling for you," he whispered. "Being proven right."

Adrian unlocked his jaw. "Absolutely. You don't think we should call for backup or anything?"

"From whom? Come on. Sunrise is due in twenty minutes. We need to be ready."

Woefully under-equipped, they lay on their fronts in the dewy grass and gorse or whatever sharp, prickly stuff covered the cliff top. Despite the discomfort to his chest and groin and damage to his silk-mix roll-neck, Adrian appreciated the view. A generous spread of beach seemed to expand as the light swelled behind them and the scene below no longer caused him eye strain. He played with the zoom of his Pentax, bringing the Chelsea Tractor to the centre of the frame. Parked in darkness on the hard standing, the driver sat smoking. He was sure because he'd seen a cigarette lighter flash. Matthew was right about these tiny lights.

He kept scanning the bay for the smugglers' boat. Not even a speck.

"Here they come." Matthew kept his tone low, but the tension hit Adrian like a whiplash.

"Where? Could I please have the binoculars for ten seconds? Just ten?"

There was no reply. Just when it seemed his request had been ignored, Matthew sat up and looped the binoculars over his head.

"You may have a full minute. I need to attend to a call of nature." He scuttled back over the gorse ridge.

The boat was miles away. What kind of boat was that, anyway? A launch? A tug? Who knew? But it had a motor, just audible, a little hut sort of affair on the front, and was heading their way at speed. A light on the shore caught his eye. The SUV door opened and an interior lamp came on. Marie Fisher stepped out, dressed in a fleece and jeans. She lit another cigarette.

He lifted the binoculars back upwards, searching for the boat. It had come a lot closer while his attention was distracted. A figure was visible at its steering wheel. White hair? Or captain's hat? He flicked down to Marie Fisher, who was smoking and watching the boat's progress. Adrian's heart rate increased and he glanced back for Matthew. The ridge, silent and empty, offered no reassurance.

Without warning, a huge floodlight hit the cliff, illuminating the beach, the road, the steep rock face and Adrian. He ducked, pressing his face into the grass. The light flicked off the next second, but Adrian remained where he was, breathing in shallow gasps. How lucky he hadn't been using the binoculars at that moment. The reflection would have been a clear giveaway. Thank his own good judgement for the black polo neck and the fact that blond had never suited him. Rustling through the undergrowth heralded Matthew's return.

"What was that flash?" he whispered.

"Get down! They've got a massive light and they flared it at the beach. They might do it again," Adrian hissed.

"I doubt it. They were probably checking the coast was clear. Our black outfits came in handy after all. Binoculars, please."

Adrian raised his head six inches, lifting the binoculars from under his chest, relieved to get his nose off the ground. The smell concerned him, country bordering on farmyard. He reached for his camera as Matthew continued his observations.

"The boat has stopped, and I can see our friend with the ponytail. He's doing something with a rope. There's another man, older, with white hair, bringing a package onto the deck." Matthew paused. "I hope to God she's on her own."

"What do you mean? No one else was in that car." Adrian snapped some shots of the men on the boat, and of Marie, waiting on the shore.

"If she had accomplices keeping watch, where would they be, do you think?"

Adrian rolled onto his back, lifted his head from the ground and scanned the lightening horizon. He sent silent thanks to his gym instructor as the position was hell on the abs. The peach-coloured sky softened the contours of the land, revealing shrubs, scrub grass and sheep. He rolled back to Matthew.

"Can't see anything."

"Quick. Get some shots of this. The two men are on the beach now. The older one has passed the package to Marie. No, it's a bag, with handles. She's put it on the ground and is looking inside. It looks more like a basket, you know, but she's blocking my view. I can't see what's in there."

Adrian tweaked the zoom, and began clicking the shutter. He watched Marie Fisher's movements. She was not happy. From her crouching position over the goods, she jabbed her finger at both men, making short, angry gestures to the basket and back to them. If only they could hear her. The men's faces grew more distinct in the growing light and a seagull cried, as plaintive and haunting as the wail of a baby.

As if aware of her visibility, Marie picked up the basket, placed it on the passenger seat and got back behind the wheel.

"Quick!" Matthew crawled backwards, keeping his head low.

"What now?"

"Let's get back to the car, we have to follow her."

"Oh my God."

"Adrian, don't go all wet on me now. You've been a great sport so far."

"It's not that. I've been lying in sheep shit."

Adrian glanced at the speedometer. 95 miles per hour. Matthew sat rigidly, clenching the steering wheel. Adrian sighed.

"Slow down. We've lost her. Either she turned off somewhere, or picked up speed as soon as she was out of sight. She's gone."

The vehicle dropped back to the speed limit and Matthew exhaled. "My fault. You were right. I should have stayed closer. I was over-cautious about her noticing us."

Adrian shook his head. Matthew was such a thoroughly decent man. "Actually, I think you were probably nearer the mark. She'd spotted us and decided to ditch her tail at the first opportunity."

"Perhaps she thought we were the police. Her driving was impeccable, sticking just under seventy and always indicating to overtake, despite the paucity of traffic."

"So what now?" Disappointed and tired, Adrian's enthusiasm was running low.

"Well, first priority is to clean you up. I'm going to pull in at that garage, and you're going to dispose of that jumper. The stink is truly appalling."

He indicated and slowed as they approached the Esso sign. The garage was almost empty. Apart from a large black SUV.

Adrian saw it first. "Keep going! That's her. Don't pull in, Matthew. Just drive!"

Matthew's eyes flicked to the mirror. Knocking the indicator off, he picked up speed again.

"But now we're ahead of her. How will we know when she turns off?" he asked.

Matthew asking him what to do struck Adrian as absurd. Neither of them had a clue what they were playing at. They needed Beatrice.

He feigned a laid-back tone. "We know where she's going, roughly. We'll do as she does. Stick around seventy, or just over, and keep her in our sights. Then, after we get onto the motorway, nearer to Cardiff, we let her overtake and tail her again. From her perspective, it won't look suspicious because there'll be a lot more traffic as we approach the city."

Matthew spent the next ninety minutes checking all three mirrors repeatedly, unable to uphold his end of any conversation. Adrian observed the tension in his shoulders, brow and face. He'd be exhausted by the time they reached Cardiff.

After the turn-off to somewhere completely unpronounceable, early morning road usage increased, as Adrian had predicted, and they allowed Marie's distinctive bullish vehicle to overtake. Matthew hunched towards the windscreen, gripping the wheel with taut hands. The possibility of losing her in the flow of vehicles affected Adrian's nerves too, so he squinted ahead with determination.

He saw the indicator light and yelled, "She's turning off!"

Matthew jumped and touched the brakes.

"Sorry, got over-excited," Adrian said, without taking his eyes from the SUV. Matthew didn't reply, but drew closer as they took the slip road off the motorway. He kept close on the roundabout, but fell back again as she indicated her exit. Adrian perched on the edge of his seat and picked up his camera. Lots of almost-opportunities to grab a decent shot slipped past, so he replaced it on his lap. The orange light flashed again and she turned towards a place called St Bride's-super-Ely. They were the only two vehicles on the road, so Matthew allowed her some distance and she disappeared around a bend. They had just regained a visual as she turned left, without indication.

The bright morning light enabled them to watch the huge black beast's progress over the top of the country hedges, while remaining safely out of sight. She turned off once more, into a newly built estate of six detached houses. It reminded Adrian of the set of *Brookside*. Matthew stopped the car just after the entrance, pulling in beside a farm gate. He hopped out of the car, stood on the door chassis and trained his binoculars over the hedge. Adrian got out and listened to Matthew's low commentary.

"Out of the car, and she's heading to one of the houses. She hasn't got the drugs with her. She's looking through a bunch of keys. Now she's opened the front door of number ... seven and gone inside. She's in a foul temper, you can see that from here. What an unpleasant woman she is. I tell you what, it's lovely to have some fresh ... hello, she's back. Opening the car door, picking up the package ..."

Once more, a seagull's cry soared into the air. But this time Adrian realised he'd been mistaken. That plaintive wail was no sea bird imitating a child. It was the real thing.

Marie took the basket inside, and Matthew, dropping the binoculars onto his chest, got off the car and rested his arms on the roof. Adrian stared at him, unable to articulate a single word. Just for something to do, he delicately eased off his jumper. With a glance at the houses beyond the hedge, he opened the boot, yanked out his weekend holdall and rolled up his stinking jumper in the plastic laundry bag. Unusually for him, he didn't even wonder if the silk-cashmere mix would be salvageable. He pulled on a T-shirt while still shaking his head. A baby. It made no sense.

Matthew appeared, staring with the same uncomprehending look as before, and reached into his bag for a water bottle. He sat on the edge of the open boot and swallowed several large gulps, before turning his gaze to Adrian.

"I believe the modern expression is, *What the fuck?* Is senility assuming control so soon, or did two men sail into that bay and hand over a baby?"

"I don't understand. I'm tired and confused and can't believe what we've just seen. Matthew, my instinct is to call Beatrice."

"I wholeheartedly agree. We're out of our depth. Fetch your device and let's call the boss. Hopefully she'll still be up. She's on surveillance."

As Adrian returned to the passenger seat and located his mobile, he heard a noise. An engine approached.

Matthew hissed from the boot, "A car's coming, hide!"

It was too late. The car was following the same route they had taken, and when it turned the corner, its occupants would have a clear view of them both and their vehicle. But it didn't turn the corner. The car slowed almost to a halt and pulled into the driveway of the cul-de-sac. Adrian snatched his camera, and stepped up onto the bumper of the Focus, using the wild hedge as a screen. Matthew repositioned himself in the doorway, leaning back against the roof, binoculars in hand.

The hesitant approach suggested this was the driver's first visit. Unlike Marie, who'd clearly known exactly where she was going. After parking on the drive behind the SUV, both the front doors opened. Adrian's nerves hummed and he took a second to check that no one had crept up on them while their attention was focused elsewhere. Apart from the ruckus created by birds, insects and wind, the lane was silent.

The driver, wearing jeans and a rugby shirt, came around the car to meet the passenger, a woman. Taking her hand, he leant to look into her face, as if concerned. She had blonde highlights, and was a good foot shorter than him. Adrian's lens followed them up the path, and caught Marie as she opened the door. He got shots of every single thing.

He removed the camera and looked at Matthew. "What

now?"

"Did you take a photograph of the number plate?"

"Several. Let's call HQ."

Beatrice was not happy about being woken after a 'bloody wretched night'. Her terse tone persuaded Adrian to hand the phone directly to Matthew. Adrian resumed his perch on the vehicle and waited to catch someone coming out of the house, while trying to pick up the drift of what Matthew was saying. Both efforts were fruitless. Finally, Matthew returned with his phone.

"She wants to talk to you." They swapped places and Matthew trained his sights on the close.

"Adrian, listen to me. Leave now. You have photographs, a vehicle registration and plenty of evidence for us to work with. If there really is a child involved, you have no choice but to report this to the South Wales police. Leave now, please, and go to the nearest police station. If either party in that house suspects you of watching them, you are in serious danger. I don't need to tell you what the consequences could be and I'm not there to watch your neck. Adrian, are you listening?"

He was, mostly. But his attention was drawn by Matthew, who stood alert as a meercat. Adrian hopped onto the bumper beside him and raised his camera.

"Absolutely. Understood. We're going now. Call you later!"

Adrian caught a few shots of the couple placing the now-silent basket in their car and swung into his seat. Marie remained out of sight.

Matthew rushed to the driver's side, waiting till he heard the other vehicle's engine before starting the car and pulling away with minimum noise. They continued in the direction of Cardiff, both constantly checking the mirrors. After a mile or so, Adrian saw a farm track, and suggested a stop. Matthew drove in for several yards, so they couldn't be seen from the road. A few seconds digging in the glove compartment provided

Adrian with a map, and thus a good reason to be there, which he unfolded across the dashboard. They returned their attention to the mirrors. Three minutes passed. Five. Seven.

"They must have gone back the way they came," Adrian suggested.

"Yes, it looks that way." Matthew made no move.

Adrian sighed. "I don't know about you but I think we should find the nearest Prêt-a-Manger and indulge in a ..."

"Hang on a sec! Here she is."

Marie's vehicle rumbled past and continued into the dappled shadows of the tree-lined lane.

"Right, come on then." Adrian folded up the map but Matthew shook his head.

"We can't follow her. Not any further. Firstly, we promised Beatrice. Secondly, if she sees the car again, she will certainly suspect observation. No, we've done our bit."

"So what now? Should we locate the nearest police station?" Despite his tiredness and discomfort, Adrian's adrenalin was still pumping.

"Hmm. You know, I wonder if it might be more diplomatic to deliver our evidence to the Pembrokeshire force. After all, it is their territory and might just redeem Beatrice in the eyes of the local inspector. We'll need to make statements and possibly accompany them to the scene."

Adrian gasped. "You know what we could do? Go to the pub!" He sat up, energised by the thought.

"It's a little early for me."

"Not now. Tonight. Those men hang about all day and go to the pub in the evening, remember? They'll be there this evening. Listen, why don't we check into a hotel? Then I can clean myself up, send these photos to Beatrice and we can both get some beauty sleep. Later, we'll drive back to Pembrokeshire and give our evidence to the local police. Tonight, we could lie in wait at the pub and identify them to the undercover officers. We could actually be present at the arrest!"

Matthew glanced at him, with a growing smile. "That's not a bad idea. It does seem a shame to miss the excitement of the final scene, after we've done all the donkey work. It would be foolish to pass up such an opportunity. Very well. There's a Travelodge a few miles back. But we ought to tell Beatrice what we're doing."

Adrian clapped his hands together. "Hell, yes. And we'll promise to be careful, not take risks, etcetera. I can shower, shave and perform other necessary ablutions, and possibly even call my friend the barman. Turn around! To the Travelodge!"

With a smile, Matthew began reversing. "I wonder if I should buy a hat?"

"Sorry?"

"A hat, to obscure my identity. The ponytailed chap has seen me before, albeit briefly, but if he were to recognise me, it could complicate matters. He might put two and two together and make a run for it."

Opportunities were falling into Adrian's lap like ripe fruit.

"You know, a half-decent haircut would probably be a better disguise. We'll see if the hotel has a proper pair of scissors."

Chapter 32

The sense of triumphant purpose and excited discussions as to the possible outcome of the evening, which accompanied the drive west, came to an abrupt halt. Fishguard police station was closed. Matthew and Adrian stood in front of the door and read the notice detailing opening hours.

Adrian was shocked. "I can't believe it actually closes! It's not even five o'clock. What happens if there's an emergency?"

"One dials 999, naturally. Emergency Services. These rural police stations don't need to be open around the clock. Crime rates hardly match London's and the expense is unjustified."

"Well, we have to call the emergency line. We can't let them get away."

"Hmm. Could we really say this is an emergency? All we'd planned to do was hand over our evidence, give statements and assist the police in identifying potential suspects. Which wouldn't even be necessary when they have photographs," said Matthew.

Adrian's Have-A-Go Hero headlines were fading fast. "But what about the arrest? If we don't grab them tonight, they'll sail out of here and we've lost them. All because the station is closed. It's ridiculous!"

"I suggest we stick to the plan. We go to the pub, keep our ears open, glean what we can and add that to our report. Then we return here in the morning, with a full dossier. The police can subsequently use our information to apprehend these men. All is not lost, Adrian."

Adrian hesitated. "Apart from us missing out on the action. Oh hell, you're right. Let's go back to the B&B. Do we have to tell Beatrice?" He caught Matthew's expression, sighed and reached for his phone.

The two men sat on the harbour wall in Porthgain, processing their orders. DI Stubbs had laid down the law. Adrian tried every which way to maintain his indignation, but had to admit the justice of her argument. Matthew was to go nowhere near Ponytail and his associate. As far as Beatrice was concerned, the passage of time, the black polo neck, black moleskin trousers and the short back and sides, which showed off his silvery temples in contrast with the rest of his thick black hair all counted for nothing; he could still be recognised. That meant endangering themselves, or wrecking any investigation if these people chose to move their operation elsewhere.

She granted permission for Adrian to go to the pub, to observe and keep his ears open, but forced him to promise several times to do nothing risky, nothing to draw attention to himself. As if he would.

"And whether you hear anything or not, first thing tomorrow morning, you go to the local police and tell them everything. You must. I've left a message for Inspector Howells and given him your number. Adrian, I really don't have time to deal with this, so I'm relying on you two to do things properly. This is now out of your hands."

"We will. First thing. But Beatrice, you needn't worry. I've got a natural skill for covert people-watching. I do it all the time." A brighter thought crossed his mind. He could now spend the evening chatting to Lyndon without neglecting Matthew. Luck was on his side once again.

He handed the phone to Matthew to say his goodbyes and wandered along the sea wall. He spent several minutes watching a large boat pitching and swaying with the movement of the waves. Sailing didn't look all that much fun. *Strike world cruise from the To-Do list.*

Matthew approached. "She's not budging. Looks like you're on your own this evening." He handed back the mobile.

"It seems totally unfair, but I have to say she's right. You can't risk being spotted. So what will you do with yourself tonight?" asked Adrian.

"Oh, I'll be fine. I shall head over to the fish restaurant and indulge myself. I feel more concerned for you, sitting alone in a busy pub, trying to overhear any information about a pair of shady characters. Part of the fun of this is the teamwork and now I have to leave you to it." His expression gave away sincere concern.

"Matthew, you've forgotten my barman. My evening might turn out to be a tiny bit more than spying and surveillance."

"Of course! The chap with the cheekbones. In fact, that's even better, because you can sit at the bar and talk to him. You'll be able to eavesdrop on any conversations as they order their drinks. Well, this has all come out rather well!"

Adrian laughed and turned his mind to the next problem. *Your sartorial challenge, should you wish to accept it, is as follows: to dress like a nondescript tourist, while still demonstrating style and class to those who count. How to stand out while fading away?*

The clientele of The Clipper Inn on a Saturday night was a varied bunch in terms of dress and age, but all were uniformly loud. Adrian sat on a bar stool, drinking a spritzer, pretending to read the local paper and exchanging shy grins with Lyndon. They were able to have a few brief conversations at first, but as the pub filled, Lyndon had no time for anything but pouring beer, wrestling with the till and rushing to the next customer. Adrian's perch allowed him the full view of the low room. The smugglers had not made an appearance.

Just after nine, Adrian began to get bored. The paper was a typical local rag, so if you didn't know these people who'd won scholarships to Aberystwyth, or been elected to the County Council, all you could do was criticise their choice of clothes. And even that was shooting fish in a barrel. Crossword completed, even if a few answers didn't quite fit, he'd exhausted the paper and had no one to talk to.

He sighed, the door opened, and in they came. Ponytail and a truly grim-looking older guy gave the room a quick scan, then made straight for the bar. Although he stood several feet away, Adrian could hear his accent as he ordered two pints of lager. Irish, certainly, but there was something else, a guttural sound which made his voice unusual. Propping themselves against the bar, they turned inwards, their backs to the rest of the customers. This gave Adrian the perfect opportunity to note details.

Beatrice was right. That hair was utterly horrific. From the front: a sharp face with an unfortunate chin, framed by dark brown hair. Short sides, floppy fringe. All perfectly acceptable until you noticed the harshly bleached fronds splayed across his shoulders. He wore dark jeans, a faded black hooded sweatshirt and battered trainers. His accomplice looked worse. White-grey hair cut short and the dour, miserable lines on the man's face made Adrian think of a US Army drill sergeant. Some faces bear the imprint of their most frequent expressions; you can recognise a veteran smiler, just as you can spot someone used to frowning. This man's face had spent far too long showing contempt. His green Army surplus shirt and black combat trousers indicated a man inordinately fond of pockets.

Lyndon shot Adrian a significant look as he spotted them and the next chance he had, he came along the bar under the pretence of retrieving some ice.

"Have you had a word?" Lyndon asked.

"No. And I don't intend to. I just want to find out a bit about them. See if you can serve them next time, get into conversation, you know."

Lyndon shrugged. "I'll try. But I've served these two before." He indicated the stuffed pike in its glass case above the fire. "I've had more fun talking to him. By the way, what you doing later?"

The chef appeared through the kitchen door. "Lyndon!"

Lyndon took his ice bucket and scooted back into the fray.

It took another twenty-two minutes. Eventually, Adrian watched the older man signal to the barmaid and elbow his colleague. Lyndon ducked in front of the approaching girl and picked up their glasses. The guy was quick, Adrian had to admit. Ponytail leant onto his right buttock and reached around to pull his wallet from his back pocket. An idea began to form in Adrian's mind. Ponytail paid for the drinks and replaced his wallet in his jeans. The 'conversation' wasn't going well. Lyndon made another comment, but received nothing more than a blank stare. He shrugged and moved off to serve some shrill Italians.

Lyndon spoke from the corner of his mouth next time he hurried by.

"Nothing. Miserable sods. You going to have a go?"

Adrian shook his head. "No. But I'm going to lift his wallet. When you ring the bell for last orders, ask them a question or spill their drinks or something. With the rush to the bar as well, that should cover me. Can I borrow one of your little waiter's pads?"

"You serious? First time anyone's asked me to create a distraction. You be careful, right? If you get smacked in the puss, I'm not taking you home tonight. Here you go. I want it back after, mind."

Adrian grinned, masking his nerves. Would Beatrice approve of his picking the pocket of a child trafficker? The thought made him pause. But a good detective should seize every opportunity. He'd be careful. He wasn't stupid and here was a chance to prove it. Professional athletes rehearse their moves in their minds, over and over until the sequence is perfect. No reason why a wine-merchant, rich tenor and part-time detective couldn't do the same.

Lyndon directed several meaningful stares across the bar as the clock ticked closer to eleven, but Adrian refused to be distracted. He kept as still as possible, not drinking, not watching, but focusing on his inner picture of a successful lift.

"Last orders, ladies and gents, last orders." The landlord, stupid git, came out of the kitchen and rang the bell, taking both Adrian and Lyndon by surprise. Adrian slid from the stool and hurried along the bar, with the rest of the 'just one more' crowd. Lyndon shifted into position and picked up the two almost empty glasses from their targets.

"Oi! We haven't finished those!" The older man's arm shot out and grabbed Lyndon's wrist.

Adrian rushed forward, pressing himself against Ponytail and slipping out the wallet with his left hand, apologising all the while.

"Shit, I'm *so* sorry. Are you okay? Did I spill your drink? Everyone's in such a hurry tonight. That bloke shoved me off balance." He looked over his shoulder in disgust at some imaginary figure. Ponytail frowned but said nothing.

Lyndon apologised and replaced the drinks, offering to serve them fresh pints before the crowd. The two men agreed and Adrian slipped away to the bathroom, with his booty. He sat on the toilet seat, and flicked through the wallet. Cash in both Euros and sterling, a driving licence in the name of Eoin – *how on earth was he supposed to pronounce that* – Connor, and a set of business cards. Lannagh Farm, Kilmore Road, Ballyharty.

Adrian debated calling Beatrice's mobile, but if she was busy entrapping a flasher, she might not appreciate it. Instead, he sent her a text message and wrote the address on Lyndon's notepad before replacing everything in the wallet. Afterwards, he switched his phone to silent. He was thorough, just as Beatrice had taught him. While he was there, he relieved the pressure on his bladder and congratulated himself on a fine piece of work. Ponytail wouldn't miss his wallet, as it was the older guy's round, and Adrian could 'find' it for him on the way back. Lyndon certainly deserved some kind of reward for his assistance, which was unlikely to be a chore. A coup de théâtre, indeed.

The two men hadn't moved from their positions, hunched at the bar, already nearing the end of their pints.

"Whoops. There's a wallet on the floor here. Does it belong to either of you?"

They both turned. Ponytail eyed Adrian and the wallet with suspicion before taking it. "It's mine."

"Must have fallen down when I bumped into you. Listen, I am sorry about that. Can I make amends by buying you both a beer? Or how about a chaser?"

Ponytail looked to his companion, who shook his head without even acknowledging the offer.

Ponytail shrugged. "No, you're all right. It's closing time anyway. Thanks anyway." He drained his pint and climbed off the stool. "Goodnight to you."

"Oh, goodnight."

They shouldered their way towards the door. Adrian returned to his stool and scanned the room for Lyndon.

"What did you find out?"

The voice at his elbow made him jump. His nerves were a little stretched. Lyndon ducked back behind the bar, carrying a tower of empty pint glasses, face expectant.

"Name, address and occupation. Not bad for an amateur. Is it too late to get a glass of wine? I feel safe enough to dispense with the soda now. And I'd like to buy you a drink, for your help and all." He tore off the address and tucked it in his wallet, handing the pad back to Lyndon.

Lyndon took it, with an impressed nod. "Not bad at all. How about we share a bottle? I've put one in to chill, so as soon as I've finished, we can go back to my place. If you like?"

"I like." Adrian's grin spread. Naturally lucky. He couldn't help it.

"Only you'll have to wait outside for me. We need to clear the pub by quarter past. Sorry. Why don't you sit on one of the benches outside? I'll be with you in two shakes of a lamb's tail."

"Better still, why don't I wait by the harbour? Absorb the view."

The glow from the pub windows faded as Adrian traced his way down the stony track to the sounds of the sea. The cold air made him wish he'd brought a jacket. He rubbed his arms, absorbing the relaxing ebb and flow of the water, the metallic clinks and clangs of boats moving with the tide, and the black, white and grey perspective afforded by the moon. He could have been in a Truffaut film. To his left stood the quarry hoppers, massive constructions of the Industrial Age, supported by a vast brick wall. Their sheer scale, not to mention dangerous edges, depths and harsh surfaces sent another chill over his shoulders. He chose to look to the right, at the moonlit water, the spots of light coming from distant cottages and the huge black solidity of the landmass which dropped to the sea.

He heard a footstep. Quicker than he expected, but there was no doubting the guy was eager. It would be perfect if Lyndon's house had a sea view. With a smile, he turned to greet him. The shock of seeing Ponytail caused his face to fall. Before he could open his mouth, someone came up behind him and wrenched his arm painfully behind his back.

That strange accent. "Right, you're coming with us."

Chapter 33

"You must be out of your mind. Did you not hear what I said in there?" Virginia jerked her head in the direction of the briefing room.

"I don't have a choice. If there are no more officers available, we have to take some of the people off Harrison. I don't like that anymore than you do, but we can't put all our eggs in one blanket when there's just as much evidence to incriminate Bennett. I want people watching him."

"Beatrice, I'm sorry, but I can't agree. We've put Harrison into a vulnerable position. You were the one lecturing me on treating the girl with respect. You sat there with me today and we both assured her of our total support. And now you want to renege on our promise to keep her as safe as we possibly can."

Beatrice clenched her teeth. "I have a duty to all the women in this city, and no plans to renege on any of the promises I made. There's nothing specific in our case to make Avery more of a suspect than Bennett. As Grant pointed out ..."

Virginia groaned. "Grant? Oh please. See this for what it is. An attention-seeking exercise from a detective hungry for promotion. All eyes are on Harrison, and he doesn't like it. He tried talking me into this wild goose chase but I had the sense to look behind the 'I-worked-all-night-and-I-think-I-found-something-ma'am' bullshit. Basically, I've been ignoring him, and this is just another technique to put himself centre stage."

The woman's ego was astounding. Beatrice took two deep breaths, determined to remain in control of her temper.

"As a matter of fact, Virginia, this is not all about you. I believe our detective work has been shoddy, and we've leapt to conclusions. We have two suspects and should be watching both equally hard. Karen Harrison seems to be an object of interest to either or both. Given that we are exposing her to a potential assault, I agree that the majority of our force should be with her. But in addition to a team of two on Avery, I want the same on Bennett. Which means taking two people off Harrison."

"No. We can investigate Bennett in more detail tomorrow, but tonight, all hands on deck for our set-up. Let's face it, you don't even know where Bennett is."

Beatrice had heard enough of Virginia's patronising tone. "We will. I've briefed the Surveillance Centre to inform us if he appears on camera. Grant and I plan to locate him, follow him, talk to his wife and find out everything we can."

"Leaving me to manage the Harrison operation single-handed?"

"Exactly. Totally on your own, backed up by a mere twenty-six officers. Which makes fifty-two hands."

Virginia's expression was hard and cold. "I find this extremely unprofessional, I have to say. We're supposed to operate as a team, not run off on different tangents. You're being pig-headed."

"And you're being blinkered. We have the same objective at heart. Just differing opinions of how to achieve it. I want to turn every stone to find this reptile. I'll report back as and when I find something."

Grant's gratitude for her support manifested itself in a non-stop justification of himself on the drive to Crouch End.

"... which is why I approached you, because even if I rate her as a senior officer, all the personal stuff has clouded the issue, although for some reason she's definitely keeping me at arm's length now, which is fine, plenty more fish and all that, but she should still see the difference when I'm trying to get her attention for a genuine issue, and I think part of the reason she's slapping me down is because she knows I want to transfer to the Met, but the way I see it, in situations like this, we should rise above politics ..."

Eventually, Beatrice shut him up. "I appreciate everything you've said, Grant, and your candour is reassuring. So I'll be equally honest and tell you that if another woman is assaulted in the Finsbury Park area, the Met intend to replace me on this investigation. Thus my motives for keeping an eye on Bennett are as much self-preservation as anything else. Now, what say we leave both the personal and the politics out of this and just concentrate on finding the bloke?"

"Fair enough, ma'am. Sorry. Still heard nothing back from Fitch on the mobile trace. So you want to hit the gym first, or visit his wife?" He checked the mirror as he indicated right into Hornsey Road.

"The gym's likely to be rather crowded, isn't it? Post-work rush. Let's visit his wife. What does she do?"

"Works at various sports centres, including *CrossTrain*. She's on the books as a qualified physio but mainly teaches classes. She's the Pilates instructor. And a bit of yoga, spinning, that sort of thing."

Beatrice glanced at Grant, irritated by his absurd mirrored sunglasses. Was he aspiring to join the CIA? "How do we know she's not at work?"

"I checked her schedule. She teaches mornings only. Bored housewives and all that."

"What is 'spinning'?" she asked, ignoring the chauvinism.

"Sort of cycling on a stationary bike. Cardio-intensive but boring as hell. Not my sort of thing."

"Nor mine. Then again, nor is rugby. All that scrumming and tackling and grabbing and ending up under a pile of none-too-fragrant bruisers."

A proud smile spread over Grant's face. "It's a man's game,

all right."

Beatrice wrinkled her nose and chose not to respond. She looked out the window. "Good Lord, look at this. Crouch End is a world away from Finsbury Park, isn't it? Mothers in Birkenstocks, fathers with pushchairs, wine bars, delis, and I bet it would take us less than five minutes to find a child called Imogen."

"London's like that. Here we are. Lightfoot Road. How do you want to play it?"

"By ear. But if he's there, would you be so good as to loom?"

"No sweat. I'm good at looming."

"I can well imagine."

Suzanne Bennett's thighs were no broader than Beatrice's forearm. She opened the door wearing an all-white tracksuit, full make-up and a perky ponytail.

"Good afternoon, Mrs Bennett. My name is Detective Inspector Beatrice Stubbs, and this is Detective Sergeant Ty Grant of the London Transport Police. We wondered if we could have a word with your husband. He's helping us with an investigation, you see."

Grant turned his head to her. He'd obviously noted how she phrased their introduction, thereby avoiding mention of the Met.

The woman laughed and rolled her eyes. "Talk about the left hand not knowing what the right's up to. He's in work. They called him in last minute, 'cos someone's off sick. Again."

Beatrice did not look at Grant, but could feel him tense. "Oh that is stupid of me. I should have checked. In that case, we'll catch up with him back at base. But while we're here, I don't suppose I could have a few minutes of your time, could I?"

Suzanne Bennett stepped back and gestured inside. "Sure. But I've got book club in twenty-five minutes. It's only the other side of the park, but I have to leave in quarter of an hour."

"Thank you. We won't delay you. Which book are you

discussing tonight?"

"*Kitchen Roll or Toilet Paper*. Have you read it?"

"I've not heard of that one."

"Well, get yourself a copy. It's brilliant. A self-help manual for women who can't see the difference between Nanny and Nurse when dealing with husbands, bosses, children, neighbours, friends and all that. One of them books where you just go 'Oh yeah', all the way through, you know what I mean?"

The terraced house, like most in the area, possessed an impressive depth. The spotless living room stretched all the way back to the neat little garden. White décor gave the room a spacious feel despite the fact that every surface was covered with photographs of the happy couple. Suzanne chattered away as she poured glasses of mineral water and Beatrice sensed that with some skilled questioning, they could find out a great deal from this painfully thin female. However, whether anything was possible in fifteen minutes remained to be seen.

Beatrice shifted forward on the sofa, while Grant stood by the mantelpiece. "After that passionate recommendation, I'll have to read it. Now, Mrs Bennett, not to waste too much of your time ..."

"Will you call me Suzanne? I hate Mrs Bennett. Makes me feel like something out of Jane Austen."

"Certainly. And you can call me Beatrice. I wonder if I can ask you how Nathan feels about being called into work at such short notice? You can speak freely, as I have no control over staffing rotas."

She cocked her head like a small bird. "Can't lie to you, he's not happy. I mean, once in a while is fair enough. But as he says, it's getting ridiculous. Over the summer, almost every week when he's off, he gets a call. He's not complaining about the extra money, course not, but it spoils any plans we've made."

"I see. Yes, that must be a nuisance. And this has become worse over the summer?"

"Yeah. It happened a couple of times before we went on

holiday. But since then, it's been once a month, easy. Sometimes twice. This month, he's been called in three times."

Beatrice shook her head. "That's unacceptable. Not least because we cannot expect our staff to operate at peak performance if they're tired or demotivated."

"Yeah, he is looking tired. And today he left his mobile at home again. That's happening more and more. I reckon he's getting forgetful under all the pressure."

Beatrice glanced at Grant. "Listen, Suzanne, I might be able to do something to help. If you could you let me have the dates he was called in unexpectedly, I'll have a quiet word with the powers-that-be. See if we can't make this system a little fairer."

"Ooh, now you're asking! Let me have a look at the calendar. That's where I usually make notes." She bounced off towards the kitchen and was back before Grant had finished raising his eyebrows.

"Here we go. This is nowhere near all of them, but I can give you some of them in the last couple of months." She began scribbling dates on the back of an envelope. Beatrice scanned the calendar as she waited.

"That's very helpful of you. And, Suzanne, why don't we keep this visit to ourselves? So when his life starts to change, he'll never know how much his clever wife is responsible."

Suzanne beamed, Grant stared and Beatrice sipped her water.

Chapter 34

At Finsbury Park Control Centre, Beatrice and Grant showed Kalpana Joshi the matching dates against the pattern of attacks.

"He told his wife he was working overtime and went out to sexually harass other women? I just cannot believe Nathan Bennett capable of that. He's not the type." Kalpana gazed at the screen. "But he is, isn't he?"

Grant shrugged. "Seems you can't tell who's the type just by looking."

"What I find even stranger is that they're trying to have children," added Beatrice.

Grant gawped at her. "When did she tell you that? Or was it just feminine intuition?"

"On her calendar, she'd marked five little red asterisks each month. And approximately a week and a half later, a block of days highlighted in pink."

Kalpana nodded. "Ovulation. Her fertile days. In that case, do you think he's on strict rations?"

"Even if he's only allowed to hump her once a year, that's still no excuse for what he's done," Grant huffed.

"Quite. And delicately put," agreed Beatrice. "The problem we have now is how to find him. Every member of our team is on surveillance, watching Paul Avery and our police decoy. Bennett may go after her, too. After all, we can't be sure who it is that follows her on camera every night. If it's Bennett, and he does go for Karen, he'll walk right into the same trap."

Kalpana pressed her palms together and rested her chin on her fingertips. "But if he's got someone else in mind, where do we start?"

"On the street. He conveniently left his mobile at home so we can't trace him that way," said Grant.

"Our operation is all over the Finsbury Park area," said Beatrice. "Grant and I taking off in another direction is a politically unpopular move, so we can't get any more officers as support. But we hoped you might be able to provide us with a few extra pairs of eyes to search for Bennett."

"One. One pair of eyes. I can't swing any more officers, but for what it's worth, I'm at your disposal."

One. One bright, experienced senior officer on their side. It was better than they could have hoped.

Kalpana left to change, Grant went outside to make some personal calls and Beatrice rang Hamilton. She knew Virginia had his ear and would have reported Beatrice's decision to change tactic as soon as she was able. It was a wonder Hamilton hadn't been roaring at her already.

"Stubbs? What do you want now?" Even for Hamilton, the tone was especially irascible.

"I apologise for the disturbance, sir. I just wanted to inform you that the investigation has widened somewhat. DI Lowe is supervising the lure and surveillance pairs. DI Joshi, DS Grant and I are following up another potential lead."

"I understood you had your man marked and it was simply a matter of catching him in the act, so to speak. Why are you chasing another lead?"

Beatrice acknowledged her boss's precise grasp of events. No matter how many cases ran simultaneously, Hamilton had an overview of every one. She used to think he was checking up on her. Now she saw it as the mark of an excellent manager.

"Your information is correct, sir. But look at it this way: we're

98% sure of our suspect, therefore we've allocated the giant's share of the manpower to observing him. And the female officer he's been watching. Yet there is an outside chance of another man having slipped the net. Just to cover every base, sir, three senior officers are going to locate him, observe him and question him."

Hamilton's voice dropped. "Are you telling me the whole joint effort involving a staggering amount of expenditure and overtime has been barking up the wrong tree?"

"No sir, we can't be sure ..."

"You can't be sure. And did I comprehend you correctly? You don't know where your second suspect is?"

"As of yet, sir, we're uncertain of his whereabouts."

"Don't doublespeak me, Stubbs. You think you've buggered up the ID, you've set the dogs on the wrong man and now you and Lowe are haring all over North London hoping to find a needle in a bloody haystack."

"Not DI Lowe, sir. She's supervising the Finsbury Park op. DI Joshi is assisting, along with DS Grant, both of BTP. Grant's the sergeant who brought the possible anomaly to my attention."

Hamilton paused. "Can I suggest, DI Stubbs, in the strongest possible terms, that you stick to your remit? A collaborative effort with the BTP to apprehend a potential rapist. I have less interest in your relations with DI Lowe than the outcome of *The X Factor*, but I vainly hoped for professionalism, selflessness and an arrest. If you can manage neither of the first two, I'll settle for the third. Depending on the outcome of your adventures this evening, I suggest a meeting tomorrow. Good evening, Stubbs."

"Good evening, sir."

Hamilton's exasperation depressed Beatrice less than it should. He had no idea she'd split from the main team, which meant Virginia had said nothing. That could be interpreted as loyalty. She picked up the phone again.

Virginia might be loyal, but she was stubborn. Despite the strong evidence to support their pursuit of Bennett, Virginia's tone was dismissive and short. She was convinced of the target and the lure was cast. Harrison in place, all officers prepared, the two officers tailing Avery awaiting his emergence from his flat, everything was set. Nothing would dissuade her from seeing this through. After agreeing to update every hour, Beatrice wished her colleague luck with the evening's operation. With some reluctance, Virginia did likewise.

Adrian's mobile was still switched off. Beatrice didn't leave a message, trusting him to call when he had news. She wondered if they were still enjoying playing detectives. So long as they were playing it safe. And having more fun than she was. She allowed herself a fond smile.

Kalpana returned from her office wearing cut-off trousers, a long-sleeved T-shirt and her hair loose. She looked about sixteen years old. Beatrice realised how vital the severe bun, smart suits and serious shoes were to maintaining her authority at work.

Kalpana gave her a tight smile. "Ready?"

Beatrice nodded. "Yes. I still can't get hold of my men-folk, but I'll just have to trust them to keep out of trouble. Are you all sorted regarding domestic arrangements?"

"Yep. The neighbour feeds my cat if I'm called away like this. Moira's an animal-loving, widowed telly addict and he's an greedy, attention-seeking, ginger gigolo. They adore each other. I often think if it happens too often, Scaramanga will pack his catty bags and move round there permanently."

"Wonderful name for a cat."

"It suits him."

While Ty Grant patrolled the Hornsey and Crouch Hill region alone, Beatrice joined Kalpana in her Toyota to scour Crouch End. Between them, they covered the whole area between Bennett's home and Finsbury Park. Hours of tension solidified Beatrice's shoulders into setting cement. The radio informed them Harrison left 'her flat' and made the journey to Leicester Square without incident, while Paul Avery was in the Snooker Club.

Kalpana seemed tired, so the two women made little small talk, apart from enquiries as to the other's state of comfort. At five to eleven, Beatrice received a text message. Adrian.

Got an ID for Ponytail. Eoin Connor, Lannagh Farm, Kilmore Road, Ballyharty. Elementary, my dear Stubbs. Ax

She smiled, more relieved than she'd expected to hear they were safe, but instantly began worrying about how he'd got hold of the information.

The next update from Ty provided nothing new and Beatrice's eyelids started to droop. She scrunched up her face and rubbed her eyes.

Kalpana noticed. "Me too. Shall we pull onto the High Street and get some coffee? I need a shot of caffeine."

The High Street had a selection of bistros, tapas bars and pubs, but all the coffee shops had long closed. They drove up and down without success. Finally, Kalpana pulled over outside the newsagents and released her seatbelt.

"Right, so two cans of Red Bull instead. Anything else? You hungry?"

Beatrice shook her head. "Entirely against character, I'm not. Have we given up on coffee, then?"

"Coffee at this time of night means a nasty takeaway or kebab shop. And this is Crouch End. So we're in the wrong place." She closed the door and headed into the fluorescent-lit shop.

Beatrice's head jerked up. *We're in the wrong place.* Bennett never attacked near his middle-class home. He targeted poorer Finsbury Park. None of his victims had been glossy Jemimas on their way home from the wine bar, but exhausted Janines on their way home from a twelve-hour shift. He watched his victims carefully, selecting those he thought he could intimidate, grooming those he thought would capitulate. He wouldn't find many of those round here. Plus the fact these people were his neighbours. It would be soiling his own doorstep.

When Kalpana got back in the car with drinks and samosas, Beatrice explained her thinking. Kalpana got it right away, and drove them back in the direction of Harringay, while tearing into a samosa. Beatrice informed Grant of their change in location, but agreed he was better stationed where he was.

At half past eleven, they parked on Lordship Park. All ears strained to pick up every detail of the commentary from the radio. Harrison had caught the Tube and was heading north. Everyone was in position and poised for action. Avery was still in the middle of a game, a fact that was relayed to Harrison. Virginia's voice advised her to delay returning to the flat. Harrison exited the station, stood by the bus stop sending a text message and finally headed towards the Snooker Club.

"She can hear us, then?" Kalpana asked.

"Oh yes. And we can hear her. One of the reasons for the title of 'Operation Robert' is because that's her alarm word. If she says 'Robert', in any context, we mobilise."

"Is that in homage to Robert Peel?"

Beatrice beamed. "You are the first person who hasn't required an explanation. Well done. The thing is, I am completely torn. If she gets home safely, I'll be delighted. And almost equally disappointed. It means he's still out there somewhere."

"I get it. Sometimes, you just get sick of waiting."

PC Fitzgerald informed them that Paul Avery had left the club and was heading in the direction of his own flat. Karen Harrison anticipated his route and walked ahead of him on Blackstock Road. He seemed to be following her and gaining. Virginia's voice warned all units that Harrison was turning onto Somerfield Road, approaching the police flat. To Beatrice, it seemed even the radio was holding its breath. However,

Avery continued along Blackstock Road, heading for home and showing no interest in following the lure. No one spoke until Harrison arrived at the police flat and the applause and whistles began.

"You see, we're all confused. Harrison got home without incident. Hooray. But we failed. He didn't pick up our lure and rather than banging him into a cell tonight ..."

Kalpana picked up her thought. "... we have to do this all over again."

"You don't. You've done enough. In fact, you could head off home now, if you like. Other officers will be available to support Grant and me."

"I'll stick with you for another hour. If all's still quiet, I'll leave you to it."

Virginia's mood seemed a similar mix of disappointment and relief, but she agreed easily to Beatrice's request. She offered to alert the Control Centre to scan all footage for Bennett's presence and sent ten officers to patrol with Beatrice and Grant. Another two already stood watch outside Avery's flat. Beatrice handed coordination duties to Grant, both out of respect and exhaustion. With a guilty twinge, she remembered the sergeant had lost sleep too.

Conversation became easier after Harrison's safe arrival, or possibly due to the caffeine. Driving around the suburban streets, Kalpana talked about growing up in Hackney, in a culture of respect, obedience and cooperation. "So the police seemed a natural choice. My parents weren't keen, and I had a hard time getting accepted, not because I was Asian or female. The problem was being such a shortarse. But when I came home with my first uniform, my folks almost burst with pride. Even my brothers couldn't stop boasting, and they make a living out of things that fall off the back of a lorry."

"You've certainly made a success of it. And I noticed how much respect you command from your team. That can't have been easy," Beatrice said.

"Thank you. I appreciate a compliment like that coming from you. I fought some battles, but I was the middle girl of the family. Two brothers older, two younger. I was used to holding my own. But things were easier for my generation because of women like you. You carved a path through the force long before the words 'women' and 'career' were ever heard in the same sentence."

Beatrice inclined her head, accepting the compliment. "My turn to thank you. Although I'm not flattered by the allusion to mediaeval times. I was born in 1954, you know."

"Like I said. The fifties. Before career women. Before female detectives. Probably before fish fingers."

Beatrice's laughter was interrupted by the radio. Quarter to one. Nothing to report. Avery's lights were out, no sign of Bennett.

Beatrice turned to Kalpana. "Why don't you knock off?"

"You sure? I'm happy to hang on."

"No, Kalpana. You've been a great help. Where do you live?"

"Still in Hackney. But *not* with my Mum and Dad."

"Glad to hear it. If you could drop me at Finsbury Park, I'll join Ty Grant and keep watch for another few hours. Bennett will have to go home then, as his supposed shift finishes at six. Once he's in his own house, I'll feel able to get some sleep."

Kalpana yawned widely, setting Beatrice off. "OK. Only because I have a meeting at half eight. But call me if anything happens."

"Fair enough. And would you let me know when you get in? Just so I know you didn't nod off at the wheel and drive into a reservoir."

"No chance. As soon as I've dropped you off, I'm going to listen to break core all the way home."

"I don't think I like the sound of that. Women my age are much more at home with a fourteenth century madrigal."

Kalpana's face creased with laughter and she looked

remarkably pretty.

Quarter past one and fatigue was beginning to show. Frustrated by the lack of urgency demonstrated by the remainder of the team, Grant became flushed and inarticulate. The pairs dispersed to search the streets for Bennett, but Beatrice had her suspicions that most of them would spend the next four-and-a-half hours moaning about Ty Grant. He'd had enough. So had she. But Nathan Bennett hadn't.

She joined Grant and they drove for the twelfth time up Green Lanes.

Chapter 35

As she swung into Sutton Square, Kalpana turned down the sounds of *Venetian Snares*. Drum beats from passing vehicles were part of Hackney life, but on this quiet square, she chose to keep her neighbours sweet. She parked the car on the tiny forecourt and noted the time in luminous digits on the dashboard. Twenty-five past one. She had to be up again in five hours.

So what? There was only one decent course of action and she'd done the right thing, out of a sense of obligation to Beatrice and her team. A member of her own staff was responsible for these attacks. She had a duty to help catch him.

She locked the car and identified her front door key, glancing two doors down to Moira's house. As if she was likely to see him now. He'd be curled up in a ginger ball on Moira's bed, purring like a chainsaw.

She smiled to herself, opened the front door and reached for the light. In the few seconds before she hit the hall carpet, she registered three things. The rapid crunching sound of footsteps on gravel, a hand shoving her forcefully into the house and a strong smell of feet.

The heels of her hands suffered carpet burns as she broke her fall. Adrenalin pulsing, she rolled onto her backside, ready to defend herself as the light came on. Nathan Bennett stood smiling at her, wearing a baseball cap and carrying a backpack.

"Here I am, ma'am. Just like you asked."

The stench was nauseating. Bennett sat opposite her, forearms on his knees, peeling the label from his beer bottle, with a permanent grin playing across his face. Kalpana was tempted to take a swig from her Pilsner, just to block out the odour for a second, but needed to keep her mind as sharp as it could be. She had to work out what the hell he was thinking. He acted as if he'd turned up as a result of an invitation, accepted the offer of a beer, refused anything to eat, all with the casual demeanour of a friend popping round. Nothing about his behaviour was threatening, apart from pushing her into the house at two in the morning, and he seemed relaxed, sober and pleased to be there. Kalpana knew her best hope of getting out of this unscathed would be to talk. Tidal waves of terror made this an awkward prospect, but she had no other ideas.

"So, it's nice of you to come round. I was just wondering ... to what do I owe the honour?" Her voice sounded girlish and false.

He exhaled through his nose, a dry laugh. "I should be asking you that question. Why did you choose me?" He reddened and a jolt of alarm shot through her as she realised he was blushing.

His eyes remained on the ground. "Look, it sounds like I'm fishing for compliments, which I suppose I am. But I really would like to know. Why me, Kalpana?"

Kalpana frowned at the familiar address and her tone was impatient. "Why you what? What are you talking about, Bennett?"

His face darkened and his mouth pinched into a bitter line. "Don't call me that! I have two perfectly good first names."

She stiffened and waited till he seemed to gain control of his temper. He was muttering.

He looked up at her and sighed. "Sorry. I didn't mean to bite your head off. But seriously, what kind of relationship are we going to have if you still treat me as if we're at work?"

Kalpana's nails dug into the upholstery, as he gave her a conciliatory smile.

"It took me a while. I have to hand it to you, you're subtle. No one at work could ever have guessed. And when I did cotton on, I couldn't believe you'd pick me."

You have a choice, Kalpana told herself. Try forcing him back to reality, or enter his skewed view of the world. The risks of both are enormous. Just by using the correct form of address, he'd flared up, ugly and angry. If he lost it and hit her, she had a feeling her self-defence training wouldn't help much. Or she could play along, discover what twisted thinking had made him decide to visit her, wait for her and physically shove her into her house. She had no idea what he'd done with the key. And she wondered, as the surges of dread threatened to overwhelm her, what the hell was in that backpack?

"When did you 'cotton on'?" she asked, her voice unsteady.

His grin was shy and pleased. "It wasn't like one big revelation. More little clues. Like just recently, when you told me that with my ambition, I could go far, in *that* voice. But at first, I told myself I was imagining it."

You were, you twisted fucking loser. You were! Kalpana clamped her lips together, refusing to allow her thoughts to tip the balance.

"You know, you're the first female boss I've had. And it seemed such a cliché, the office romance. I tried not to think about it, but the tension was driving me insane. I had to do some stuff, let off steam. Yeah, that shit was all your fault," he laughed, his tone teasing.

That shit? Kalpana searched for some kind of appropriate response. None came.

His colour heightened and he shifted forward to the edge of the sofa. A foul whiff of cheese and sweat triggered another wave of sickening fear in Kalpana's stomach.

"I'll be honest, pretty soon I couldn't think about anything else. You, in your pinstriped suits. I could just imagine what you had on underneath. Those cute little heels, your tied-up hair, I fantasised, time and time again about taking your hair down ..."

His breath was short and his colour high. He was aroused. Kalpana panicked.

"But you're married ..." she couldn't call him Nathan. It would only add to his deluded sense of intimacy. "What about your wife?"

His grin spread. "The wedding. That was when I first started to believe it. You came to the evening do, you kissed me and you whispered in my ear, remember?"

"I remember kissing you both on the cheek and saying congratulations."

"I know. I got it. That was when you told me you were giving yourself to me as a present. From then on, I watched the signs. I kept a diary of all those little signals, all the little messages you sent. Every one. And finally, you made your move."

Kalpana's fear took on a new shape and tears built as she saw the extent of the psychosis in front of her. "My move?"

The phone rang, making them both start. Kalpana lost her grip on her beer bottle. It slipped to the floor and spilt over the carpet. Bennett looked at her and wagged a forbidding finger. The machine clicked in.

"Leave a message after the tone. Please speak clearly."

"Kalpana, it's Beatrice. If you are already in bed, then I apologise. No news at this end, but you did promise to call when you got in. It's now quarter past two and I've heard nothing. Could you please give me a quick call or text, otherwise I will have to come round, or send a patrol car to check that you're all right. Call me a Mother Hen, but ..."

Bennett scowled, grabbed his bag and with a jerk of his head, indicated the phone. She moved to answer it, feeling Bennett press himself against her, one arm around her waist, the other holding a large blade just under her left ear. Cold steel and the foul stench made her flesh crawl.

"Tell her you're home and put it down," he whispered, and

reached down to press the speakerphone.

Kalpana picked up. "Beatrice! Sorry, I completely forgot to call. Yes, I got home safely."

"Oh, you *are* there. Good. That's all I wanted to know. I'll let you get some sleep."

She was going to ring off, leaving Kalpana alone with a mentally unstable deviant, who'd chosen to bring a hunting knife to his imaginary date. What else had he got in his bag? Her hands shook and she felt Bennett's arm tighten around her waist, pressing his erection into her back.

"Thanks for calling, Beatrice. I really appreciate it."

"No problem. See you tomorrow. Give my love to Scaramanga."

The pressure on her neck increased, bringing with it an instant of inspiration.

"I will. Give my love to Robert. Good nig..."

Bennett cut her off.

He released her and stood back, grinning broadly. "Well done. I like it when an officer obeys orders."

Kalpana turned with a tearful smile. "So, how about another drink? And then you can finish telling me how you worked it all out?"

He stared at her, eyes tracing her form, all the way down her body.

"I think I'm done talking. You didn't invite me round here to talk. What the fuck are you wearing? Those clothes are ugly. I thought you'd have made more effort for me tonight." His face was cold and hard.

She shook her head, unable to speak, tears falling freely.

He picked up his backpack. "Fortunately, I've brought you some presents."

Chapter 36

Beatrice pressed End Call and sat back in her seat, yawning.

"All OK?" asked Grant.

"Yes, she just forgot, that's all. Seems paranoia is my constant companion these days."

"That's understandable, ma'am. Where to now?"

That's understandable? Another of those comments. Beatrice decided this was her opportunity to ask Grant exactly what he knew. He had made far too many references to her condition, indicating a distinct familiarity with the subject. She would pressure him until she found out how widespread the knowledge of her breakdown had become.

"Where are we?"

"Clissold Park. Who's Scaramanga?"

"Let's do Green Lanes again. It's the name of her cat. You don't know Scaramanga? He's a Bond villain, played by Christopher ... oh my God."

Beatrice reacted as if she'd jumped into freezing water; her skin tightened, her stomach contracted and she gasped short breaths.

Grant braked instinctively, scanning the street for danger. "What?"

"Bennett's there! After I said, 'Give my love to Scaramanga,' she said, 'Give my love to Robert.' Bloody hell, Grant, it's the alarm signal, I told her about it tonight. He's there! He's got her.

Drive to Hackney! Now! I have to find her address."

He executed a rapid U-turn and drove at speed down Green Lanes and onto Balls Pond Road. All sense of tiredness evaporated as Beatrice made a series of emergency calls. When she'd got confirmation of Kalpana's address from the Control Centre, Beatrice called the team. "We need all officers to 91 Sutton Square, off Urswick Road. Approach with stealth, we don't want him to know we're there."

She informed Virginia, who promised to meet them at the scene. Her question frightened Beatrice. *Why Kalpana?* Why indeed? Was she the last in the line? In which case, what did he plan for his final assault? As they drove up Dalston Lane, Beatrice felt pathetically inadequate. How to get Kalpana out of there without injury?

"What would you do in this situation, Grant?"

His face seemed pale in the occasional oncoming headlight. "Scope the place and make a decision fast. Every second we waste ..."

Beatrice scrunched up her toes, unable to imagine what a delay would mean to Kalpana. She had to get this right, first time. She picked up the phone again and requested authorisation for body armour and firearms.

Although barging in heavy-handed might provoke a disproportionate reaction to being threatened, she knew he was likely to be carrying weapons. Attempts to negotiate presupposed an ability to get him to talk. Ideally, they could get into the house silently, wait for their moment and grab Bennett with no danger to Kalpana. But how were they to get in, unless through the cat-flap?

The cat.

Kalpana said her neighbour took care of him if she worked late. Something Scottish ... Moira! In order to get the cat, Moira must have a key.

"How much farther now?"

"It's over there, ma'am. This is Urswick Road, and that's Sutton

Square on the right. I'll park here."

Beatrice fumbled with her belt and scrambled out. "We need to contact her neighbour who has a key, but let's find number 91 first."

As soon as they entered the square, Grant identified the numbering pattern and indicated that the second house on the opposite side was 91. They navigated a path around the ornamental pond, keeping their eyes fixed on the modern terraced house. A light was on downstairs, but the curtains were drawn. A movement to their right indicated the arrival of PC Fitzgerald and PC Hyen. Beatrice joined them under the laburnum bush which screened them from view.

"Check the houses either side and a couple more further down. She has a neighbour, Moira something, who looks after her cat and has a key. Don't be alarmist, just explain we need access to Inspector Joshi's house, and it must be now. Grant will try to see what's going on in there, and I'll wait here to meet the others." Her voice surprised her. She sounded calm and in control, conveying no reflection of the frantic cramps in her stomach.

Grant nodded and squeezed past Kalpana's Toyota, taking care to remain on paving stones and not to tread on the gravel. He moved with impressive speed and grace for such a great lump of a man and Beatrice's admiration surfaced above the barely controlled panic. A light went on upstairs and Beatrice froze.

"Ma'am?"

Two other teams had arrived and waited in the darkness. Beatrice raised a finger for patience and returned her attention to the house. Grant stood in the porch, peering through the curtain into the still-lit front room. No one moved. Minutes ticked past. Grant moved to the front door, lifted the letterbox and craned forward, as if listening. The upstairs light went off again and the curtains moved a fraction, as if a gust of air had caught them. Grant slid back past the vehicle towards the team. Beatrice turned to see the remaining four officers and Virginia joining the group. She motioned them back behind the bush. No sign of Fitzgerald and Hyen yet.

Grant acknowledged his colleagues with a nod. "Sounds like he's in the front room and he's sent her upstairs to get something. I heard him shout, 'I'm waiting', but I didn't hear a thing out of her."

Virginia winced. "So why are we all standing around here? Let's get in there and arrest him before he goes any further."

"DI Lowe, I sent two officers to retrieve a key from the neighbour. I'd rather not go in all guns blazing, just in case the fear factor provokes him. We need to surround the house completely. Some of you will need to find the back alley which must run behind these gardens. Grant, can you allocate places for six of the team in case he tries to run?"

Beatrice took Virginia to one side. "When we get the key, I suggest we get Grant and Fitzgerald in body armour in there to overpower him. We'll follow right behind, backed up by four more officers. Everyone else remains out here as a safety precaution ... here's PC Fitzgerald."

Fitch held up a key. "Moira Hilliard. Three doors down. Hyen stayed with the old girl, she's off on one. But this is the key to the front door."

Virginia seemed to wake up. "Right. Ty, Fitch, get your kit on. You're going in first."

They left the team in position, while Beatrice followed Virginia and the two men to the vehicles. Despite her revulsion towards firearms, her training enabled her to ready her gun automatically, leaving her brain free to think. As they prepared themselves, Virginia spoke. "Listen up, we're going to brief you as you dress. Time is crucial. DI Stubbs?"

Beatrice swallowed her surprise and donned her holster. She gave in to her impatience to take control.

"Don't take any chances. Wait for the right moment when he can't get to her before you get to him. Disarm him, get him in cuffs and no more. We'll be right behind you, ready to back you up. Use of weapons, as always, only in extreme circumstances. Injuries to yourselves, Inspector Joshi or even him in this operation are unacceptable."

Two heads nodded and Beatrice handed Grant the key. Scurrying back to the house, Virginia silently pointed out the order of officers to follow. Beatrice and Virginia were two and three. The team assumed positions. Grant and Fitzgerald were already at the door, Grant turning the key imperceptibly and listening. It opened and the two men crept inside. Beatrice and Virginia slid alongside the car, ears alert for any sound.

Entering the hallway, Beatrice saw the outlines of Grant and Fitzgerald pressed against either side of the living-room door. A faint voice, almost chanting, could be heard. Grant's hand on the doorknob moved in millimetres, and Beatrice's breath had become so short it barely reached her lungs. Grant crouched and pushed open the door gently. The voice continued.

"... told you to do it slowly. Now turn round. Good. And now bend over. Bend over and touch your toes. Look at me. Look at me between your legs."

She heard Virginia exhale and an uneven shiver crawled over her own skin. Grant eased his head into the room, then kicked open the door, shouting, "Freeze! Hands in the air!"

Fitzgerald dashed after him and Beatrice heard the release of the safety catch from his weapon. Beatrice, Virginia and their support officers rushed in to see the backs of Grant and Mitchell aiming their guns directly ahead; Kalpana Joshi in underwear, standing on a heap of pinstripes on the coffee table; and Nathan Bennett sitting in the armchair, with both hands up, trousers down and a fast-deflating penis. A foul smell of feet filled the air.

Virginia holstered her weapon and approached Bennett, kicking away the knife at his feet. The movement seemed to snap him back to reality. He narrowed his eyes at Kalpana.

"What the fuck is this? How did you call them? What did you do, you dirty slut? I took your phone, for fuck's sake! How did you do it? You lying, sly little bitch!"

Kalpana stood there, half-naked, staring at him with a look of profound revulsion.

As Fitzgerald read Bennett his rights and Grant put on the cuffs, Beatrice picked up the sofa throw to cover Kalpana. Virginia informed the officers waiting outside of the successful arrest. Bennett's voice rose, insistent and ugly. Easing Kalpana from the glass table, Beatrice could feel the woman's trembles through the chenille. Bennett was shouting over Fitzgerald as Grant pulled him to his feet and yanked up his trousers.

"You can't arrest me! She fucking invited me, the prick-tease! Ask her!"

Kalpana turned to face him, her face livid. The shakes were not, as Beatrice assumed, born of fear, but of barely-controlled temper.

"Get out of my house, Bennett. You disgust me. And you fucking stink."

Grant and Fitzgerald led him from the room, still hurling abuse at his superior officer. Virginia snapped gloves to pick up the knife and bag it, casting sympathetic glances at Kalpana's slight form.

"Kalpana? Can we call anyone for you? PC Hyen says your neighbour is outside."

"Thanks, Virginia. Could you let Moira in? I'd like to reassure her."

Virginia ducked out into the square, taking the evidence with her. Kalpana looked at Beatrice.

"Thank God for Beatrice Stubbs. I wasn't sure you'd got it."

Beatrice shook her head. "I didn't for a moment. I'm still shocked he came after you."

"It seems I was his ultimate target. The rest of them? Just him exercising his frustrations, apparently. So in his dysfunctional logic, it's all my fault those other woman suffered unwanted attention."

Beatrice blinked, trying to imagine being in Bennett's mind.

It must be rather like a William Burroughs' novel.

"Had you never noticed his foot odour before?"

Kalpana shook her head with emphasis. "He wears a uniform at work and I'm strict about presentation. I assume it was those revolting trainers. And you know what? He was the one who complained about Paul Avery's breath."

Virginia returned with Grant and an older woman in a quilted dressing-gown.

"Oh God, Kalpana, I'm so glad to see you! I was worried out of my mind, the police arriving in the small hours and demanding your key, I just couldn't imagine, Scaramanga's hidden under my bed, I had no idea what was going on and they wouldn't let me come round at first ..."

While Moira was speaking, Grant reached behind the armchair and retrieved Bennett's backpack. His face, on seeing the contents, attracted Virginia's attention. She glanced into the bag and Beatrice saw her eyes darken.

The charge in atmosphere caused Kalpana to look up. Her eyes flicked from one to the other and back to the bag.

"What was it? What did he have in there? Tell me, I want to know what he was planning ..."

Virginia interrupted, taking hold of the backpack. "No, you don't, Kalpana. Not now. Trust me." She motioned to Grant and they left the room, taking the backpack.

Kalpana covered her eyes with her hand.

"How about a nice cup of tea?" Moira sat beside her and patted her knee.

Beatrice stood. "We need to get back and start processing Bennett. Do you think you'll feel up to making a statement tomorrow?"

With a bitter exhalation, Kalpana looked up. "You try and stop me."

Chapter 37

His ankle was the worst. His jaw still throbbed, his shoulders were stiff and aching from sitting so long with his hands tied behind him and he was colder than he could ever remember being. The initial vomiting caused by the constant heaving of the boat had dissipated, but it left him weak and shaky. But the pain in Adrian's wrenched ankle was searing. Exhaustion swept over him several times and he almost dozed once or twice, especially after Ponytail Man – Eoin – had draped a blanket over his shoulders. He knew how to pronounce it now. 'Owen', as in Clive. And the other one was called Sammy.

He'd learnt their names from the furious whispered conversation they'd had behind the Porthgain quarry hoppers.

After dragging him out of sight, they searched his bag, finding the photographs, the camera, Adrian's notebook and horribly, the key to the B&B. Surely they wouldn't go after Matthew? But the key didn't seem to interest them. What really caught their attention were the pictures on the Pentax. The beach, the packages, Marie's vehicle in the cul-de-sac. Sammy stood over him, demanding to know who he was. Adrian wondered why they hadn't checked his jeans. They would have discovered not only his wallet, containing ID, but also his mobile phone. That was when Sammy hit him.

The shock of the blow totally disorientated Adrian and the taste of blood made him nauseous. Sammy grabbed his jumper and hauled his face close.

"I'll ask you again. Who the fuck are you?"

He had to lie, but was hopeless at making things up under pressure. He fell back on the only pre-fabricated story he had.

"Andrew Ramos. I'm a private investigator. I was asked to watch this beach for signs of illegal activity and report back with whatever I found."

"Who asked you?" Sammy kicked out at him. His hard boot connected with Adrian's thigh. Pain radiated through his body and he squeezed his eyes shut for a couple of seconds.

When he opened them, Sammy was waiting.

Eoin, whose face was in darkness, made a small sound of exasperation. "Sammy, would you ever stop with the fists and the feet? Let the man talk."

Adrian breathed for a second, until the pain lessened. "Professor Michael Bryant. He and his wife stayed here on the Bank Holiday weekend. After his wife's bag was stolen and their cottage burgled, he suspected something dubious was behind it. He asked me to check. So here I am."

The silence stretched out. Sammy staring at Adrian, Eoin staring at Sammy.

Finally, Eoin spoke. "What did I tell you? What did I say? Trying to get the fecking photographs back is what's caused the problem. Not the pictures. Jesus, Sammy, this is what your paranoia's done."

Sammy stared into the darkness at Eoin, until the sounds of customers leaving the pub carried up to them. Sammy shook his head, like a dog with a flea, and reached into his jeans pocket. He pulled out a mobile and opened the flap. The pale blue glow highlighted his sour expression.

Eoin's voice, low and nervous, came out of the dark. "Who're you calling?"

"We have to make a decision. What do we do with yer man?" Sammy pointed the phone towards Adrian like a weapon.

"Call Marie. She'd get here in a couple of hours."

"Fuck that. I want to talk to someone with sense. I'm calling the Mammy."

Eoin exhaled through his teeth. Sammy pressed some buttons and paced away up the slope. For a few seconds, Adrian felt eyes on him. Whichever way you looked at it, he was a massive inconvenience to these men. This quiet observation from the shadows was an assessment. What exactly to do with him? Adrian heard footsteps move away in the direction of Sammy's murmurs. If they found his wallet, he was lost. Name, address, not to mention sexuality stated on various membership cards, none of which matched what he'd told them. All he could do was to leave it here in these industrial ruins, hoping it would not expose Beatrice. And it was a long shot, but it someone might find it and raise the alarm. He wriggled and winkled the flat leather packet from his back pocket, leant forward and threw it as far as his roped wrists allowed. All he had now was his mobile, switched to silent since the text message to Beatrice. His head fell back against the brick wall. He'd screwed everything up.

Sorry, Beatrice. Sorry, Matthew. Sorry, Lyndon.

Whatever 'the Mammy' said provoked Sammy into an even greater rage. He dragged Adrian to his feet and searched him as roughly as possible. He found the phone in seconds, threw it to the ground with an unintelligible curse and smashed it with his boot. Once the village was quiet, Eoin guided him down to the harbour, Sammy striding ahead. The difficulty of getting Adrian on board the small boat seemed to push Sammy over the edge. He swore, this time in English, and hauled him from the jetty like a sack of coal. Adrian's thighs whacked onto the side of the boat and he was still gasping with pain when Sammy shoved him hard down the steps to the cabin. His foot caught and he fell heavily on his side, wrenching his ankle and winding himself. That was when he passed out.

When he came round, he vomited immediately. Adrian's companion in the tiny under-deck area was a slim, dark-haired, hard-eyed woman, whose arrival he'd missed. The girl sat opposite, arms folded, giving him the occasional wary look. Eoin came down and offered him water after the puking session. He cleared up without comment, gave him the blanket and untied him long enough for a visit to the toilet. Hoping for a lockable door and the chance of a few minutes alone to assess the damage, Adrian could have cried when he saw he had to piss into a bucket. But after he'd finished, Eoin re-tied his hands behind him, placing his limbs in the same agonising position. Adrian groaned in pain, and without a word, Eoin adjusted the rope so that his arms were slightly more relaxed.

Eoin's ministrations were discreet, as if it might not meet with Sammy's approval. Without a word, he offered the girl a bottle of water and once she'd taken it, hurried to return back on deck.

Adrian tried to talk to his fellow captive. "Are you OK?"

She looked away.

"They didn't hurt you, did they?"

She kept her head turned from him.

"My name is Adrian."

Recognition lit her expression and she faced him. "My name is Katya."

"Hello, Katya. Do you know where they're taking us?"

She shook her head and waved her hands in a 'no pictures, please' gesture, wrapped her blanket around herself and curled up on the bench.

Leaving Adrian to shiver and suffer and second-guess their plans.

The unbearable night of pain, cold and misery had to come to an end sometime. Finally, the sky through the portholes grew lighter. Noise above deck focused his attention, and the movement of the boat slowed. Dull pain and an undercurrent of dread switched places and Adrian's fear tasted as real as the coppery flavour of his own blood. His stomach heaved again but had nothing left to throw up.

Eoin came down the steps and beckoned Katya, who unfolded and heaved herself to her feet. The careful movements and recognisable stance spelt out her condition even before she turned sideways, giving Adrian a clear view of the bump. Eoin helped her up the steps, which took some time. It was like manoeuvring a heifer up a ladder. As he heaved her onto the deck, Eoin jumped back down and motioned for Adrian to follow. Shuffling forward, Adrian attempted to rise but the awkward position and white heat of his ankle made it impossible. He fell backwards, an excruciating tear shooting across his shoulders as his muscles protested against the forced position.

Eoin stooped to support him by lifting his upper arm, but Adrian's ankle would not take his weight. Shoving, leaning, struggling and with gritted teeth, the two men navigated the steep steps and emerged onto deck. Sammy waited beside the girl, shaking his head with disbelief.

"Eoin, you idiot, how long does it take?"

Despite his pain, Adrian noted the accent. A hint of Russian in those dark vowels?

Eoin ensured Adrian was stable against the handrail before withdrawing his arm to wipe the sweat from his lip. "Woulda been a lot fucking quicker if you'd not twisted his ankle. Now I'm taking off the rope. Fecker can't even walk, leave alone run. So shut it, gobshite, and let's get to the car."

The release of his arms brought tears to Adrian's eyes. As feeling returned, as if to frozen fingers, the relief and the pain seemed equally torturous. Sammy leapt into the water, helped Katya down the ladder and escorted her towards the shore without a single look backwards. The light grew stronger and to Adrian's eyes, the beach seemed hardly different to the one he'd been watching the previous morning.

Eoin watched the retreating back and looked at Adrian. A downward twist of his mouth conveyed an apology as he grabbed Adrian in a fireman's lift and struggled down the ladder. It hurt like hell. Remember the details, Beatrice had said. Hanging upside down over Eoin's shoulder, he mentally described the smell. A dampness, slightly meaty, unsubtly disguised by something artificial, like air-freshener. And what good would this do him? Tears of despair, frustration and pain rolled down Adrian's forehead into his hair.

When they reached their destination, Eoin had to lift him again. Not a pleasant task. Rattling around in the back seat of a Jeep, hands tied in front of him, and wearing some sort of blindfold at Sammy's insistence, Adrian's stomach had found something after all. So when he was hefted over Eoin's shoulder once again, his sense of smell picked up nothing more than his own vomit. He never saw what happened to Katya.

Eoin yanked the material off his head and Adrian's eyes adjusted quickly. He'd been dumped on a pile of straw in some sort of stable. Stone walls and floor, a damp chill and precious little light. Through the open door, Adrian saw a rutted farm track and more outbuildings. Eoin released his hands, fetched a towel from outside the door and threw it onto Adrian's lap. The large wooden door slammed closed, bolts shot home and Adrian was left alone. He rubbed his face and lay on his side, shivering and sore, knowing that sooner or later, he had to start thinking. But not yet. Not just yet.

During his doze, the top half of the door opened several times. He squinted against the sunlight and saw backlit silhouettes staring in. The door closed again. Adrian kept his eyes closed, concentrating on his pain and the smell of sick all over him. But each time someone came to look, another stink seeped in through the open door. It was foul and rotten with chemical overtones. He'd never smelt anything like it before, but somehow he recognised the stench of death.

When he next awoke, he felt a presence. He looked around the room. Apart from some sort of hay-holder and a metal bucket, the room was empty. The sound of someone sucking their teeth came from above. The wall to his left did not reach all the way to the ceiling. It ended some three feet below, and in the gap sat a large girl, legs either side, as if astride a horse.

She pressed her fingers to her lips and whispered, "I'm not allowed in here."

Adrian stared, unable to speak.

"But they're all arguing in the kitchen, so who's to know?" She dipped her hand into her pinafore pocket and drew out a carton of Ribena.

"I brought you a drink. And a sandwich. Well, it's not a sanger yet, you'll have to put it together yourself. But I brought bread with butter on it, and some rashers. The Mammy usually sees everything, but today her head is somewhere else so you were lucky. Are you ever coming over here, or what?"

Adrian's mouth was dry and sour and he craved liquid. His voice sounded cracked. "Thank you. You're very kind. But I don't think I can move. I hurt my ankle."

"Is that right? I did my wrist a while back. I had bandages and one of them yokes goes round your neck. Maybe I can make one for you. Right so, if you can't walk, you'll have to drag yourself over here. I can't just chuck this food on the floor, there's bound to be some horseshit down there. Come here to me, like this ..."

She demonstrated a buttock walk along the wall, looking precarious.

Adrian lifted his swollen ankle off the floor and began a painful shuffle across the six feet of stone floor to sit beneath her.

"Good man yourself! You ready now? I'll chuck your drink down first, and when you finish, lob it back up here, or they'll find the packet and know it was me."

She dropped the carton down into his lap, followed by two large slices of bacon wrapped in kitchen roll, and two thick slices of bread. The latter had been wrapped in nothing at all, but simply stuffed into the girl's apron pocket. Fortunately, the buttered sides stuck together but they were still covered in bits of grey fluff. Despite the nauseating smell seeping through the air, it was the most delicious food Adrian had ever tasted. The girl kept up a cheerful monologue as he ate his sandwich and gulped down the blackcurrant drink.

"... been to the hospital that often they say I should have a season ticket. Clumsy's her middle name, that's what the Mammy says. You finished already? Jaysis, you musta been hungry. Well, I don't know your name so I think I'll call you Gannet. Suits you right enough."

"My name's ... you can call me Gannet if you like. Thank you so much for bringing me some food and drink. Can I ask your name?"

"Sure you can, Gannet. I'm Teagan. Pleased to meet you. Now would you throw that old carton back up here to me? I have to push off before I'm missed. I'll pop back after dinner, maybe. Bring you something else."

Adrian panicked, terrified of being left alone. "Teagan, can I ask you something?"

"Putting in requests now, are you? Look, I'll get what I can. Could be steak and chips, could be dog biscuits. But I promise not to bring fish, I understand why you're sick of that."

Adrian looked up at the open face, taking in her bunches, thick calves, work-boots and cleaner's pinny. This was no child. She had crows' feet, distinct jowls and a tell-tale delta of lines across her décolletage. This was a large-breasted, middle-aged woman, who talked and dressed like a child.

"Fish? Why would I be sick of fish?"

She laughed with a hoot and clapped both hands over her mouth. "Sugar! I forgot I was supposed to keep quiet. Fish!" she hissed, more quietly. "Samir and Eoin just hooked you out of the sea, so you must be sick of them. First time they ever come back off one of their trips with a catch like you. Plenty of girls, and today, for the first time, a fine-lookin' fella. But never a single fish."

Samir? What kind of name was that?

"Teagan, can you tell me where we are?" Adrian pleaded.

She cast a worried look over her shoulder. "OK, Gannet. I'll tell you where we are. But then I have to go. Don't run away, I'll be back before you know it."

One more glance behind her and she leant down further than was safe.

"We're on the farm."

She swung her leg over the wall, landed with a thump the other side and was gone.

Chapter 38

Beatrice stepped out of the shower, wrapped herself in the bathrobe and yawned. Four hours' sleep. The average woman usually indulged in at least eight. Unless she was Margaret Thatcher. Well, a *normal* woman usually indulged in at least eight. Beatrice frowned. She was too old for all this, and the only thing likely to get her through the morning was a full-strength espresso.

The machine bubbled and spat as she dressed and gave up on styling her hair. She poured the coffee, already invigorated by the smell, and added a drop of cold milk. The telephone rang. Taking her first sip, she returned to the living room and spotted the flashing light indicating messages. Had she slept that deeply? The incoming call number was unfamiliar.

"Hello?"

"Beatrice, it's Matthew. How are you?"

"Matthew. At long bloody last. I'm absolutely fine. I've been worried about you two, so it's a relief to hear your voice. But the good news is that last night we got him! He's now in custody. The nasty part about it ..."

"Sorry to interrupt, Beatrice, but the thing is, I've lost Adrian."

"What on earth do you mean by that? Lost him how?"

"He went to the pub alone last night and didn't come back to the B&B. I waited up till gone midnight, so I presumed he'd gone off with his barman. He seemed rather keen on the chap. But the young man in question came round here this morning, determined to have it out with Adrian. According to Lyndon, they arranged to meet after the pub closed. But when he got down to the harbour, there was no sign of Adrian at all."

The cold grip of dread tightened Beatrice's scalp. "You've checked his room?"

"I'm an amateur, Beatrice, not an idiot. He's not there, and we've looked everywhere we can think of. Lyndon is worried. So am I. Apparently Adrian lifted the wallet of our ponytailed smuggler last night. Lyndon thinks he may have fallen into the sea, but my fears are more prosaic."

Beatrice dropped her head into her palm. "He lifted a wallet? I don't believe it. The man is an arse. Didn't I tell him? This was such a stupid idea. Why didn't you go to the police? I should have forced you. Matthew, we have to find him, fast. If the men from the boat have him, they also have evidence they're being watched. That is dangerous for everyone, but Adrian as the messenger is in genuine physical peril. Stay at the B&B, keep Lyndon with you. I'll mobilise the local force who will interview you first. Tell the truth, Matthew, and impress upon Lyndon the importance of doing the same. I will be there as soon as I possibly can. Is this the number of the B&B?"

"No. We're at the pub. The landlord has been most helpful now he knows of our connection. Gary sends his regards."

"In that case, stay there. The police will be there soon. Have you tried Adrian's mobile?"

"Naturally. Lyndon's been calling all night. It says number unobtainable."

"Hellfire! Stay where I can reach you and I'll call as soon as I know more."

Mobilising both Met, Welsh and Irish local forces needed authorisation from the top. Hamilton. She dialled the emergency number with unsteady fingers, her other hand clenched into a fist.

Trying to get anything out of him under ordinary circumstances was like pulling teeth from a stone. She had her trump card – Bennett in a cell with a willing confession. Hamilton had his rule book – one job at a time. But he *had* to help. With a normal human being, the personal involvement would tip the balance, but Hamilton's view of emotions was similar to his attitude to foreign languages. Highly suspicious. The phone clicked and buzzed, and began ringing. If he didn't agree to providing assistance, she'd go it alone. Simple as that. And then she'd file an official complaint against him when she got back, regardless of the consequences.

"Metropolitan Police, DI Rangarajan speaking. How can I help?"

"Ranga? Where's Hamilton?"

"Hello Beatrice! Good to hear your voice. And well done on that arrest. That was a nasty one. Hamilton's in hospital. Silly old sod wouldn't go to the dentist and now he's got an impacted wisdom tooth. They're taking it out today. So I'm his substitute."

"Thank God. Oh, that is such good news. Ranga, listen. I need a favour."

On leaving home for the office, Beatrice's mind raced so hard she was almost able to ignore her fear. But she'd forgotten she had to pass Adrian's flat. The pain of not knowing where he was, not knowing what they were doing to him, not knowing how he felt, not even knowing if he was still alive cut into her like a Stanley knife. The memory of his proud message *Elementary, my dear Stubbs* relating the Irish address twisted the blade. She practically ran to the Tube station, listing through the positives as she went. She had all the photographic evidence Adrian had sent on her memory stick. Clear images of these men and this woman, who had to be somehow identifiable. Ranga had not only authorised Met involvement with the case, but offered a senior detective to assist – Dawn Whittaker. Beatrice could have cried with relief.

Inspector Howells, fully cooperative, had mobilised the Dyfed-Powys police, who were currently searching the area around Porthgain. Her apologetic phone call to BTP had resulted in both Virginia and Grant offering their services and accepting no refusal. She welled up with gratitude once more and gave herself a light tap on the cheek. Emotional exhaustion was no excuse. Next time, she warned herself, it would be a slap.

Ranga assumed the role of coordinator with diplomacy and intelligence. With typical efficiency, he rapidly indicated names and roles of the assembled personnel, before beginning his presentation.

"I'd like to say that I appreciate your being here, especially as I know some of you had very little sleep last night. As you've heard from Beatrice, two men appear to be smuggling packages onto a remote beach in South Wales. We have every reason to believe the contents of these packages could be children. Babies, to be precise. From what we already know, four locations require investigation.

"One is already in hand. The Welsh police are searching the area around the beach and the village of Porthgain, assisted by Professor Bailey and the last people to see Adrian Harvey. The next two are connected. Marie Fisher, based in Cardiff, is the woman who receives the 'merchandise'. And the couple in this photograph, who seem to be the end clients. Their vehicle ID gives us an address in Chepstow. One team could deal with both of these. Finally, the farm in Ireland, believed to be the home of one of the supposed smugglers. There's a strong possibility that Mr Harvey was taken there. In my view, the Irish farm is potentially the most dangerous. I'd recommend DS Grant accompanies DI Stubbs on a flight to Cork."

Four heads nodded, absorbing the implications.

Virginia stated facts. "Leaving DI Whittaker and myself to handle the Chepstow and Cardiff line of enquiry. That makes perfect sense to me. Dawn has an outstanding reputation with sensitive situations such as this. I'd be happy to assist."

Blinking in surprise, Dawn took a moment before agreeing. "Sound logistics, Ranga. I presume you'll be involving the Garda at the Irish location? I mean, I'm glad DS Grant will be beside Beatrice, but they're going to need backup from the local force."

Ranga smiled. "No need to worry, Dawn. You get out there and I'll make sure you've got every kind of support there is. Don't forget, I'm one of you."

In an effort to swallow the lump in her throat, Beatrice squeezed her eyes shut and vowed to slap herself later, in the privacy of the bathroom.

Chapter 39

"Gannet? You awake?"

Adrian jumped. For such a hefty female, Teagan could creep around. He'd been straining his ears for any sound and heard nothing.

"Yes," he whispered. "I have no idea what time it is."

"Nor me. I never do. It's either before-breakfast or after-breakfast, before-dinner or after-dinner, before tea..."

"What is it now?"

"Before-dinner. That's why I can't stay long, but I got you some of last night's leftovers. Let's see here. An apple, two fine floury spuds, a lump of pork, and a drink of juice. Peas are too difficult to sneak out, you know what I mean?"

Adrian's stomach had been in spasm since the last time she left, and his level of dehydration was reaching a serious stage.

"Teagan, you are wonderful. Thank you so much. Just one question, do you think you could get me some water? A bottle, a jug, or even a bucket. I'm so thirsty."

She folded her arms and leant on them to look down at him. "Water? No problem at all. We have a tap right outside here. You want it now? Yeah, I'll fetch it for you now, just in case."

He managed to haul himself to a standing position against the wall, his injured foot held up behind him as if he were a horse about to be shod. *Before dinner.* Late morning, he assumed. He'd been here since dawn, so by now Matthew must have raised the alarm. But no one knew where to find him. His wallet might be found in the scrub behind the quarry hoppers, the broken bits of his mobile might cause some suspicion, but how could anyone locate him on 'the farm'? Think, Adrian, think.

"Here, I can't lift a bucket, but I filled an old bottle. You'll be pissing like a carthorse after this."

"Thank you so much. I can't tell you how grateful I am, Teagan. When I get out of here, I'm going to buy you such a fabulous present … what sort of thing would you like?"

"A present?" She folded her arms again, leant back against the beam and swung her legs, with a dreamy smile on her face. He was no expert, but this woman had certain special needs, that was clear. But whatever her problems, she was his only hope. He drank deeply from the plastic bottle, ignoring the swirling sediment.

"A present that comes in a box, or like anything at all?" she asked, scratching at her frizzy fringe.

"Anything at all. What would you like most in the world?"

She answered before he'd finished speaking. "A babby. But one I can keep. This time I want to keep him. Or her. One of them was a little girl. I'd like a girl."

Adrian's breaths came short and shallow. "You couldn't keep the other ones?"

Her dejected face became impatient. "Course not! None of us can, that's the rule. And you know it from the off so there's no point whining. The babbies go to a better place, we know that and it's best. The Mammy told us. They all go to university and Oxford and London and abroad. They have presents all the time."

He put down the bottle, sensing the tightrope he trod. "Best for the … babbies, but it must be hard for you. For the mothers."

Teagan rocked gently from side to side. "Some takes it harder. But when you come to Lannagh, you know what to expect." She burst into a surprisingly good rendition of Abba's *The Name of the Game*. "Everyone knows the name of the game. Or if they don't, they soon cop themselves on. Are you going to eat your food?"

Lannagh. The name on Eoin's business card. So there was a possibility that Beatrice did know where he was. Adrian bit into a cold potato, savouring the dry, crumbly mouthful. "Delicious. You're a good singer. I can tell."

"It's not just Abba I can do ...

So if your man is nice, take my advice
Hug him in the morning, kiss him at night
Give him plenty love madam, treat your man right
'Cause a good man nowadays sure is hard to find ..."

"Sssh, Teagan, that's brilliant, but I think we should keep quiet. You really do have an impressive voice. Who was that? Ella Fitzgerald?"

"No idea, Gannet. It's off a record, that's all I know. Your turn."

"OK, but quietly." He flicked through his repertoire and chose something appropriate to time, place and audience.

"*I dream of Teagan with the light brown hair*
Borne, like a vapour, on the summer air
I see her tripping where the bright streams play
Happy as the daisies that dance on her way."

Teagan rested her head on her shoulder and gazed at him as he sang softly. When he'd finished, she clapped with enthusiasm, although her palms never quite met.

"Is that a real song or did you make it up?"

"It's a real song, but I changed the name. Just for you."

Her smiling cheeks shone like autumn apples. "You have a voice on you, you creature. Oh, it's a crying shame. I'd love to keep you. But no. They take them all away. That's the rule."

The potato wouldn't go down. Adrian swigged more water.

"Take me away? They wouldn't do that, surely?"

Teagan's regretful expression was that of someone looking into an open coffin. "Ah, they would, you know. That was decided first thing. The row that's gone on all the morning was only about how to get rid of you once it's done. You're not exactly what they're used to. But Samir's persuaded the Mammy." Her imitation of the harsh voice was exact. "*Everything we need right here, and we've had no problems so far. I'll sort it after dinner.* Oh aye, Gannet, they're going to take you away."

Adrian swallowed the piece of potato, which felt like a house brick. "When you say 'not what they're used to', why am I different?"

"C'mon, you know yourself, most creatures are already dead when they get here."

Adrian couldn't speak, couldn't think and focused all his attention on breathing. *In. Out. In. Out.* There had to be a way of out of this.

"Teagan, I know someone who can help. Help both of us. All I need to do is call her. Or maybe you could call her for me. I think you'd like her."

Her open face soured into a pout. "Your girlfriend?"

"No, my ... boss. She's much older than me, but a very nice person. I think she'd like to hear from you. Would it be difficult for you to call a number and leave a message? I don't want to get you in trouble."

"I dunno, Gannet. I'm not good with the telephone. But I'll have a go. What do I have to do? If you don't want that pork, I'll have it. I've always got room for more."

"I do want it. I'm starving and my stomach is growling like a mad dog. But this is more important, Teagan. What you need to do is dial 999 and ask for Detective Stubbs of the Metropolitan Police. Tell her I'm here and give her this address. Can you remember ...?"

"Police, Gannet? You're a sandwich short of a picnic, you are. We can't have the Garda round here! Am I not after telling you the rules? I'll bring you something after dinner, if you're still here." She jumped off the wall, landing with a thud on the other side of the partition.

"Teagan!"

He heard her tut and sigh, before the adjoining stable door creaked open. The male voice made him jump.

"Teagan! What the feck were you doing in there?"

"Jesus, Eoin, you scared me half to death! I just wanted to have a look at your man. Being nosy is all."

"Get back to the house. Dinner's nearly ready. And if I catch you hanging round here again, I'll tell the Mammy. You know what'll happen then."

"Ah don't, Eoin. I'll not do it again. Promise. I'll go in and help with the dishing-up, will I? What you got there? You taking him some food?" Teagan's voice switched from humble to curious in a second.

"What did I just tell you about sticking your beak in? Now piss off back to the house."

Adrian stuffed the water bottle under the straw, along with the scraps of food, and sat with his injured ankle stretched out in front of him. The door creaked open, and bright afternoon sunshine lit the stable until Eoin slid in and shut the door behind him, bringing a fresh wave of the unbearable stench.

"Brought you something. You'll be thirsty enough, after all the puking, I'd say. And a couple of sandwiches, if your stomach can face it. Cheese and pickle, and pork with apple sauce. Brought you a jacket an' all. Gets cold enough at night."

Adrian took the foil-wrapped package and bottle of water. Eoin laid the jacket over his knees. "Thank you. Look, it's kind of you to bring me some food, but I'd like to know when I can leave."

"Won't be long. But when exactly, well, that's up to Samir. But I think you'll be out of here soon enough. Right, I need to get back. How's your ankle?"

"Painful."

"Good. So you won't be trying to take off anywhere."

"Unlikely. My ankle is sprained."

"Teagan had that. My sister, the one who's been poking her nose over the wall. But when she got hold of a crutch, you couldn't stop her. She was moving about fast enough."

Adrian couldn't believe the man. Small talk when they'd already decided to dispose of him. "I'm so glad she's better. Thanks for the sandwiches."

"Get them down you. And whatever it was Teagan brought you. You're gonna need your strength." His expression was in shadow as he closed the door behind him.

Adrian heard the bolt shoot home and the turn of the key in a padlock. Heavy footsteps crunched away.

So he knew Teagan had brought him food. He swigged some water and picked up the foil package. Of course, it could be drugged. Maybe he should stick with Teagan's rations. Funny how he mentioned her ankle. She'd told him it was her wrist. A shaft of light played across the straw-littered stable. Light from the doorway. Eoin had shot the bolt and padlocked it, but the door wasn't closed. He could get out.

Adrian struggled to his foot. How could he escape in such a state? He slipped on the jacket, shoving the sandwiches and water into his pocket, and hopped towards the light. The door creaked open at his touch. He surveyed the track down towards the house. No one about. He turned to check the uphill section and saw it immediately. An upturned broom against the wall. He checked again.

Eoin had brought him food, drink and clothes, put the idea of a crutch in his mind and left the door open. He was trying to help him escape. The smell made him pause, but he knew he had to get away.

Far enough from the house, so no one would be likely see him, especially if they were all eating lunch. He reached for the broom, shoved the bristly end under his armpit and hobbled his way behind the stable block. Every single movement jarred through his leg, but he chanted encouragement to himself. Keep going, you can do it, another step, don't stop. All he had to do was make for the road, flag down a vehicle and get to the nearest police station.

He rounded the corner of the stables, peering into the forest for a path. A shadow crossed the corner of his vision. Adrian had only half-turned before the blow caught him on the back of his head, buckling his knees and snapping the broom. His face hit the ground, all squashy and covered in pine needles, and his last conscious thought was an appreciation of the nice smell.

Chapter 40

And for One Million Pounds, Dawn Whittaker, where do you think you'll be at nine a.m. on Sunday morning?

A: In bed with toast and a mug of tea

B: Doing some half-hearted yoga

C: Cleaning up after the kids

D: Driving down the M4 with the woman who wrecked my marriage to apprehend some baby-traffickers.

Virginia couldn't have been more accommodating.

"Would you prefer to drive, Dawn?"

"Let me know if you'd like to stop for a coffee or anything."

"Is the air-con a bit strong? I'll turn it off for a while."

Dawn gave monosyllabic replies and reviewed the situation several times. Virginia was out of order treating her like a maiden aunt. She was not an invalid, nor a widow, but a divorcee. A woman whose husband had been unfaithful. After thirteen years of happy marriage, at the ceremony where she was due to receive her first policing award, Ian had gone into the toilets with this woman and made the name Dawn Whittaker synonymous with sniggers for police forces across the country.

After an hour of silence, Virginia spoke. "Do you want to talk about the obvious, or would you rather not?"

"By the obvious, you mean my husband's penis in your mouth?"

"That's the one. I'm happy to apologise, take the verbals, or you can slap me in the face, if you like. Just let me pull onto the hard shoulder first."

Dawn stared ahead, wondering what she did want. "I don't think I want revenge. It's more a case of wanting to understand. Why did you do it? You smashed up a family, a marriage, four lives, and left two children with a broken home."

Virginia drove for some miles without speaking. Finally, she cleared her throat.

"I don't think I did all that. That happened, I'm not denying it, as a result of the PBA 'event'. But none of that was my intention. I didn't know he was married."

"Would it have made a difference if you had?" Dawn faced her.

"Probably not, if I'm honest. The thing is, my selfish opportunism threw a curveball into your marriage. I'm sorry for that. But the inability to cope with it, the divorce and the resultant traumas? I can only accept so much responsibility."

Dawn turned to the window, fighting the truth of the statement. Ian had tried to repair her faith; he'd wanted to work at resolving the crisis. Still did. She refused. Once a philanderer ... it was only a matter of time before he humiliated her again. And the shame of all her colleagues knowing, laughing; she had no choice but to act. Taking him back would have been the worst kind of weakness. She despised that politician's wife kind of behaviour. Forgive and forget. How could she ever forget?

Virginia's voice was low and conciliatory. "Dawn? Saying this is a pointless exercise, but I'm actually sorry. I wish it hadn't happened. I'm older now and not all that proud of how I used to behave. So despite what you think of me, can we work together, do you think?"

Dawn gritted her teeth. "For Beatrice's sake, we'll have to. And in the circumstances, what's the alternative? Shall I take the lead in Chepstow, and let you handle Ms Fisher of Cardiff?"

"Sounds good to me. How about putting in a call to Ranga, see if he's found out which car hire firm she's using?"

"OK. And I also want to know what time Social Services are meeting us. I must have some time to talk to this couple first."

Dawn dialled, curious about how easily she'd let this marriage-wrecker off the hook. Not even a pejorative name had been used in anger. Maybe it was time to move forward. Maybe it was time to speak to Ian. Three years later, she still refused to speak to him directly. It wouldn't hurt to attempt a conciliatory gesture next week. Just a call. Or perhaps a Hi-how-are-you email. For the kids' sake. The trouble with harbouring a grudge was the time and energy it took to maintain. And who knows, if she stopped seeing herself as a victim, others might follow suit.

She was about to end the call when Ranga answered.

The terrace was on a steep slope, like something out of a Yorkshire soap opera. Virginia parked the Volvo opposite and checked the names again.

"Yvonne and Gerry Nicholls. What do you want me to do? Hang about in the background, interview neighbours, or join in and back you up?"

Dawn considered for a moment. "Why don't you see what you can find out from neighbours, wait for Social Services and ask them to hang on for half an hour. Then ring the bell. If I need more time, I'll say. But if they're still holding out, you can bring in the big guns."

"Will do. Good luck."

The door opened. Dawn offered a reassuring smile, whilst taking in every detail. Late thirties, tired and without make-up, permanent worry lines, velour leisure bottoms and stained grey T-shirt. Every inch the new mother.

"Yes?"

"Mrs Yvonne Nicholls? I'm Detective Inspector Dawn Whittaker from the Metropolitan Police. Sorry to disturb you on a Sunday, but I wonder if I could ask you a few questions. May I come in?"

As Yvonne announced 'a detective from the police', Gerry Nicholls turned from his position at the window, a tense concern dragging on his mouth as he gently rubbed the back of the tiny infant held to his chest. Dawn smiled and moved behind him to look at the crumpled sleeping face. A blue Babygro.

"How old is he?" she asked, in a quiet voice. He was undoubtedly premature, probably jaundiced and should be in hospital.

"Three weeks," Gerry answered, his eyes darting from his wife to Dawn. "He's away now, so I'll put him down."

Dawn's objective was to cause the minimum of embarrassment. The tension emanating from Yvonne Nicholls told Dawn it wouldn't take much to get full disclosure. So she accepted tea and waited for Gerry Nicholls to rejoin them.

"What's your baby's name, Mrs Nicholls?"

"Liam. We liked it because it's sort of old and modern at the same time, and it has a sort of solid sound to it. We did think about Edward, after Gerry's dad, but that's become a bit common now so ..." Her husband returned and she petered out.

He shook hands with forced levity. "So, Detective, can you tell us what all this is about?" He sat opposite Dawn at the dining table, beside his wife. Another one on a hair trigger.

Actions speak louder than words. Dawn spread the 8x4s of the Welsh cul-de-sac across the coffee table and sipped her tea. Pictures of them entering the house, pictures of them leaving with the basket. She didn't need to say a word. Yvonne cracked instantly.

"Oh God, Gerry, oh God. They're going to take him away, I

can't bear this, I can't."

White-faced, he rubbed his wife's back, unconsciously repeating his earlier gesture of comfort and staring at Dawn in abject misery.

"Mr Nicholls, I'd prefer to hear your side of the story. The evidence only gives us so much."

"I should have known. Nothing ever works out for us. Everything we try and do turns to shit. Every-fucking-thing." His face contorted into a rictus of a smile, he covered his eyes with his palm and his shoulders shook silently. Dawn sat opposite the weeping pair and reached for a packet of Wet Wipes from the sideboard. He recovered and brushed away the tears with the heel of his hand.

"We can't have kids. No reason why not, nothing wrong with either of us, but it just doesn't work. We've tried hormone injections, zinc tablets, fertility cycle management, ovulation tests and three series of IVF. All we got was a big fat disappointment, every time. So we faced facts and applied for adoption."

Yvonne blotted her face with a Wet Wipe and looked at Dawn, red-eyed and desperate. "We wanted to do it properly. We did try."

Gerry continued, with a nod. "She's right. We're not criminals, Detective. But I'm self-employed. The Greenery Guy. I provide and maintain plants in offices. Or I did. After the credit crunch, lots of companies dropped me and several major bills went unpaid. I filed for bankruptcy in 2009. So we gave up on any chance of an official adoption."

"I'm sorry to hear that. So you felt you had no alternative but to adopt through other channels?"

Yvonne's voice was harsh. "There was no other way! You tell me what else we could have done?"

Dawn shook her head. "I don't know, Mrs Nicholls. But I'd like you to know that I am not here to judge you. I just want to understand the steps that brought you to this situation, and if possible, try to help. Can you tell me how you contacted the people who provided Liam?"

"They contacted us!" Gerry's voice was indignant. "They got in touch after our first cycle of IVF. This woman came round one day, explained their service and gave us her card. We said no thanks. We wanted to do it properly. I have the card here."

He pulled a dog-eared business card from his wallet.

Dream-Makers: dreams can come true. Sienna Smith. Not even a website. Only a mobile number.

"I see. So when you'd reached the end of your tether, you called Miss Smith."

Yvonne nodded. "Exactly. She told us about all these unwanted babies from Eastern Europe and how people put their kids in the orphanage if they can't afford to keep them. And Gerry and me, well, we haven't got much, but we're getting back on our feet, and we'd love a child more than anything."

"I don't imagine this service came cheap."

Yvonne glanced at her husband and looked down at the crumpled Wet Wipe in her hands.

Gerry shrugged. "Fifteen grand. And he's worth every penny."

"I have to ask, Mr Nicholls. How does a recently bankrupt, unemployed man gather fifteen thousand pounds?"

"I'm not unemployed. I do two jobs. Deliveries for Waitrose and horticulture work for the Council."

"That still ..."

Yvonne broke in. "We borrowed it. My parents and his brother gave us the money. We'll pay them back."

Dawn nodded. "So you handed over the cash to Sienna Smith, and ...?"

"No, we're not that naïve. We only handed over the money when we received Liam. But we made an agreement, gave her a deposit and prepared for having a baby. We moved here, where no one knew us. Yvonne wore a pregnancy pad under her clothes for months. We put off any visitors and told the neighbours we preferred to stick with our family GP in Salisbury. All we had to do was to make sure she didn't get ill. We couldn't risk a trip to any doctor. Then we got the nod. Sienna told us where to go and when."

Dawn rested her chin on her clasped hands. "And yesterday morning, you got your little boy. Did you know the name of the woman who handed him over?"

"No, we only knew her as Scarlett," Yvonne said. "We were worried because Liam was crying so much. She was so rude, wasn't she, Gerry?"

"Downright unpleasant. Fortunately we had all the equipment with us. Dry nappy, baby food, Calpol. Poor little sod was in a right state. How could they treat a child like that? But they've got us over a barrel. Who's going to report them?"

"You are, I'm afraid. Mr and Mrs Nicholls, your child is a case of illegal adoption. Social Services are on their way and they will help you take this through the proper channels. Liam will have to be taken into care, pending an official investigation. If the parents of the child are willing and the authorities have no reason to refuse you, there's every chance you can adopt baby Liam. The fact that you've taken good care of him will work in your favour. But the proper procedures must be observed. I promise to do everything in my power to help you."

Yvonne began to sob quietly, but Gerry narrowed his eyes. "Why would you do that? We've committed a crime."

"As a matter of fact, I see you as victims, not perpetrators. Not only that, but if you can assist me in catching these traffickers, it'll make a positive impression on those who make the decisions. Listen, Gerry, Yvonne. You seem like good parents. Why would I want to destroy that? All we have to be sure is that the birth mother gave him up voluntarily, that there was no coercion, no rape, and no associated crimes such as blackmail involved."

The doorbell rang.

"Oh my God!" Yvonne's sobs restarted. Gerry embraced his wife as Dawn got up to answer.

Virginia, slightly bedraggled after summer rain, stood with

a small bald man, who was wearing jeans and an anorak. "Mr Horniman, this is DI Whittaker. Dawn, this is Jason Horniman from Social Services, Adoption Advisor. Can we come in? It's wet out here."

After leaving the Nicholls's house, Dawn retreated into silence on the journey to Cardiff, but this time for less selfish reasons. Absorbed by thoughts of what that couple and poor little Liam had undergone, anger and sympathy filled her chest. She'd call them next week and offer her continued support. The thought of that tiny little person, carried across the sea, cold, wet and hungry when he should have been in an incubator. Whoever was responsible was going down for this.

She felt Virginia glance at her as they sped down the M4. "Hey, the social worker will look after them. They might well get him back if the investigation doesn't show up involvement in a paedophile ring or anything dodgy on their records."

"I know. I was just trying to imagine what they've been through. What the baby's been through. No, I agree with you. They're in capable hands and the social worker seemed like a decent guy. Even if he doesn't live up to his name."

Virginia took her eyes off the motorway to shoot her a puzzled frown.

Dawn deadpanned. "I could have sworn you introduced him as Horniman. Well, not in my book he ain't."

Virginia laughed loudly and shook her head. "Nor mine."

And that would do as an olive branch for now. Time to get to business.

"Right. Now for Ms Marie, or should I say Scarlett, Fisher. Do we head for Docklands Rentals or pick her up at her address?"

Virginia's eyes flicked to the clock. "The rental firm told Ranga the return was due between twelve and one. We could make that easily, with time for a sandwich stop. We're going for an arrest, right?"

"Too right. This is obviously one hard-nosed little bitch and we've got ample evidence. Take her in, lean on her and find out where they've taken Adrian Harvey." Dawn yanked up her bag from the foot well. "I'm going to update Beatrice and then see how Heddlu de Cymru want to play it."

"And I'll keep my eyes peeled for food and caffeine."

Docklands Rentals had a Portakabin as its office. Virginia pulled up onto the forecourt, positioning the vehicle parallel to the front fence, facing the line of returned cars and went in to announce their presence. Dawn finished her water, observing the traffic entering and leaving the superstore on the other side of Newport Road. She dialled the number again. He must be back by now.

"Ah, hello. DI Whittaker again. Just wondering if your duty sergeant is back at his desk? Thank you. Hello, Detective Sergeant Harris, DI Whittaker here. I called before but you were out at lunch."

"Good afternoon to you, DI Whittaker. No, I'm afraid lunch is on hold. I've been talking to DI Rangarajan and DI Stubbs just now. We're happy for you to take the lead on this arrest and I've already checked we have the necessary force to back you up, if you need us."

"Oh, I see. Well, that's good of you, but we're not expecting any trouble. So if it's all right with you, we'll make the arrest and bring her to Cardiff Bay. Would there be an interview room available?"

"Not a problem. Like I say, give us a shout if you need any help."

"Thank you, DS Harris. And I think you'll be safe enough to have your lunch now."

"Kettle's already boiled, DI Whittaker. Beef and tomato Pot Noodle today. See, I'm a traditionalist at heart. Look forward to meeting you later."

Dawn ended the call with a smile and was adjusting the radio to Cardiff Eastern frequency when Virginia returned.

"Right, as I expected. The office is staffed by two adolescents who'll keep their traps shut, but I think we should lift her as soon as she gets out of the car."

"I agree. The Cardiff force is ready with backup."

Virginia rested her head on the back of the seat. "I'm so tired, I daren't close my eyes. Not even for a second. Did you say backup? Do you think that's necessary?"

"Can't be too careful. Are you OK? Do you want my coffee?"

Virginia yawned, stretching her long, lean arms over the steering wheel. "I need some kind of kick. Adrenalin, amphetamine, I'm not fussy. Don't answer that. You know what?" She jerked her head at the Portakabin. "Behind the reception desk is one of those one-way mirrors and when I looked into it, you know what I saw? Bruce Forsyth in a Boden dress."

Dawn laughed and was about to make a complimentary comment on chins when an SUV drove past, curved around and parked in an empty space, a hundred yards in front. The driver's door opened and a slight, dark-haired woman slid out.

As Dawn put on her sunglasses, she noted Virginia doing the same. "Come on then, Brucie. Let's take her."

They opened their doors in unison and the Fisher woman's head whipped around. Her eyes moved from one to another as they approached. Calmly and with no sudden movements, Marie Fisher turned and got back into the car. Dawn stopped and looked at Virginia.

"She's not ..."

An engine roared and gravel spat from beneath the wheels.

"She fucking is. In the car!"

The SUV had already shot out of the entrance by the time Dawn buckled her belt and started the siren. She grabbed the radio and alerted Cardiff HQ as to Marie Fisher's vehicle description, plates and direction as Virginia hurled the Volvo into traffic. Poor Sergeant Harris and his Pot Noodle.

"Taking a left, and again, no indication, stupid bitch, thinks she can throw me ..." Virginia kept up a muttered monologue as she threw the vehicle after their target. Marie knew where she was going, that much was clear. Racing to a junction, cutting up other vehicles, hacking left or right without warning, she certainly gave the impression of trying to outrun her pursuers.

Dawn clenched her handset, tensing herself against the seat as if it would offer protection, and relayed as much information as she could to the operator.

"Broadway, headed south west, past The Royal Oak pub."

Cars, buses, lorries, even bikes slowed and made room for the siren, which unfortunately aided Marie Fisher in weaving a determined path down the back streets. The red light of a pelican crossing indicated pedestrian priority and a mother stepped out with a pushchair. Both Dawn's feet hit the carpet but Virginia slammed her hand to the horn, causing the startled woman to leap backwards.

Passing Cyril Street on the right, another siren joined them. A patrol car pulled in behind and Virginia's momentary glance away from the road meant she didn't see Fisher's handbrake turn.

"Left! Left here! Now!" Dawn shrieked.

Virginia hit the brakes, ramming the gearstick upwards and swinging the wheel a full circle, before changing into second and accelerating once more. Flung against the door, Dawn felt sick but kept up her continual commentary.

"We've taken a left, don't know the name but we're passing Sapphire Street, Emerald Street, Copper Street ... is this some sort of joke? Taking a left. Next is ... oh shit!"

Passengers leaving a bus had just finished crossing the road as it pulled out of the stop. Marie overtook, bouncing up on the pavement, perilously close to a pair of elderly ladies, but just made it past. Virginia swung left into the bus bay, hit the accelerator, climbed the kerb and overtook the bus on the inside. The bus driver braked and honked his horn, but the Volvo was already swinging back into position, closing on Marie Fisher. Dawn's buttocks were clenched so hard, her bum took up half its usual space.

Virginia changed down a gear and the engine whined as she gained on Fisher's rear. She leant forward, neck muscles taut, forearms tensed and eyes scanning the scene ahead. Dawn compared her own stance: hands gripping the radio, whole body clenched and thrust as far back as physically possible. She realised the radio was squeaking at her and resumed her relay.

"Sorry, lost it for a moment there. Now on Splott Road, heading south. She's doing fifty, fifty-five on a residential street."

"More backup on its way."

"Suspect on South Park Road, no, taken a right, Seawall Road, heading south-east. We're on an industrial estate, and she's picking up speed. Reading sixty-five. She's keen to get away. Is there another way into this place? We might be able to ..."

The black vehicle lost it on the bend, swerving madly from one side to the next, but Marie managed to hold it and sped on. Virginia handled the curve far better, braking, turning and picking up speed all at the perfect moment. They gained several seconds and could almost see the outline of Fisher's head. Virginia flashed her lights and motioned to pull over. Marie indicated, braked and slowed and Dawn inhaled a deep breath of relief. Then the SUV took off again at speed, spitting back stones and dust. Virginia roared with rage, changed into second and Dawn's head bounced off the back of the seat.

Seawall Road straightened and as they tore past the school, Dawn gave thanks it was a Sunday. At the end of the road was a roundabout, with two possible exits. Virginia was closing the gap and Marie's choices were decreasing. Another siren joined the cacophony. A second patrol car approached from the right exit, lights flashing. Marie didn't hesitate, taking a screeching left.

"Left. Repeat. Suspect took a left off roundabout at end of Seawall Road. Second police vehicle in support."

Virginia tore the wheel to the left and Dawn's head hit the window again, before she was thrown forward into her seatbelt as Virginia slammed on the anchors. Marie's SUV was stationary, brake lights on. The road was nothing more than a track to an industrial wasteland. Ahead: a dead end. Marie Fisher had run out of choices.

They waited for several seconds. Virginia tensed as the reverse lights came on, but Fisher killed the engine. South Wales police officers fanned out around them as Dawn and Virginia stepped out of the car. Dawn's legs were unreliable, so she leant, nonchalantly, on the bonnet.

The door of the SUV opened and Virginia stepped forward to make the arrest. Marie gave no reaction. Dawn watched as two officers clipped on cuffs and guided her into the patrol car.

Virginia strode back towards Dawn with a broad grin. "Well, that woke me up. To the station for a light bout of interrogation?"

Dawn shook her head and sighed. "To think I could be watching Eastenders."

Chapter 41

Beatrice and Inspector Crean sheltered from the shower under the eaves of the Cork Airport terminal until Grant ended his call and came across the tarmac to join them.

His face looked dreadful; there were dark shadows under his eyes and he clearly bore bad news.

"Dyfed-Powys police found Adrian Harvey's wallet near Porthgain harbour. They've searched the whole area, a disused industrial site, but found nothing else."

Beatrice's last vestige of hope died: that Adrian had got lost, met someone else, fallen asleep or anything other than being taken by suspected child-traffickers.

"I see. Inspector Crean, let me introduce DS Ty Grant. The Inspector's going to escort us to the farm. A team's already there, conducting a search."

"How are you, Ty?" Inspector Crean offered a large hand and generous smile. "It'll take us around forty minutes to get there, so I can give you all the background along the way."

Beatrice nodded, hiding her impatience. She had a feeling this gentle, slow-moving man would drive like a grandma. While Adrian lay in the hands of human traffickers who treat people like animals, using them for what they can get.

Thankfully, Crean had a police driver, who was efficient and fast, albeit monosyllabic. The inspector sat in the passenger seat, twisting round to address herself and Grant.

"Now then, Lannagh Farm. Well, first thing you should know is that it's not really a farm. It's a rendering facility."

Beatrice gave Grant an enquiring glance, but he shook his head.

"I always assumed rendering was something you did to walls," she said.

The inspector had turned his attention to the road. Banners, bikes and significant numbers of spectators announced a cycle race. Beatrice dug her nails into her upper arms, noting the time on the dashboard as twelve-fifteen. The inspector finished advising the driver as to an alternative route and turned back to them.

"So, rendering. Not one of the most pleasant jobs you can do. That's why the farm is so remote. Terrible stink. They take waste products from slaughterhouses and farms; diseased animals, or the bits not fit for human consumption and so on. A rendering plant divides it into stuff that must be disposed of safely, and the rest it processes."

Beatrice clenched her jaw. "Processes into what?"

"Fertiliser, soap, animal food, that sort of thing."

Grant met her eyes and Beatrice closed hers.

The smell grew as they bumped their way up the long rough track which led to Lannagh Farm. The Inspector wasn't exaggerating; that reek was repulsive. A young sergeant waited outside the farm buildings and an ambulance stood with its doors open on the opposite side of the yard.

Beatrice's heart pulsed with fear. She released her seatbelt and opened her door before the car had come to a halt, hurrying over to the young officer.

"DI Stubbs of the Met. Is the emergency vehicle for Mr Harvey?"

"Sergeant Sullivan. No, ma'am. We've not yet located Mr Harvey. My colleagues are still searching. It's a big place, unfortunately. We've taken Brigid Connor, her family and three employees to the station. That includes Eoin Connor, your man with the ponytail from your pictures."

"Has he given you any information as to the whereabouts of Mr Harvey?"

"No, ma'am. Mrs Connor told them all to say nothing until they speak to a solicitor."

Inspector Crean and Grant joined them.

"Good afternoon, sir. I was just explaining that we've taken most of the family and farm staff in for questioning. But Mrs Connor's husband, Samir Lasku, is out doing a job on the farm somewhere. No one seems to know what or where. So far, we haven't located Mr Harvey."

Grant jerked his head at the ambulance. "So this is just a precaution?"

"No, it's for one of the girls. Look, this is a bit complicated. Do you want to come through here?"

Grant gestured for Beatrice to go inside. "You go ahead, I'll take a look around."

While Beatrice and Inspector Crean sat, the young sergeant stood at the end of the kitchen table, as if he were Head Boy about to deliver assembly.

"We've searched the farm and most of the outbuildings, but we haven't started on the plant yet. It's a huge area, full of bits of dead animals, so it'll take a while. The Inspector has asked them to shut the processes down, but they can't, so we're going to have to work around them. They're on lunch right at the moment, but the machines will start up again in around half an hour."

Inspector Crean smiled and nodded. "Good work, Sullivan. What else is there?"

"Upstairs in this house, we found four young women, all in different stages of pregnancy. Brigid Connor says they all work here. Three of them are at the station but one's still upstairs, bleeding heavily. It looks like she's having a miscarriage. I called an ambulance to take her to hospital, but she doesn't speak much English, so the crew are having some difficulties persuading her to go."

The inspector shook his head in amazement. "Do we know where she's from?"

"No clue, sir, sorry. Don't recognise her language and she has no ID that we can find."

"Were the other pregnant girls also foreigners?" asked Beatrice.

Sergeant Sullivan consulted his notepad. "No, Ma'am. All Irish girls, but none local."

Grant ducked under the low doorway, a frown darkening his face.

"Anything?" he asked.

Beatrice shook her head. "No sign of Adrian yet. The local officers are starting to search the plant."

Grant stood with his back to the window, making his expression hard to read. But his voice was tight and angry. "Let's be realistic. Why bring him back here? Because he had evidence, and they wanted to get shot of him. The most logical place to get rid of a body is in with all the others. We need to search the rendering area, but there are still trucks arriving. Why hasn't the plant been shut down?"

Inspector Crean sat back and gave a patient smile. "We've tried, Sergeant Grant. To shut the place down, we'd need a court order. Under Department of Agriculture rules, it runs continuously to prevent contamination."

His easy-going manner infuriated Beatrice. "Inspector, if there's a dead body in that factory, everything will be contaminated. I have to ask you to prevent any more vehicles entering the plant for the time being."

Sergeant Sullivan cleared his throat. "Inspector, we can actually close that first section. It's already inactive while the crew have their lunch. The first two parts of the process are only kept moving so as to minimise decay. The only section that needs a court order is the rendering equipment, where the raw material is heated and sterilised. We can halt the deliveries right now."

Beatrice turned to give Grant the order, but he was already out the door.

"Inspector, if Sergeant Sullivan accompanies Grant and myself to the plant, could you ask your men to prevent any more lorries from arriving. Is that acceptable to you?"

His eyebrows floated upwards, but he gave a gentle smile. "It is, DI Stubbs. Wild horses wouldn't drag me up there. I'll leave the best man to the job. Sullivan, let the officers know DI Stubbs has my full support."

"Sergeant Sullivan, could you walk with me? I'd like to ask you a few questions."

Receiving a benevolent nod from Crean, the sergeant picked up his notebook and followed Beatrice outside. He indicated a path curving away to the right and they began walking towards the origin of the all-pervading stink.

"You seem to know a lot about this rendering business," she began.

"A bit. My uncle has a slaughterhouse and used to bring his waste here. I did work experience with him, only for a few months, but learned about what happens to the bits we don't eat." The sergeant's high colour could have been due to embarrassment, enthusiasm or genetics. Beatrice was unfussed.

"Can you talk me through it? I'm not squeamish."

"Sure I can. Take a left here now and we're onto the main track up to the plant. This is a Category Three facility. Animal by-products fall into three categories; the first two are the diseased or toxic carcasses, which you've got to keep out of the food chain, or process them properly, as I expect you know. Category Three includes the bits of the animal we don't eat; hooves, snouts, tails, ears, guts, well, you get the picture. Slaughterhouses can only use about half a cow. The rest is sent here. This category also includes gone-off meat from shops, put-down pets from vets and animal shelters and downed animals from local farms."

Beatrice decided she did feel squeamish after all. "So to summarise, this is one of the less dangerous facilities."

"Right enough. Anything dangerous is separated and treated at another plant. They don't have the equipment here to cope with infectious diseases. So lorries deliver the bits of meat, cat corpses, poultry feathers and so on, which they call the 'raw'. It's all tipped onto the plant floor and then it's reduced before processing."

"And that would be the first two stages? Delivery and reduction. I don't think I really want to know this, but can you explain 'reduction'?"

"Ah, it's not all that complicated. Two massive rollers crush the whole lot to a pulp. After that, it's treated with the sterilising chemicals, dried out and separated into fat or bone meal. Are you feeling all right there, ma'am?"

The smell, the images and her own fragile emotions stopped Beatrice in her tracks. Heat swelled her neck and the blood-rush in her ears made balance a struggle. Sullivan held her elbow, peering at her face.

Adrian.

She opened her eyes and concentrated on the job.

"Thank you, sergeant. We can move on now. Tell me, have you lived in this area long?"

Chapter 42

Good cop, bad cop. No one needed to discuss it.

Dawn assumed her practised you-can-tell-me-anything expression, softened with slow blinks and beatific smiles. Virginia's tiredness and impatience made itself manifest in the atmosphere, like the unease before a thunderstorm. Her scornful lightning strikes lit up the room against Dawn's calm, kindly patience.

Yet Marie Fisher, or Mairead Connor, as her passport showed, remained unmoved. A WPC stood in the corner of the room, observing proceedings. Her presence for the sake of protocol allowed Virginia to make frequent exits. The lawyer had not yet arrived, so Dawn and Mairead sat in silence. Dawn allowed her gaze to rest on the grey table and breathed herself gently into a semi-meditative state. Addressing each discomfort in turn, she acknowledged her own tensions, her fears for Beatrice and Adrian, her need for peace and emotional processing time, her hunger, and her impatience with this witness. She politely asked each urge to wait in the queue.

The door swung open and Virginia was back, pressing the record button on the monitoring device and smiling.

"DI Lowe has returned. So Mairead, you may as well start now. Your lawyer is still en route, but your family have already coughed up the story. It's a shame, but the charges are stacking up now that the foreign girl's gone to hospital. Negligence at best, but I'm pushing for attempted murder."

Mairead's deliberately unimpressed look at Virginia slid away to the wall, reminding Dawn of her own teenage son.

Virginia's eyes shone. "Not going to give us your side? Because they're not sparing you, I'll tell you that. The whole baby farm was your idea, you organised the network of recruiters and it was your decision to use your retarded sister as a guinea-pig."

Mairead's head snapped round. "Fuck you! She's not retarded. Minor learning difficulties is all. And she's never been a guinea-pig."

Dawn flashed a look at Virginia and lowered her voice from the confrontational tone. "What's your sister's name?"

"Teagan. She's forty-five but still acts like a kid. She's not developed the way the rest of us have. But we never took advantage of the fact she's a bit innocent. God knows, others did. More than once. But we're her family, so we always helped her out. Not like we had a choice."

"You're telling me she got pregnant accidentally?" Virginia demanded.

Mairead's eyes flicked to Virginia and away in contempt. Dawn tried a softer tack.

"That must have been a shock for you all. And I'm guessing you didn't find out till quite late on."

Mairead gave a brief nod. "No. She didn't realise herself till the Mammy spotted it. But Ceana, that's my other sister, she's a nurse. She was working in Birmingham back then. She knew of a couple, infertile and desperate for kids, so it seemed obvious. Teagan couldn't even take care of herself, leave alone a baby. What we did was a kindness."

Virginia raised her eyebrows. "How much did you charge them for this 'kindness'?"

Mairead didn't even look at her, but continued talking to Dawn. "It was a one-off. But our eldest sister ..."

"Can I interrupt, Mairead? I just need to get the facts clear in my mind. When did you give Teagan's baby away?" Dawn asked.

"Ninety-four. My father died the same year, before we found out about Teagan, thanks be to God."

"That must have been tough for your mother, running the farm alone."

"She had Samir. And Eoin could be useful if he just copped himself on. He's lazy, soft-hearted and no kind of asset on a farm. But Samir's not afraid of hard work. He came over as a refugee from Albania with his daughter. One of the first out the country as soon as they opened the borders. He kept the place going all right. We owe him a lot."

Virginia slid behind Mairead and made a speeding-up motion with her hand, indicating her watch. Dawn nodded once.

"I think your story is going to be very important to this case, so I want you to take your time. The problem is, we need to find Adrian Harvey, the man Eoin and Samir abducted from Pembrokeshire. As a matter of urgency. If you can help us locate Mr Harvey, it will do you a real favour when this comes to court. A jury is always better inclined to a cooperative witness. Can you help us, Mairead?"

Mairead threaded her fingers together and pressed her forehead to her hands, as if she was praying. Minutes ticked past. Virginia shifted from foot to foot, glowering at the silent woman. Dawn held up a hand, asking for patience.

Mairead looked up. "The guy had photographs. Pictures of me, the last deal we did, the boat ... he told them he was a private detective, so we thought he was working alone. We couldn't have let him go, he'd have blown the whole thing open. So Samir decided to deal with it. Disappear him."

Virginia sat beside Dawn, her voice hard. "By 'disappear him', you mean you planned to kill him."

Mairead stared at Virginia with naked dislike. "I just said, Samir decided. He was going to do it and dump him with the rest of the carcasses at the plant."

"How can you be sure a human body wouldn't be spotted

among the animals?" asked Dawn.

Mairead leant back with a sigh. "Because we've done it before."

When Dawn got back from the bathroom, Virginia was still on the phone to the Cork Constabulary. She looked up and indicated the interview room, mouthing the word 'lawyer'.

"Thanks for your help, Detective. Call you back within the hour. Bye now." She replaced the receiver. "They haven't found Adrian. And no sign of Samir Lasku either, which isn't reassuring. But seems Eoin Connor has made a full confession and claims he tried to help Adrian get away. The girls and Teagan are spilling all over the place, but nothing from Brigid. Otherwise known as the Mammy. They're searching the factory now. Rather them than me." She lifted her shoulders and rolled her neck from side to side.

Dawn grimaced. "If he's in the factory, he's already dead."

Virginia stopped her stretching and looked up. "You're right. Oh God, poor Beatrice."

"Come on, let's go and hear Mairead's side."

Dawn's headache tightened. "Let's go back. I can see how you found prospective parents, through Ceana's job at the hospital fertility clinic. But locating the girls ..."

Virginia looked like death warmed up and the lawyer was picking at his nails.

Mairead sighed with impatience. "As already I said, we have two routes. Niamh, she's the oldest, has good contacts at IFPA, the Irish Family Planning Association. They tip her off about girls looking for an abortion. She does a bit of research and approaches them with a proposition. Her code name is Sandy. All of us begin with an S. Scarlett, Sienna, Saffron. Memorable names, see."

"So one recruitment channel was through your older sister in

Ireland. And the other?" asked Dawn.

"The other route was through Elira. I told you Samir and Elira came to us as Albanian refugees. Now Elira works with asylum-seekers in London and has an eye for girls in trouble. She offers them six months' work and a solution to the problem. It's like I keep saying. We're doing people a favour. The mothers, the kids, the new parents; everyone's happy." Mairead's saintly expression was nowhere near genuine.

Dawn's instinct told her it was time to puncture that smug surface. "Was Teagan happy when you sold her twins?"

Mairead's back hit the chair and she placed her palms on the edge of the table. "Do I have to repeat everything for you people? Teagan is under-developed. She can't look after anything. We had to take the twins away and give them a proper family. Of course she didn't like it, she gets easily attached. But for everyone's sake, it was better that way."

Her expression had changed. Defensive, as opposed to indignant. There was something else. "Who got her pregnant, Mairead?" asked Dawn.

"Jesus, Mary and Joseph, how the feck do I know? I live in Cardiff, I don't follow my little sister around all day, making sure no one takes advantage. How do you expect ...?"

Virginia's voice, low and deliberate, interrupted. "Who do you think it was? There's a limited pool of sperm donors on the farm."

"I don't know! I have no idea! There are up to seventy lorries a day coming in and out of the plant, it could have been anyone. As if I'd know." Her cheeks were a stark binary pattern of white and red.

Virginia turned to Dawn and the disbelief in her eyes was clear. Internally, Dawn agreed. Whoever it was, Mairead knew. The silence swelled with implications.

Mairead's voice changed from shrill to persuasive. "Look, we wanted to help people. Unwanted kids, childless parents. All we did was find a supply to meet a demand."

"The fact remains, despite your altruistic motives, you sold children. How much, Mairead? How much did Teagan's first baby go for?" asked Virginia.

"I told you already, that was a one-off."

"Apart from the twins you flogged later. How much?"

"Five grand. But that was in ninety-four. There was one other girl in ninety-six, which was more of a favour than anything. But in ninety-eight, the fallout from Mad Cow disease hit the factory and we had cash-flow problems. But we also had a way of raising money. So we put the price up."

Dawn tilted her head and smiled, struggling to stay sympathetic. Virginia folded her arms and closed her eyes.

"Yes. I hear fifteen grand is the going rate nowadays. And that's when the 'business' started in earnest?" asked Dawn.

Mairead shrugged. "Yeah. By 2000, we had a waiting list of parents. It was complicated, but we were very, very careful. The parents won't say anything because they might lose the child. The girls have a job for six months, a solution to their problem and a cash payoff at the end. No one knows what they've done and so long as they keep it shut, no one will tell."

Virginia opened her eyes. "How much did you pay 'the girls'? How much of fifteen grand do they see?"

"We take all the risks, so we keep the majority. They get five hundred Euro and should be grateful. It's enough for them to start off again."

No one spoke. Dawn breathed deeply and gazed at the grey surface once more, willing herself to find calm. She couldn't even attempt to communicate with Virginia, who scraped back her chair and left the room. Dawn informed the recording device of the change in personnel and returned her attention to Mairead.

"You mentioned earlier that human cadavers had been disposed of at the factory. Could you explain?"

Mairead glanced at the lawyer, who scribbled something on his pad for her to read.

"In the spirit of cooperation and full disclosure, I'll tell you.

We lost three babies, and one of the mothers died in childbirth. All those bodies went into the crusher."

"And no one noticed? None of your employees saw a human cadaver? No one missed this girl?"

"She was a refugee. No one really knew where she came from, so there was no one to miss her. It was a shame, a sad situation, but the easiest thing all round was to clear up any trail. And as for the plant workers, no. Look, when carcasses are unloaded onto the rendering floor, they aim for the conveyor in the middle. Two machines push the raw from the edges onto the conveyor. If something strange was on the outer edges, it's possible someone might see it. If you just make sure your waste is in the middle, the conveyor feeds it directly to the crusher."

"Detective Inspector Whittaker is leaving the room. Interview suspended at twelve-fifty."

Chapter 43

Grant advanced towards the man, his gestures short and stabbing. Dawn's urgent tones from the mobile in her ear and Grant's threatening manner towards the group of employees combined to release a thin wail of panic inside Beatrice. Closing her phone, she approached Grant and the crowd of disgruntled lorry drivers, uniformed factory staff and their stubborn-looking boss.

"DI Stubbs, we have a problem. Mr Donelly here is the foreman and he refuses to stop the plant operations ..."

Without waiting for Grant to finish, she began issuing orders. "Sergeant Grant, first priority. Ensure the conveyor belt on the rendering floor remains inactive until I give alternative instructions. Clear all personnel from the floor and the crushers. Mr Donelly will show you how, or he'll be placed under arrest and charged with obstructing justice. Go, now! Sergeant Sullivan, please remove all these people from the scene and tape the area. All workers in stages one and two of the rendering process are requested to leave the premises until further notice as this is now a serious crime scene. You may all be called as witnesses."

Donelly spat behind him, several workers mumbled abuse but Beatrice was more than ready for a fight. Scanning each face with a stony expression, watching each pair of eyes slide away, she made her mark. With a brisk nod, she marched after Grant and Donelly, towards the huge ramps used by the trucks to dump their waste. The stink waves of rotting flesh, putrefying matter and decay grew stronger until it became almost physical. Every cell in her body screamed at her to flee, her stomach bucked and heaved, but she strode on, head down, into the pit.

Donelly's attitude improved in a direct ratio to how sick she and Grant became. As they donned their protective clothing, along with wellingtons, gloves and masks, Beatrice knew her face reflected the same green pallor of Grant's. He attempted a smile but immediately tore off his mask and vomited into the toilet of the staff changing room. Donelly seemed pleased. Beatrice vowed not to chuck up her breakfast, but if it proved essential, she would bestow most of it on Mr Donelly.

Detective Sullivan and PC Hegarty, similarly clad, awaited them as they emerged to climb the stone steps to the rendering floor.

"Right. When we get onto the floor, I want Grant and Sullivan on the right side of the belt, taking half each. Hegarty's with me, taking the other side. Grant, let's start closest to the crusher. We've wasted a lot of time, so that end is our danger zone. Sullivan, keep an eye on him. OK, this is not going to be pleasant, but do your best."

Donelly opened the door to the processing plant and Beatrice forced out short breaths from her nose, a futile attempt at expelling the stench. She stamped up the concrete steps after Grant and followed him through the sliding doors. The reek of decomposition instantly caused her to gag, affecting Grant the same way. PC Hegarty couldn't even enter the room, heaving and hunched over his knees at the top of the steps. She ordered him back to the changing rooms. He would be no help.

Beatrice averted her eyes from the piles around her and pressed on towards the centre of the huge barn. Grant's retching and choking from the corner continued. Observing his spasmodic vomiting, she realised she and Sullivan would be working alone. She waved at Grant, indicating the exit with her thumb, releasing him from a duty he simply couldn't perform. He held up a gloved hand, helpless, and staggered away.

Orientation was not an issue. The vast maw at the other end gaped across the mounds of animal flesh. Beatrice, battling her stomach convulsions by repeating the word *Adrian* like a mantra, made her way to the opposite side. Sullivan traced a parallel route to her right, apparently unfazed by the atmosphere. Beatrice stared at the scene. Fur, tails, eyes, ears with tags, teeth, bone, feathers, flesh, hooves, blood, supermarket packaging, clawed paws, entrails and effervescent patches of maggots culminated in a scene of utter horror. The room was eerily quiet, but she only had to imagine the noise of the relentless conveyor, the drone of small earthmovers and the cacophonous grinding of relentless crushing rollers, to envisage one of Dante's Inner Circles of Hell.

They approached the central section, bending, lifting, kicking and examining. Beatrice couldn't see. Tears flooded her eyes as she accepted the fact they were looking for Adrian's body. No one could survive this. The lachrymose taste, unfortunately, could not repel the stench of rotting death. She got to work.

Beginning at the end of the belt nearest the inert crushers, she shifted several feet of dead sheep, checking beneath each carcass, finding nothing but more dead sheep. The next section was more varied. Poultry. Feet, beaks, heads and feathers. Pure force of will forced down her bile as she recalled Adrian's chicken cacciatore. After an area of unidentifiable innards, she came across the dogs. A pile of Jack Russells, a German Shepherd tangled up with several collies, on top of which lay two Westies, one of whose paws were crossed against its chest. He still had his collar on. Beatrice's chest was already heaving as she reached for the name tag. That was when she saw the arm.

Stepping over the dogs, she cautiously batted aside a pile of feathers to reveal Adrian's face. Bloodstained, eyes closed and skin white, he lay on his side with vomit trailing from his mouth.

"He's here! Sullivan, he's under here!"

Sullivan scrambled over the landscape of cadavers and body parts in her direction, digging under his overall for his phone.

Beatrice's tears flowed over her mask as she pressed two fingers to his neck.

"He's got a pulse!" Her cry ricocheted around the room. "I've got a pulse. Ambulance, Sullivan, now! We've found him!"

"Already on its way. The same one's still down at the farm. Don't move him, ma'am, we don't know how badly he's hurt."

She lowered her face to Adrian's, listening for any sign of breath. In the fetid, foul air, the sweetest sound blew into her ear. He was still breathing!

Sullivan arrived beside her, clearing the bloody detritus from Adrian's prone form with pragmatic ease and checking him for injury. Adrian gave no reaction as the detective's hands pressed and pushed his joints. Beatrice swiped at her face and scooped up Adrian's hand.

"Adrian, we've got you. You'll be fine. An ambulance is coming. We're here, we'll look after you, but you must be strong. Adrian, listen to me, you must be strong for me."

The Irish officer worked his way down Adrian's legs, as Beatrice gently patted his face. Once Sullivan reached the ankles, Adrian's body convulsed and his eyes opened for a second.

"Adrian? Adrian! He's gone again. It must be his leg. Sullivan? The ambulance?"

"It'll be here in less than one minute, Ma'am. Coming from the farm, see? That girl wouldn't budge, so today's our lucky day."

Beatrice could remember luckier days.

The showers were communal, so Beatrice decided to leave the men to clean up while she accompanied Adrian to the hospital. After all, one person humming of dead animals is not all that different to two. The ambulance staff diagnosed Adrian with shock, dehydration, a head wound and a sprained ankle, along with minor lacerations and bruises. None of which gave them serious cause for concern. Once he'd been whisked away into A&E, the ambulance woman kindly took her to the hospital showers and provided her with a set of whites.

She scrubbed for ages. The sticky stench of death seemed to have woven its way into her pores, her hair, under her nails. Eventually, she turned off the water and stood there, steaming. Adrian was alive. Most of the traffickers were in custody. Matthew was back in London, awaiting her return. Nathan Bennett could harass no more women. Dawn and Virginia were speaking to each other. Everything was fine. Except that Adrian had been dumped into that pile of carcasses, to be crushed alive. She sat on the floor of the shower stall, so appalled by the depths of human nature she could not even cry.

Chapter 44

Keys clattering against the door dragged Beatrice back to the present. With a disbelieving glance at the clock, she saw forty minutes had elapsed while she'd been staring out the window, dwelling on the past. The front door closed and Matthew called out.

"I'm back!"

"So I gathered. What took you so long?" Beatrice forced her attention back to the computer. She was nearly there.

"Oh, just chatting, you know what Adrian's like. I don't think he's stopped talking long enough to draw a breath. Now he's demanding a celebratory glass of something because he's off painkillers. I said we'd pop down with something special in a while."

"In a while. Yes, that's a nice, vague sort of term. I'm almost done here, so let's take him some of that champagne you bought in Reims."

Beatrice re-read the document for the last time, sighed and pressed Send. All done. She stretched her arms above her head. "How's his leg today?"

"Up. He's recumbent on the chaise longue in his pyjamas and looks exactly like Noel Coward."

September clouds parted, permitting autumn sunshine to flood the room. The low light cast a pinkish glow over the room, enriching her green tablecloth to a jewel-bright emerald and highlighting the dust. Matthew clattered about in the bathroom, raising his voice as he turned on the taps.

"How did you get on this afternoon?" he yelled.

Such a noisy man. Beatrice stood in the bathroom doorway and watched him rub shaving foam all over his jaw.

"I managed to finish it, despite the disturbance from downstairs. What on earth were you doing down there? It sounded like you were playing skittles with concrete bollards."

"Jared and I rearranged the entire flat so that Adrian barely has to move. Remote controls, books, phone and a bowlful of organic fruit are all at his fingertips."

Beatrice envisaged the pampered patient and forcibly obliterated the reminder of Adrian's pale, bloodied, feather-stuck skin under fluorescent light. The urge to hurry downstairs and check on him tugged at her for the hundredth time that week.

"Why are you bothering to shave now?" she asked.

"May as well make an effort. I plan to change too, but fear not. I won't wear black."

Beatrice smiled. Matthew's 'Raffles' look was now replaced by the familiar toad-brown cords, off-white shirt and bobbled sage cardigan. And his hair would grow back, eventually.

"What a fuss. Just for a drink with Adrian and Jared. Are you sure you're not on the turn?"

Matthew laughed. "I'm not but I wonder if he is. You know, I think he's becoming a Young Fogey. He uses terms such as 'damned fine idea', 'sagacious' and 'tip-top'. Is that healthy, at his age, do you think?" He picked up his razor and scraped a clean path through the foam from cheekbone to chin.

"I think you'll find the Young Fogey will wear off when he tires of his Agatha Christie persona. What are we having for dinner?"

"Lord knows. I'll cobble something together when we get back."

He'd forgotten, again. But somehow, it reassured her. Matthew lived in the present. And from now on, so would she. The past smelt bad.

"Aren't you going to change, Old Thing?" he asked. "That pullover's still got Bolognese sauce on it from lunch."

She muttered and grumbled but acquiesced, as no doubt he knew she would. In the wardrobe was the top she'd worn this time last year. Dark blue with a silver thread running through it. It might even jog his memory. A flattering cut, but more importantly suitable for her age. She'd never had a desire to look like mutton dressed as ham.

When she returned, Matthew was waiting with a bottle of Heidsieck Monopole Gold Top.

"Will I do?" she asked. "I wonder if we should take some snacks. I may get hungry."

"Jared's taken care of all that. Umm, Beatrice?"

"Yes, I know. I'll do it as soon as I find my hairbrush."

"That wasn't what I was going to say."

Beatrice looked into the mirror above the fireplace and wished she hadn't. Her hair looked as if someone had used an electric whisk on her head.

"Oh, well. It's only Adrian. What were you going to say?"

"Nothing. You look perfect, my love. Let's go."

As soon as she opened Adrian's door, her instinct told her something was off kilter.

"Happy Birthday!!"

Beatrice stopped dead in the hallway. Balloons. Music. People. A plastic banner reiterating the message. She turned to Matthew for an explanation, but he'd slipped past her to join the crowd.

Adrian, in an armchair, pulling a party popper. Virginia, raising a glass. Ty Grant, applauding. Dawn, coming forward to hand her a glass. Jared, blowing kisses. Cooper and Ranga, lifting cans of lager. Lyndon, yanking out a champagne cork. Kalpana, bringing forward a tray of cupcakes. And Matthew, laughing.

"Speech!"

"Speech, Beatrice, come on!"

"Speech! Birthday Girl!"

Beatrice blinked. This would never work. Who invited both Dawn *and* Virginia? What was Adrian thinking, putting Jared and Lyndon in the same room? Kalpana was far too fragile to be at any kind of party. Why the hell had Matthew gone along with such a ridiculous plan? He knew she abhorred surprises. And what on earth made them all look so happy? She had a choice. To laugh or to cry, and the former was far more socially acceptable.

"Thank you. As a rule, I hate surprises. And this is no exception. However, all of you helped me get Adrian back. For that reason alone, you are forgiven. Matthew, I'll deal with you later. Cheers!"

Grant and Cooper looked around in amusement as Virginia and Kalpana whooped with laughter. Jared grinned, pleased with his punch line. The sight of Kalpana wiping away tears of laughter provoked an involuntary smile from Beatrice. Matthew and Ranga were in the kitchen, presumably still discussing Keralan cuisine, while Dawn and Lyndon had gone to open more champagne.

Adrian shifted on his cushion and Beatrice moved to give him room.

"It's fine, stay where you are. Just itchy, that's all. Matthew says you finished your report this afternoon."

"Yes, I did." The grey gloom which had accompanied her all day made a brief reappearance.

"Why the long face? Isn't it good news? Seven child-traffickers behind bars. Jared thinks I'm insane to testify on behalf of Eoin, but I'm determined. And I've already made my statement on Teagan's behalf. They both tried to help me, I really believe they did."

"If that's how you choose to see it."

"Beatrice, you weren't there. Anyway, I refuse to rehash this. Especially tonight. You should be enjoying yourself and toasting your success. That's why we're here. You know, I was still on the pills when I heard they'd picked Samir up. Even so, I had a sneaky glass of Prosecco to rejoice."

Beatrice agreed. "Me too. His violence and cruelty and paranoia may have served him and Brigid Connor well over the years, but his stupidity let him down at the end. As Inspector Crean said, he came in on a boat and was bound to try getting out the same way. All they had to do was wait."

"Crean's a classic tortoise, isn't he? Nothing flashy, but in the end, he gets his man. Rather like Morse."

"Adrian, I know that face. Don't tell me you're inventing another detective persona."

"No. Despite my natural flair, I do accept that a little training does help. Now, will you stop worrying about me and start celebrating?"

"I am celebrating. Or will be as soon as Dawn gets back with my champers. But writing up such a report forces you to acknowledge your mistakes. That hurts."

"Good job I don't have to do one, in that case. As I said, I'm not going over this anymore. I'm bored of it. And if you attempt for one second to blame yourself again, I swear to God, I'll have you thrown out of this flat."

"You can't do that. I'm the birthday girl."

"And a royal pain in the arse. Here comes the fizz. Now drink and be merry. I insist."

"Right. I'm going to chat to Dawn and leave you and Lyndon to finish your argument about Sherlock Holmes. Were you winning?"

"No. It's a well-known fact about the Welsh. Stubborn as hell."

Beatrice gave him a kiss on the forehead. "Good luck."

She stood to meet Dawn and led the way to the window seat.

Beatrice accepted her glass with a smile. "You're too good to me. But then again, I am the birthday girl."

"For someone who hates birthday surprises, you can't half milk it. Sure you don't want any more cakes? There's plenty left."

Beatrice shook her head, her attention drawn by the two men sitting at the dining table. "They were delicious, really, but I know my limits. With cakes, at least. Thank you for that. I never knew you could bake."

"Don't tell Hamilton. He hates multi-taskers. Oi, what are you gawping at?"

"Just curious. Ty Grant seems to have buddied up with Cooper. I wonder what they've got in common?"

Dawn snorted with laughter. "Apart from being early-thirties, straight, single white males who play rugger? Only the fact that Grant is angling for a transfer to the Met. I'd say Cooper is being pumped for information. He's already worked on me and Ranga."

"A-ha. What are his chances?"

"As DS, highly likely, unless Hamilton takes against him. But DI, no chance. There's a queue and no one's due for retirement anytime soon."

Beatrice didn't answer, watching Grant's large shoulders and Cooper's shorter-than-short haircut. A matching pair of British Bulldogs.

"Are you and Matthew going to take a holiday now?" Dawn asked. "It's well overdue."

Beatrice wrinkled her nose. "His term starts in two weeks, so he needs to get back and plan lectures. I might potter off somewhere for a week or so, and take a proper break with him later."

"Beatrice?" Dawn's eyes were soft and concerned. "How are you feeling?"

"Tired. Bone-weary. Despite James and a full hour of therapy. You might be right, you know. I do need a holiday. And funnily enough, I think I need some more cake. Shall we?"

Upstairs, Beatrice's laptop glowed into life, emitting a blue luminosity in the empty room. A pop-up box flashed onto the screen, where it remained for thirty seconds.

One message received.

The box shrank to a small envelope, blinking in the bottom right-hand corner, leaving the last document visible.

Dear Superintendent Hamilton

It is with regret that I hereby tender my notice.

After many fulfilling years spent with the force, I have a duty to maintain the standards of excellence for which we strive.

After careful consideration of my performance in the two most recent cases to which I was assigned, I believe I have made serious errors of judgement, endangering both fellow officers and members of the public.

I now see myself as more of a liability than an asset, and therefore choose to leave my position as Detective Inspector after the formal notice period has elapsed.

On a personal note, I would like to thank you for your unstinting support and patient interest in my development.

I wish you, my colleagues and the Metropolitan Police Force every success in the future.

Yours sincerely
Beatrice Stubbs

Acknowledgements

With grateful thanks to the readers who helped shape this novel: Sheila Bugler, Jane Dixon-Smith, Gillian Hamer, Liza Perrat and Catriona Troth (Triskele Books); Sue Carver, Sharon Hutt, Geves Lafosse, Jane Hicks, Amanda Hodgkinson, Lorraine Mace, Jo Reed and Michelle Romaine (Writing Asylum); and Libby O'Loghlin (Nuance Words). I'd also like to thank Martin Horler and Sue Carver for their professional expertise; Jane Dixon-Smith and James Lane for their artistic flair; and Dominic Murcott for introducing me to Porthgain.

Also by JJ Marsh

Behind Closed Doors

"Beatrice Stubbs is a fascinating character, and a welcome addition to crime literature, in a literary and thought-provoking novel. I heartily recommend this as an exciting and intelligent read for fans of crime fiction." – Sarah Richardson, of Judging Covers

"Behind Closed Doors crackles with human interest, intrigue and atmosphere... author JJ Marsh does more than justice to the intelligent heroine who leads this exciting and absorbing chase." – Libris Reviews

"Hooked from the start and couldn't put this down. Superb, accomplished and intelligent writing. Ingenious plotting paying as much attention to detail as the killer must. Beatrice and her team are well-drawn, all individuals, involving and credible." – Book Reviews Plus

Tread Softly

"The novel oozes atmosphere and JJ Marsh captures the sights, sounds and richness of Spain in all its glory. I literally salivated as I read the descriptions of food and wine. JJ Marsh is an extremely talented author and this is a wonderful novel." – Sheila Bugler, author of *Hunting Shadows*

"There are moments of farce and irony, there are scenes of friendship, tenderness and total exasperation - and underlying it all a story of corruption, brutality, manipulation and oppression with all the elements you'd expect to find in a good thriller, including a truly chilling villain. Highly recommended". – Lorna Fergusson, *FictionFire*

Cold Pressed

Human Rites

Thank you for reading
a Triskele Book

If you loved this book and you'd like to help other readers find Triskele Books, please write a short review on the website where you bought the book. Your help in spreading the word is much appreciated and reviews make a huge difference to helping new readers find good books.

Why not try books by other Triskele authors?
Receive a complimentary ebook when you sign up
to our free newsletter at

www.triskelebooks.co.uk/signup

If you are a writer and would like more information on writing and publishing, visit http://www.triskelebooks.blogspot.com and http://www.wordswithjam.co.uk, which are packed with author and industry professional interviews, links to articles on writing, reading, libraries, the publishing industry and indie-publishing.

Connect with us:
Email admin@triskelebooks.co.uk
Twitter @triskelebooks
Facebook www.facebook.com/triskelebooks